The Best of Simple

The Best of Simple

| by LANGSTON HUGHES
Illustrated by BERNHARD NAST

HILL AND WANG
New York

Hill and Wang
A division of Farrar, Straus and Giroux
19 Union Square West, New York 10003

Library of Congress Control Number: 61014477
ISBN-13: 978-0-374-52133-2
ISBN-10: 0-374-52133-6

www.fsgbooks.com

54 56 58 60 61 59 57 55 53

To Melvin Stewart
*Broadway's genial
Simple*

| Foreword: Who Is Simple?

I CANNOT truthfully state, as some novelists do at the beginnings of their books, that these stories are about "nobody living or dead." The facts are that these tales are about a great many people—although they are stories about no specific persons as such. But it is impossible to live in Harlem and not know at least a hundred Simples, fifty Joyces, twenty-five Zaritas, a number of Boyds, and several Cousin Minnies—or reasonable facsimiles thereof.

"Simple Speaks His Mind" had hardly been published when I walked into a Harlem cafe one night and the proprietor said, "Listen, I don't know where you got that character, Jesse B. Semple, but I want you to meet one of my customers who is *just* like him." He called to a fellow at the end of the bar. "Watch how he walks," he said, "exactly like Simple. And I'll bet he won't be talking to you two minutes before he'll tell you how long he's been standing on his feet, and how much his bunions hurt—just like your book begins."

The barman was right. Even as the customer approached, he cried, "Man, my feet hurt! If you want to see me, why don't you come over here where I am? I stands on my feet all day."

"And I stand on mine all night," said the barman. Without me saying a word, a conversation began so much like the opening chapter in my book that even I was a bit amazed to see how nearly life can be like fiction—or vice versa.

Simple, as a character, originated during the war. His first words came directly out of the mouth of a young man who lived just down the block from me. One night I ran into him in a neighborhood bar and he said, "Come on back to the booth and meet my girl friend." I did and he treated me to a beer. Not knowing much about the young man, I asked where he worked. He said, "In a war plant."

I said, "What do you make?"

He said, "Cranks."

I said, "What kind of cranks?"

He said, "Oh, man, I don't know what kind of cranks."

I said, "Well, do they crank cars, tanks, buses, planes or what?"

He said, "I don't know what them cranks crank."

Whereupon, his girl friend, a little put out at this ignorance of his job, said, "You've been working there long enough. Looks like by now you ought to know what them cranks crank."

"Aw, woman," he said, "you know white folks don't tell colored folks what cranks crank."

That was the beginning of Simple. I have long since lost track of the fellow who uttered those words. But out of the mystery as to what the cranks of this world crank, to whom they belong and why, there evolved the character in this book, wondering and laughing at the numerous problems of white folks, colored folks, and just folks—including himself. He talks about the wife he used to have, the woman he loves today, and his one-time play-girl, Zarita. Usually over a glass of beer, he tells me his tales, mostly in high humor, but sometimes with a pain in his soul as sharp as the occasional hurt of that bunion on his right foot. Sometimes, as the old blues says, Simple might be "laughing to keep from crying." But even then, he keeps you laughing, too. If there were not a lot of genial souls in Harlem as talkative as Simple, I would never have these tales to write down that are "just like him." He is my ace-boy, Simple. I hope you like him, too.

LANGSTON HUGHES

New York City
August 1961

| Contents

Feet Live Their Own Life

"IF YOU want to know about my life," said Simple as he blew the foam from the top of the newly filled glass the bartender put before him, "don't look at my face, don't look at my hands. Look at my feet and see if you can tell how long I been standing on them."

"I cannot see your feet through your shoes," I said.

"You do not need to see through my shoes," said Simple. "Can't you tell by the shoes I wear—not pointed, not rocking-chair, not French-toed, not nothing but big, long, broad, and flat—that I been standing on these feet a long time and carrying some heavy burdens? They ain't flat from standing at no bar, neither, because I always sets at a bar. Can't you tell that? You know I do not hang out in a bar unless it has stools, don't you?"

"That I have observed," I said, "but I did not connect it with your past life."

"Everything I do is connected up with my past life," said Simple. "From Virginia to Joyce, from my wife to Zarita, from my mother's milk to this glass of beer, everything is connected up."

"I trust you will connect up with that dollar I just loaned you when you get paid," I said. "And who is Virginia? You never told me about her."

"Virginia is where I was borned," said Simple. "I would be borned in a state named after a woman. From that day on, women never give me no peace."

"You, I fear, are boasting. If the women were running after you as much as you run after them, you would not be able to sit here on this bar stool in peace. I don't see any women coming to call you out to go home, as some of these fellows' wives do around here."

"Joyce better not come in no bar looking for me," said Simple. "That is why me and my wife busted up—one reason. I do not like to be called out of no bar by a female. It's a man's perogative to just set and drink sometimes."

"How do you connect that prerogative with your past?" I asked.

"When I was a wee small child," said Simple, "I had no place to set and think in, being as how I was raised up with three brothers, two sisters, seven cousins, one married aunt, a common-law uncle, and the minister's grandchild—and the house only had four rooms. I never had no place just to set and think. Neither to set and drink—not even much my milk before some hongry child snatched it out of my hand. I were not the youngest, neither a girl, nor the cutest. I don't know why, but I don't think nobody liked me much. Which is why I was afraid to like anybody for a long time myself. When I did like somebody, I was full-grown and then I picked out the wrong woman because I had no practice in liking anybody before that. We did not get along."

"Is that when you took to drink?"

"Drink took to me," said Simple. "Whiskey just naturally likes me but beer likes me better. By the time I got married I had got to the point where a cold bottle was almost as good as a warm bed, especially when the bottle could not talk and the bed-warmer could. I do not like a woman to talk to me too much —I mean about me. Which is why I like Joyce. Joyce most in generally talks about herself."

"I am still looking at your feet," I said, "and I swear they do not reveal your life to me. Your feet are no open book."

"You have eyes but you see not," said Simple. "These feet have stood on every rock from the Rock of Ages to 135th and Lenox. These feet have supported everything from a cotton bale to a hongry woman. These feet have walked ten thousand miles working for white folks and another ten thousand keeping up with colored. These feet have stood at altars, crap tables, free lunches, bars, graves, kitchen doors, betting windows, hospital clinics, WPA desks, social security railings, and in all kinds of lines from soup lines to the draft. If I just had four feet, I could have stood in more places longer. As it is, I done wore out seven hundred pairs of shoes, eighty-nine tennis shoes, twelve summer sandals, also six loafers. The socks that these feet have bought could build a knitting mill. The corns I've cut away would dull a German razor. The bunions I forgot would make you ache from now till Judgment Day. If anybody was to write the history of my life, they should start with my feet."

"Your feet are not all that extraordinary," I said. "Besides, everything you are saying is general. Tell me specifically some one thing your feet have done that makes them different from any other feet in the world, just one."

"Do you see that window in that white man's store across the street?" asked Simple. "Well, this right foot of mine broke out that window in the Harlem riots right smack in the middle. Didn't no other foot in the world break that window but mine. And this left foot carried me off running as soon as my right foot came down. Nobody else's feet saved me from the cops that night but these *two* feet right here. Don't tell me these feet ain't had a life of their own."

"For shame," I said, "going around kicking out windows. Why?"

"Why?" said Simple. "You have to ask my great-great-grandpa why. He must of been simple—else why did he let them capture him in Africa and sell him for a slave to breed my great-grandpa in slavery to breed my grandpa in slavery to breed my pa to breed me to look at that window and say, 'It ain't mine! Bam-mmm-mm-m!' and kick it out?"

"This bar glass is not yours either," I said. "Why don't you smash it?"

"It's got my beer in it," said Simple.

Just then Zarita came in wearing her Thursday-night rabbit-skin coat. She didn't stop at the bar, being dressed up, but went straight back to a booth. Simple's hand went up, his beer went down, and the glass back to its wet spot on the bar.

"Excuse me a minute," he said, sliding off the stool.

Just to give him pause, the dozens, that old verbal game of maligning a friend's female relatives, came to mind. "Wait," I said. "You have told me about what to ask your great-great-grandpa. But I want to know what to ask your great-great-grand*ma*."

"I don't play the dozens that far back," said Simple, following Zarita into the smoky juke-box blue of the back room.

Landladies

THE next time I saw him, he was hot under the collar, but only incidentally about Zarita. Before the bartender had even put the glasses down he groaned, "I do not understand landladies."

"Now what?" I asked. "A landlady is a woman, isn't she? And, according to your declarations, you know how to handle women."

"I know how to handle women who act like ladies, but my landlady ain't no lady. Sometimes I even wish I was living with my wife again so I could have my own place and not have no landladies," said Simple.

"Landladies are practically always landladies," I said.

"But in New York they are landladies *plus!*" declared Simple.

"For instance?"

"For a instant, my landlady said to me one night when I come in, said, 'Third Floor Rear?'"

"I said, 'Yes'm.'"

"She says, 'You pays no attention to my notices I puts up, does you?'"

"I said, 'No'm.'"

"She says, 'I know you don't. You had company in your room after ten o'clock last night in spite of my rule.'"

"'No, ma'am. That was in the room next to mine.'"

"'Yes, but you was in there with your company, Mr. Simple.' Zarita can't keep her voice down when she goes calling. 'You and you-all's company and Mr. Boyd's was raising sand. I heard you way down here.'"

"'What you heard was the Fourth Floor Back snoring, madam. We went out of here at ten-thirty and I didn't come back till two and I come back alone.'"

"'Four this morning, you mean! And you slammed the door!'"

"'Madam, you sure can hear good that late.'"

"'I am not deaf. I also was raised in a decent home. And I would like you to respect my place.'"

" 'Yes, ma'am,' I said, because I owed her a half week's rent and I did not want to argue right then, although I was mad. But when I went upstairs and saw that sign over them little old pink towels she hangs there in the bathroom, Lord knows for what, I got madder. Sign says:

GUEST TOWELS—ROOMERS DO NOT USE

"But when even a guest of mine uses them, she jumps salty. So for what are they there? Then I saw that other little old sign up over the sink:

WASH FACE ONLY IN BOWL—NO SOX

And a sign over the tub says:

DO NOT WASH CLOTHES IN HEAR

Another sign out in the hall says:

TURN OUT LIGHT—COSTS MONEY

As if it wasn't money I'm paying for my rent! And there's still and yet another sign in my room which states:

NO COOKING, DRINKING, NO ROWDYISMS

As if I can cook without a stove or be rowdy by myself. And then right over my bed:

NO CO. AFTER 10

Just like a man can get along in this world alone. But it were part Zarita's fault talking so loud. Anyhow when I saw all them signs I got madder than I had ever been before, and I tore them all down.

"Landladies must think roomers is uncivilized and don't know how to behave themselves. Well, I do. I was also raised in a decent home. My mama made us respect our home. And I have never been known yet to wash my socks in no face bowl. So I tore them signs down.

"The next evening when I come in from work, before I even hit the steps, the landlady yells from the parlor, 'Third Floor Rear?'

"I said, 'Yes, this is the Third Floor Rear.'

"She says, 'Does you know who tore my signs down in the bathroom and in the hall? Also your room?'

"I said, 'I tore your signs down, madam. I have been looking at them signs for three months, so I know 'em by heart.'

"She says, 'You will put them back, or else move.'

"I said, 'I not only tore them signs down, I also tore them *up!*'

"She says, 'When you have paid me my rent, you move.'

"I said, 'I will move now.'

"She said, 'You will not take your trunk now.'

"I said, 'What's to keep me?'

"She said, 'Your room door is locked.'

"I said, 'Lady, I got a date tonight. I got to get in to change my clothes.'

"She says, 'You'll get in when you pay your rent.'

"So I had to take the money for my date that night—that I was intending to take out Joyce—and pay up my room rent. The next week I didn't have enough to move, so I am still there."

"Did you put back the signs?" I asked.

"Sure," said Simple. "I even writ a new sign for her which says:

**DON'T NOBODY NO TIME TEAR DOWN
THESE SIGNS—ELSE MOVE"**

| Simple Prays A Prayer

IT WAS a hot night. Simple was sitting on his landlady's stoop reading a newspaper by streetlight. When he saw me coming, he threw the paper down.

"Good evening," I said.

"Good evening nothing," he answered. "It's too hot to be any good evening. Besides, this paper's full of nothing but atom bombs and bad news, wars and rumors of wars, airplane crashes, murders, fightings, wife-whippings, and killings from the Balkans to Brooklyn. Do you know one thing? If I was a praying man, I would pray a prayer for this world right now."

"What kind of prayer would you pray, friend?"

"I would pray a don't-want-to-have-no-more-wars prayer, and it would go like this: 'Lord,' I would say, I would ask Him, 'Lord, kindly please, take the blood off of my hands and off of my brothers' hands, and make us shake hands *clean* and not be afraid. Neither let me nor them have no knives behind our backs, Lord, nor up our sleeves, nor no bombs piled out yonder in a desert. Let's forget about bygones. Too many mens and womens are dead. The fault is mine and theirs, too. So teach us *all* to do right, Lord, *please*, and to get along together with that atom bomb on this earth—because I do not want it to fall on me—nor Thee—nor anybody living. Amen!' "

"I didn't know you could pray like that," I said.

"It ain't much," said Simple, "but that girl friend of mine, Joyce, drug me to church last Sunday where the man was preaching and praying about peace, so I don't see why I shouldn't make myself up a prayer, too. I figure God will listen to me as well as the next one."

"You certainly don't have to be a minister to pray," I said, "and you have composed a good prayer. But now it's up to you to help God bring it into being, since God is created in your image."

"I thought it was the other way around," said Simple.

"However that may be," I said, "according to the Bible, God can bring things about on this earth only through man. You are a man, so you must help God make a good world."

"I am willing to help Him," said Simple, "but I do not know much what to do. The folks who run this world are going to run it in the ground in spite of all, throwing people out of work and then saying, 'Peace, it's wonderful!' Peace ain't wonderful when folks ain't got no job."

"Certainly a good job is essential to one's well-being," I said.

"It is essential to me," said Simple, "if I do not want to live off of Joyce. And I do *not* want to live off of no woman. A woman will take advantage of you, if you live off of her."

"If a woman loves you, she does not mind sharing with you,"
I said. "Share and share alike."

"Until times get hard!" said Simple. "But when there is not
much to share, *loving* is one thing, and *sharing* is another. Often
they parts company. I know because I have both loved and
shared. As long as I shared *mine*, all was well, but when my wife
started sharing, skippy!

"My wife said, 'Baby, when is you going to work?'

"I said, 'When I find a job.'

"She said, 'Well, it better be soon because I'm giving out.'

"And, man, I felt bad. You know how long and how hard it
took to get on WPA. Many a good man lost his woman in them
dark days when that stuff about 'I can't give you anything but
love' didn't go far. Now it looks like love is all I am going to
have to share again. Do you reckon depression days is coming
back?"

"I don't know," I said. "I am not a sociologist."

"You's colleged," said Simple. "Anyhow, it looks like every
time I gets a little start, something happens. I was doing right
well pulling down that *fine* defense check all during the war,
then all of a sudden the war had to jump up and end!"

"If you wanted the war to continue just on your account, you
are certainly looking at things from a selfish viewpoint."

"Selfish!" said Simple. "You may *think* I am selfish when the
facts is *I am just hongry* if I didn't have a job. It looks like in
peace time nobody works as much or gets paid as much as in
a war. Is that clear?"

"Clear, but not right," I said.

"Of course, it's not right to be out of work and hongry," said
Simple, "just like it's not right to want to fight. That's why I
prayed my prayer. I prayed for white folks, too, even though a
lot of them don't believe in religion. If they did, they couldn't
act the way they do.

"Last Sunday morning when I was laying in bed drowsing
and resting, I turned on the radio on my dresser and got a church
—by accident. I was trying to get the Duke on records, but I
turned into the wrong station. I got some white man preaching
a sermon. He was talking about peace on earth, good will to

men, and all such things, and he said Christ was born to bring
this peace he was talking about. He said mankind has sinned!
But that we have got to get ready for the Second Coming of
Christ—because Christ will be back! That is what started me to
wondering."

"Wondering what?" I asked.

"Wondering what all these prejudiced white folks would do if
Christ did come back. I always thought Christ believed in folks'
treating people right."

"He did," I said.

"Well, if He did," said Simple, "what will all these white
folks do who believe in Jim Crow? Jesus said, 'Love one another,'
didn't He? But they don't love me, do they?"

"Some do not," I said.

"Jesus said, 'Do unto others as you would have others do unto
you.' But they don't do that way unto me, do they?"

"I suppose not," I said.

"You know not," said Simple. "They Jim Crow me and lynch
me any time they want to. Suppose I was to do unto them as
they does unto me? Suppose I was to lynch and Jim Crow white
folks, where would I be? Huh?"

"In jail."

"You can bet your boots I would! But these are *Christian*
white folks that does such things to me. At least, they call themselves Christians in my home. They got more churches down
South than they got up North. They read more Bibles and sing
more hymns. I hope when Christ comes back, He comes back
down South. My folks need Him down there to tell them Ku
Kluxers where to head in. But I'll bet you if Christ does come
back, not only in the South but all over America, there would
be such another running and shutting and slamming of white
folks' doors in His face as you never saw! And I'll bet the Southerners couldn't get inside their Jim Crow churches fast enough
to lock the gates and keep Christ out. Christ said, 'Such as ye do
unto the least of these, ye do it unto me.' And Christ *knows*
what these white folks have been doing to old colored me all
these years."

"Of course, He knows," I said. "When Christ was here on

earth, He fought for the poor and the oppressed. But some people called Him an agitator. They cursed Him and reviled Him
and sent soldiers to lock Him up. They killed Him on the cross."

"At Calvary," said Simple, "way back in B.C. I know the Bible,
too. My Aunt Lucy read it to me. She read how He drove the
money-changers out of the Temple. Also how He changed the
loaves and fishes into many and fed the poor—which made
the rulers in their high places mad because they didn't want the
poor to eat. Well, when Christ comes back this time, I hope He
comes back *mad* His own self. I hope He drives the Jim Crowers
out of their high places, every living last one of them from Washington to Texas! I hope He smites white folks down!"

"You don't mean *all* white folks, do you?"

"No," said Simple. "I hope He lets Mrs. Roosevelt alone."

| Conversation On The Corner

It was the summer the young men in Harlem stopped wearing
their hair straightened, oiled or conked, and started having it
cut short, leaving it natural, standing up about an inch or two
in front in a kind of brush. When Simple took off his hat to fan
his brow, I saw by the light of the neon sign outside the Wishing
Well Bar that he had gotten a new haircut.

"What happened to your head?" I asked.

"Cut short," said Simple. "My baby likes to run her fingers
through it. This gives her a better chance."

"As much as you hang out on this corner," I said, "I don't see
when she has much of a chance."

"You know Joyce is a working woman," said Simple, "also
decent. She won't come to see me, so I goes to see her early. I
already paid my nightly call."

"I understand that you work also and it's midnight now.
When do you sleep?"

"In between times," Simple answered, lighting a butt and

taking a long draw. "Sleep don't worry me. I just hate to go back to my little old furnished room alone. How about you? What're you doing up so late?"

"Observing life for literary purposes. Gathering material, contemplating how people play so desperately when the stakes are so little."

"What do you mean by all that language?" asked Simple.

"I mean there are very few people of substance out late at night—mostly hustlers. And all the hustlers around here hustle for such *small* change."

"They will not hustle off of me," said Simple. "No, sir! Somebody is always trying to take disadvantage of me. The other night I went to a poker game and lost Twelve Bucks. They was playing partners, dealing seconds, stripping the deck and palming, so all I could do was lose. I could not win—so I prefer to drink it up."

"At least you'll have it *in* you," I said. "But why do you imbibe practically every night?"

"Because I like it. I also drink because I don't have anything better to do."

"Why don't you read a book," I asked, "go to a show or a dance?"

"I do not read a book because I don't understand books, daddy-o. I do not go to the show because you see nothing but white folks on the screen. And I do not go to a dance because if I do, I get in trouble with Joyce, who is one girl friend I respect."

"Trouble with Joyce?"

"Yes," said Simple, leaning on the mailbox so no one could mail a letter. "Joyce thinks every time I put my arms around a woman to dance with her, I am hugging the woman! Now, how can you dance with a woman without hugging her? I see Joyce enough as it is. I drink because I am lonesome."

"Lonesome? How can you be lonesome when you've got plenty of friends, also girl friends?"

"I'm lonesome inside myself."

"How do you explain that?"

"I do not know," said Simple, "but that is why I drink. I don't do nobody no harm, do I? You don't see me out here hustling off nobody, do you? I am not mugging and cheating and robbing, am I?"

"You're not."

"So I don't see why I shouldn't take a beer now and then."

"*When* did you say?"

"Now," said Simple.

"You said 'now and then,' which is putting it mildly."

"I meant *now*," said Simple, "*right now* since I have met up with you, old buddy, and I know you will buy a beer."

"I saw Zarita in that bar," I said, "and if we go in there, you will have to buy her more than a beer."

"No, I won't! I'm off that dame. She talks too loud—come near getting me put out of my room. Besides, she will drink you up coming and going and not try to pay you back in no way. She is one of them hustlers you was talking about always out in the street at blip-A.M."

"Most of these people where you hang out are hustlers."

"All but you and me. I came out here hoping to run across you to borrow a fin until payday."

"I regret to say that I don't have anything to lend."

"Too bad—because I was going to buy you a drink."

"Then lose the rest in a game?"

"I was not," said Simple. "You see that cat inside the bar with that long fingernail, don't you? Well, he uses that nail to mark cards with. Every time I get in a game, there is somebody dealing with a *long* fingernail. It ain't safe! I am tired of trickeration. Also I have had too many hypes laid down on me. Now I am hep."

"I'm glad to hear that," I said. "It's about time you settled down anyhow and married Joyce."

"Right. I would marry her," said Simple, "except that that gi l insists that I get a divorce first. But my wife won't pay for it. And looks like I can't get that much dough ahead myself—in my line of work, I can't grow no long fingernails because they would break off before night."

"Oh, so you would like to be a hustler, too."

"Only until I pay for my divorce from Isabel," said Simple.

"If you hadn't quit your wife, you wouldn't need a divorce," I said. "If I had a wife, I would stay with her."

"You have never been married, pal, so you do not know how hard it is sometimes to stay with a wife."

"Elucidate," I said, "while we go in the bar and have a beer."

"A wife you have to take with a grain of salt," Simple explained. "But sometimes the salt runs out."

"What do you mean by that parable?"

"Don't take serious everything a wife says. I did. For instant, I believed her when my wife said, 'Baby, I don't mind you going out. I know a man has to get out sometimes and he don't want his wife running with him everywhere he goes.'

"So I went out. I didn't take her. She got mad. I should have taken that with a grain of salt. Also take money. My wife said, 'A man is due to have his own spending change.' So every week I kept Five Dollars out of my salary. When that ran out 'long toward the end of the week, and I would ask Isabel for a quarter or so, she'd say, 'What did you do with that Five Dollars?'

"I'd say, 'I spent it.'

" 'Spent it on what?' she'd say.

" 'I drunk it up.'

" 'What did you do that for?' she'd yell. 'Why didn't you have your clothes pressed, or spend it on some good books?'

" 'I didn't want any good books.'

" 'Why didn't you send some of it to your old aunt?'

" 'Next time I will *tell* you that I sent it *all* to my old aunt.'

" 'Then you intend to lie to me?' says my wife.

" 'Anything to keep down an argument,' I says.

" 'You do not trust me,' Isabel hollers. Then she starts to quarrel. So you see how it is. A woman will get you going and coming. You can't outargue a woman. She even had the nerve to tell me, 'Why don't you buy your beer by the case and set up home here and drink it with me?'

"I said, 'Baby, I cannot set up here at home and look into your face each and every night.'

"She said, 'You took me for better or worse. Do I look worse to you now?'

"I said, 'You do not look any worse, baby, but neither does you look any better as time goes on.'

"She said, 'If you would buy me some clothes, maybe I could look like something.'

"I said, 'Honey, we ain't got our furniture paid for yet.'

"She said, 'So you care more for an old kitchen stove than you does for me?'

"I said, 'A man has to eat, and a woman can't cook on the floor.'

" 'All you got me for is to cook,' Isabel said. 'If I had knowed that, I could of stayed home with my mother.'

" 'I must admit,' I said, 'your mother cooks better than you.'

" 'Huh! I can't do nothing with them stringy old round steaks you bring home for us to eat,' she says.

" 'My money won't stretch to no T-bones,' I says. 'Anyhow, baby, no matter how tough the steak may be, you can always stick a fork in the gravy.'

"I just said that for a joke, but somehow it made her mad. She flew off the handle. I flew off the handle, too, and we had one of the biggest quarrels you ever saw. Our first battle royal—but it were not our last. Every time night fell from then on we quarreled—and night falls every night in Baltimore."

"Night does," I said.

"The first of the month falls every month, too, North or South. And them white folks who sends bills never forgets to send them—the phone bill, the furniture bill, the water bill, the gas bill, insurance, house rent. They also never forget you got their furniture in the house—and they will come and take it out if you do not pay the bill. Not only was my nose kept to the grindstone when I was married, but my bohunkus also. It were depression, too. They cut my wages down once at the foundry. They cut my wages down again. Then they cut my wages *out*, also the job. My old lady had to go cook for some rich white folks. *And don't you know Isabel wouldn't bring me home a thing to eat!* Neither would she open a can when she got home.

"I said, 'Baby, what is the matter with you? Don't you know I have to eat, too?'

"She said, 'You know what is the matter with me. Ever since

I have been with you, I have been treated like a dog for convenience. Who is paying for this furniture? Me! Who keeps up the house rent? Me! Who pays that little dime insurance of yourn? Me! And if you was to die, I would not benefit but Three Hundred Dollars. It looks like you can't even get on WPA. But you better get on something, Jess. In fact, take over or take off.'

"Then it were that I took off," said Simple.

"And ever since you've been a free man."

"Free?" said Simple. "I would have been free if I hadn't run into some old Baltimore friend boy here in Harlem who wrote and told my wife where I was at. So for the last year now she's been writing me that if I wasn't going to even give her a divorce, to at least buy her a fur coat this winter."

"Why didn't you give her a divorce when you left?" I asked.

"You can't buy no divorce on WPA. And when the war came, she was working in a war plant making just as much money as me," said Simple. "She could get her own divorce. But no! She still wanted me to pay for it. I told her to send me the money then and I would pay for it. But she wrote back and said I would never spend none of her money on Joyce. Baltimore womens is evil."

"Evidently she does not trust you."

"I would not trust myself with Three Hundred Dollars," said Simple.

"So you are just going to keep on being married then. You can't get loose if neither one of you is willing to pay for the divorce."

"I've been trying to get Joyce to pay for it," explained Simple. "Only thing is, Joyce says I will have to marry her *first*. She says she will not pay for no divorce for another woman unless I am hers beforehand."

"That would be bigamy," I said, "married to two women at once."

"It would be worse than that," said Simple. "Married to one woman is bad enough. But if I am married to two, it would be hell!"

"Legally it would be bigamy."

"Is bigamy worse than hell?"

"I have had no experience with either," I said. "But if you go in for bigamy, you will end up in the arms of justice."

"Any old arms are better than none," said Simple.

| Simple on Indian Blood

"Anybody can look at me and tell I am part Indian," said Simple.

"I see you almost every day," I said, "and I did not know it until now."

"I have Indian blood but I do not show it much," said Simple. "My uncle's cousin's great-grandma were a Cherokee. I only shows mine when I lose my temper—then my Indian blood boils. I am quick-tempered just like a Indian. If somebody does something to me, I always fights back. In fact, when I get mad, I am the toughest Negro God's got. It's my Indian blood. When I were a young man, I used to play baseball and steal bases just like Jackie. If the empire would rule me out, I would get mad and hit the empire. I had to stop playing. That Indian temper. Nowadays, though, it's mostly womens that riles me up, especially landladies, waitresses, and girl friends. To tell the truth, I believe in a woman keeping her place. Womens is beside themselves these days. They want to rule the roost."

"You have old-fashioned ideas about sex," I said. "In fact, your line of thought is based on outmoded economics."

"What?"

"In the days when women were dependent upon men for a living, you could be the boss. But now women make their own living. Some of them make more money than you do."

"True," said Simple. "During the war they got into that habit. But boss I am still due to be."

"So you think. But you can't always put your authority into effect."

"I can try," said Simple. "I can say, 'Do this!' And if she does something else, I can raise my voice, if not my hand."

"You can be sued for raising your voice," I stated, "and arrested for raising your hand."

"And she can be annihilated when I return from being arrested," said Simple. "That's my Indian blood!"

"You must believe in a woman being a squaw."

"She better not look like no squaw," said Simple. "I want a woman to look sharp when she goes out with me. No moccasins. I wants high-heel shoes and nylons, cute legs—and short dresses. But I also do not want her to talk back to me. As I said, I am the man. *Mine* is the word, and she is due to hush."

"Indians customarily expect their women to be quiet," I said.

"I do not expect mine to be *too* quiet," said Simple. "I want 'em to sweet-talk me—'Sweet baby, this,' and 'Baby, that,' and 'Baby, you's right, darling,' when they talk to me."

"In other words, you want them both old-fashioned and modern at the same time," I said. "The convolutions of your hypothesis are sometimes beyond cognizance."

"Cog hell!" said Simple. "I just do not like no old loud back-talking chick. That's the Indian in me. My grandpa on my father's side were like that, too, an Indian. He was married five times and he really ruled his roost."

"There are a mighty lot of Indians up your family tree," I said. "Did your granddad look like one?"

"Only his nose. He was dark brownskin otherwise. In fact, he were black. And the womens! Man! They was crazy about Grandpa. Every time he walked down the street, they stuck their heads out the windows and kept 'em turned South—which was where the beer parlor was."

"So your grandpa was a drinking man, too. That must be whom you take after."

"I also am named after him," said Simple. "Grandpa's name was Jess, too. So I am Jesse B. Semple."

"What does the B stand for?"

"Nothing. I just put it there myself since they didn't give me no initial when I was born. I am really Jess Semple—which the kids changed around into a nickname when I were in school. In fact, they used to tease me when I were small, calling me 'Simple Simon.' But I was right handy with my fists, and after I beat the 'Simon' out of a few of them, they let me alone. But my friends still call me 'Simple.' "

"In reality, you are Jesse Semple," I said, "colored."

"Part Indian," insisted Simple, reaching for his beer.

"Jess is certainly not an Indian name."

"No, it ain't," said Simple, "but we did have a Hiawatha in our family. She died."

"She?" I said. "Hiawatha was no she."

"She was a she in our family. And she had long coal-black hair just like a Creole. You know, I started to marry a Creole one time when I was coach-boy on the L. & N. down to New Orleans. Them Lousiana girls are bee-oou-te-ful! Man, I mean!"

"Why didn't you marry her, fellow?"

"They are more dangerous than a Indian," said Simple, "also I do not want no pretty woman. First thing you know, you fall in love with her—then you got to kill somebody about her. She'll make you so jealous you'll bust! A pretty woman will get a man in trouble. Me and my Indian blood, quick-tempered as I is. No! I do not crave a pretty woman."

"Joyce is certainly not bad-looking," I said. "You hang around her all the time."

"She is far from a Creole. Besides, she appreciates me," said Simple. "Joyce knows I got Indian blood which makes my temper bad. But we take each other as we is. I respect her and she respects me."

"That's the way it should be with the whole world," I said. "Therefore, you and Joyce are setting a fine example in these days of trials and tribulations. Everybody should take each other as they are, white, black, Indians, Creole. Then there would be no prejudice, nations would get along."

"Some folks do not see it like that," said Simple. "For instant, my landlady—and my wife. Isabel could never get along with me. That is why we are not together today."

"I'm not talking personally," I said, "so why bring in your wife?"

"Getting along starts with persons, don't it?" asked Simple. "You must include my wife. That woman got my Indian blood so riled up one day I thought I would explode."

"I still say, I'm not talking personally."

"Then stop talking," exploded Simple, "because with me it is personal. Facts, I cannot even talk about my wife if I don't get personal. That's how it is if you're part Indian—everything is personal. *Heap much personal.*"

| A Toast to Harlem

QUIET can seem unduly loud at times. Since nobody at the bar was saying a word during a lull in the bright blues-blare of the Wishing Well's usually overworked juke box, I addressed my friend Simple.

"Since you told me last night you are an Indian, explain to me how it is you find yourself living in a furnished room in Harlem, my brave buck, instead of on a reservation?"

"I am a colored Indian," said Simple.

"In other words, a Negro."

"A Black Foot Indian, daddy-o, not a red one. Anyhow, Harlem is the place I always did want to be. And if it wasn't for landladies, I would be happy. That's a fact! I love Harlem."

"What is it you love about Harlem?"

"It's so full of Negroes," said Simple. "I feel like I got protection."

"From what?"

"From white folks," said Simple. "Furthermore, I like Harlem because it belongs to me."

"Harlem does not belong to you. You don't own the houses in Harlem. They belong to white folks."

"I might not own 'em," said Simple, "but I live in 'em. It would take an atom bomb to get me out."

"Or a depression," I said.

"I would not move for no depression. No, I would not go back down South, not even to Baltimore. I am in Harlem to stay! You say the houses ain't mine. Well, the sidewalk is—and don't nobody push me off. The cops don't even say, 'Move on,' hardly

no more. They learned something from them Harlem riots.
They used to beat your head right in public, but now they only
beat it after they get you down to the stationhouse. And they
don't beat it then if they think you know a colored congressman."

"Harlem has a few Negro leaders," I said.

"Elected by my *own* vote," said Simple. "Here I ain't scared
to vote—that's another thing I like about Harlem. I also like it
because we've got subways and it does not take all day to get
downtown, neither are you Jim Crowed on the way. Why, Negroes is running some of these subway trains. This morning I
rode the A Train down to 34th Street. There were a Negro driving it, making ninety miles a hour. That cat *were really driving*
that train! Every time he flew by one of them local stations looks
like he was saying, 'Look at me! This train is mine!' That cat
were gone, ole man. Which is another reason why I like Harlem! Sometimes I run into Duke Ellington on 125th Street and
I say, 'What you know there, Duke?' Duke says, 'Solid, ole man.'
He does not know me from Adam, but he speaks. One day I saw
Lena Horne coming out of the Hotel Theresa and I said,
'Hubba! Hubba!' Lena smiled. Folks is friendly in Harlem. I
feel like I got the world in a jug and the stopper in my hand! So
drink a toast to Harlem!"

Simple lifted his glass of beer:

> "Here's to Harlem!
> They say Heaven is Paradise.
> If Harlem ain't Heaven,
> Then a mouse ain't mice!"

"Heaven is a state of mind," I commented.

"It sure is *mine*," said Simple, draining his glass. "From Central Park to 179th, from river to river, Harlem is mine! Lots of
white folks is scared to come up here, too, after dark."

"That is nothing to be proud of," I said.

"I am sorry white folks is scared to come to Harlem, but I am
scared to go around some of *them*. Why, for instant, in my home
town once before I came North to live, I was walking down the

street when a white woman jumped out of her door and said,
'Boy, get away from here because I am scared of you.'

"I said, 'Why?'

"She said, 'Because you are black.'

"I said, 'Lady, I am scared of you because you are white.' I
went on down the street, but I kept wishing I was blacker—so
I could of scared that lady to death. So help me, I did. Imagine
somebody talking about they is scared of me because I am black!
I got more reason to be scared of white folks than they have of
me."

"Right," I said.

"The white race drug me over here from Africa, slaved me,
freed me, lynched me, starved me during the depression, Jim
Crowed me during the war—then they come talking about they
is scared of me! Which is why I am glad I have got one spot to
call my own where I hold sway—Harlem. Harlem, where I
can thumb my nose at the world!"

"You talk just like a Negro nationalist," I said.

"What's that?"

"Someone who wants Negroes to be on top."

"When everybody else keeps me on the *bottom,* I don't see
why I shouldn't want to be on top. I will, too, someday."

"That's the spirit that causes wars," I said.

"I would not mind a war if I could win it. White folks fight,
lynch, and enjoy themselves."

There you go," I said. That old *race-against-race* jargon.
There'll never be peace that way. The world tomorrow ought
to be a world where everybody gets along together. The least we
can do is extend a friendly hand."

"Every time I extend my hand I get put back in my place.
You know them poetries about the black cat that tried to be
friendly with the white one:

> "The black cat said to the white cat,
> 'Let's sport around the town.'
> The white cat said to the black cat,
> 'You better set your black self down!' "

"Unfriendliness of that nature should not exist," I said. "Folks ought to live like neighbors."

"You're talking about what ought to be. But as long as what *is* is—and Georgia is Georgia—I will take Harlem for mine. At least, if trouble comes, I will have *my own window* to shoot from."

"I refuse to argue with you any more," I said. "What Harlem ought to hold out to the world from its windows is a friendly hand, not a belligerent attitude."

"It will not be my attitude I will have out my window," said Simple.

| Simple and His Sins

JUST as the street lights were coming on one warm Sunday evening in midsummer, I ran into my friend of the bar stools between Paddy's and the Wishing Well. He was wiping his brow.

"Man, I came near getting my wires crossed this afternoon," he said, "and all by accident. I told Joyce I would meet her in the park, so I was setting out there on a bench with my portable radio just bugging myself with Dizzy Gillespie, when who should come blaséing along but Zarita."

"How did she look by daylight?" I asked.

"She looked fine from the bottom up, but beat from the top down," said Simple.

"You kept your eyes down, I presume."

"No, I didn't neither," said Simple. "I looked Zarita dead in the eye and I said, 'Woman, what you doing out here in the broad-open daytime with your head looking like Zip?'

"Zarita said, 'Don't look at my hair, Jess, please. I ain't been to the beauty shop this week.'

" 'Then you ought to go,' I said. 'Besides, how are you going to get your rest staying up all night? Last thing I saw last night was you—and now you're out here in the park and it ain't hardly noon.'

" 'I could ask you the same thing,' said Zarita, 'but I ain't that concerned about your business. And I don't have to answer your questions.'

" 'You didn't mind answering them last night when I was buying you all them drinks,' I said.

" 'To be a gentleman,' said Zarita, 'you speaks too often about the money you spend. I'll bet you if your girl friend ever saw you setting up in the bar having a ball every A.M. she would lay you low.'

" 'Joyce knows all about me,' I said, 'and I would thank you to keep her name out of this. Joyce is a lady.'

" 'What do you think I am?' yells Zarita.

" 'You ain't even an imitation,' I said, 'coming out in the street with your head looking like a hurrah's nest!' "

"Why were you so hard on Zarita?" I asked. "I thought she was a friend of yours."

"She ain't nothing but a night-time friend," said Simple, "and I do not like to see her in the day. You would not like to see her neither if you had seen her this noon. I often wonders what makes some women look so bad early in the day after they have looked so sweet at night. Can you tell me?"

"You can answer that yourself."

"Well, for one thing, a woman is half make-up," said Simple, "and the other half is clothes. They got no business coming out in the morning before they fix themselves up. I said, 'Zarita, go on home and put on some face, also oil your meriney.'

" 'I can see through you,' she hollered. 'You just scared somebody will spy you talking to me out here in the broad daylight and go tell that female friend of yourn. Well, you ain't gonna drive me off with your insulting remarks. This is a public park. I aims to set right here on this bench with you, Jess Simple, and listen to that radio until the Dodgers come on. I follows Jackie.'

" 'You will have to follow Jackie on somebody else's radio,' I said. 'I will not be seen setting in the park with no uncombed woman. Neither do I know you that well, Zarita, for you to set down here with me.'

" 'I set on a bar stool with you,' says Zarita.

" 'Not on the same stool,' I says. 'Woman, unhand me and lemme go.'

"Don't you know I had trouble getting away from that girl. Zarita pitched a boogie right there in the park and she has got a voice like a steam calliope. I cut out and went up to Joyce's house.

"When I rung Joyce's bell, she comes to the door in her wrapper and says, 'Baby, I thought you was going to set in the park until I got dressed.'

"I said, 'Joyce, you took too long. Let's go to a nice air-cooled movie instead of setting in the park listening to the ball game today. I hear Jackie's twisted his ankle, anyhow.' And I put that radio down and took that woman the other way, so she would not run into Zarita."

"Your sins will find you out," I said.

"I don't care nothing about my sins finding me out," said Simple, "just so Joyce don't find out about my sins—especially when their hair ain't combed."

Temptation

"WHEN the Lord said, 'Let there be light,' and there was light, what I want to know is where was us colored people?"

"What do you mean, 'Where were we colored people?' " I said.

"We must *not* of been there," said Simple, "because we are still dark. Either He did not include me or else I were not there."

"The Lord was not referring to people when He said, 'Let there be light.' He was referring to the elements, the atmosphere, the air."

"He must have included some people," said Simple, "because white people are light, in fact, *white,* whilst I am dark. How come? I say, we were not there."

"Then where do you think we were?"

"Late as usual," said Simple, "old C. P. Time. We must have been down the road a piece and did not get back on time."

"There was no C. P. Time in those days," I said. "In fact, no people were created—so there couldn't be any Colored People's Time. The Lord God had not yet breathed the breath of life into anyone."

"No?" said Simple.

"No," said I, "because it wasn't until Genesis 2 and 7 that God 'formed man of the dust of the earth and breathed into his nostrils the breath of life and man became a living soul.' His name was Adam. Then He took one of Adam's ribs and made a woman."

"Then trouble began," said Simple. "Thank God, they was both white."

"How do you know Adam and Eve were white?" I asked.

"When I was a kid I seen them on the Sunday school cards," said Simple. "Ever since I been seeing a Sunday school card, they was white. That is why I want to know where was us Negroes when the Lord said, 'Let there be light'?"

"Oh, man, you have a color complex so bad you want to trace it back to the Bible."

"No, I don't. I just want to know how come Adam and Eve was white. If they had started out black, this world might not be in the fix it is today. Eve might not of paid that serpent no attention. I never did know a Negro yet that liked a snake."

"That snake is a symbol," I said, "a symbol of temptation and sin. And that symbol would be the same, no matter what the race."

"I am not talking about no symbol," said Simple. "I am talking about the day when Eve took that apple and Adam et. From then on the human race has been in trouble. There ain't a colored woman living what would take no apple from a snake—and she better not give no snake-apples to her husband!"

"Adam and Eve are symbols, too," I said.

"You are simple yourself," said Simple. "But I just wish we colored folks had been somewhere around at the start. I do not know where we was when Eden was a garden, but we sure didn't get in on none of the crops. If we had, we would not be so poor today. White folks started out ahead and they are still ahead. Look at me!"

"I am looking," I said.

"Made in the image of God," said Simple, "but I never did see anybody like me on a Sunday school card."

"Probably nobody looked like you in Biblical days," I said. "The American Negro did not exist in B.C. You're a product of Caucasia and Africa, Harlem and Dixie. You've been conditioned entirely by our environment, our modern times."

"Times have been hard," said Simple, "but still I am a child of God."

"In the cosmic sense, we are all children of God."

"I have been baptized," said Simple, "also anointed with oil. When I were a child I come through at the mourners' bench. I was converted. I have listened to Daddy Grace and et with Father Divine, moaned with Elder Lawson and prayed with Adam Powell. Also I have been to the Episcopalians with Joyce. But if a snake were to come up to me and offer me an apple, I would say, 'Varmint, be on your way! No fruit today! Bud, you got the wrong stud now, so get along somehow, be off down the road because you're lower than a toad!' Then that serpent would respect me as a wise man—and this world would not be where it is—all on account of an apple. That apple has turned into an atom now."

"To hear you talk, if you had been in the Garden of Eden, the world would still be a Paradise," I said. "Man would not have fallen into sin."

"Not this man," said Simple. "I would have stayed in that garden making grape wine, singing like Crosby, and feeling fine! I would not be scuffling out in this rough world, neither would I be in Harlem. If I was Adam I would just stay in Eden in that garden with no rent to pay, no landladies to dodge, no time clock to punch—and my picture on a Sunday school card. I'd be a real gone guy even if I didn't have but one name—Adam—and no initials."

"You would be real gone all right. But you were not there.

So, my dear fellow, I trust you will not let your rather late arrival on our contemporary stage distort your perspective."

"No," said Simple.

| Wooing the Muse

"HEY, now!" said Simple one hot Monday evening. "Man, I had a *fine* week end."

"What did you do?"

"Me and Joyce went to Orchard Beach."

"Good bathing?"

"I don't know. I didn't take a bath. I don't take to cold water."

"What did you do then, just lie in the sun?"

"I did not," said Simple. "I don't like violent rays tampering with my complexion. I just laid back in the shade while Joyce sported on the beach wetting her toes to show off her pretty white bathing suit."

"In other words, you relaxed."

"Relaxed is right," said Simple. "I had myself a great big nice cool quart of beer so I just laid back in the shade and relaxed. I also wrote myself some poetries."

"Poetry!" I said.

"Yes," said Simple. "Want to hear it?"

"Indeed I do."

"I will read you Number One. Here it is:

> *Sitting under the trees*
> *With the birds and the bees*
> *Watching the girls go by.*

How do you like it?"

"Is that all?"

"That's enough!" said Simple.

"You ought to have another rhyme," I said. "*By* ought to rhyme with *sky* or something."

"I was not looking at no sky, as I told you in the poem. I was looking at the girls."

"Well, anyhow, what else did you write?"

"This next one is a killer," said Simple. "It's serious. I got to thinking about how if I didn't have to ride Jim Crow, I might go down home for my vacation. And I looked around me out yonder at Orchard Beach and almost everybody on that beach, besides me and Joyce, was foreigners—New York foreigners. They was speaking Italian, German, Yiddish, Spanish, Puerto Rican, and everything but English. So I got to thinking how any one of them foreigners could visit my home state down South and ride anywhere they want to on the trains—except with me. So I wrote this poem which I will now read it to you. Listen:

> I wonder how it can be
> That Greeks, Germans, Jews,
> Italians, Mexicans,
> And everybody but me
> Down South can ride in the trains,
> Streetcars and busses
> Without any fusses.
>
> But when I come along—
> Pure American—
> They got a sign up
> For me to ride behind:
>
> COLORED
>
> My folks and my folks' folkses
> And their folkses before
> Have been here 300 years or more—
> Yet any foreigner from Polish to Dutch
> Rides anywhere he wants to
> And is not subject to such
> Treatments as my fellow-men give me
> In this Land of the Free.
>
> Dixie, you ought to get wise
> And be civilized!
> And take down that COLORED sign
> For Americans to ride behind!

Signed, *Jesse B. Semple*. How do you like that?"

"Did you write it yourself, or did Joyce help you?"

"Every word of it I writ myself," said Simple. "Joyce wanted me to change *folkses* and say *peoples,* but I did not have an eraser. It would have been longer, too, but Joyce made me stop and go with her to get some hot dogs."

"It's long enough," I said.

"It's not as long as Jim Crow," said Simple.

"You didn't write any nature poems at all?" I asked.

"What do you mean, nature poems?"

"I mean about the great out-of-doors—the flowers, the birds, the trees, the country."

"To tell the truth, I never was much on country," said Simple. "I had enough of it when I was down home. Besides, in the country flies bother you, bees sting you, mosquitoes bite you, and snakes hide in the grass. No, I do not like the country—except a riverbank to fish near town."

"It's better than staying in the city," I said, "and spending your money around these Harlem bars."

"At least I am welcome in these bars—run by white folks though they are," said Simple, "but I do not know no place in the country where I am welcome. If you're driving, every little roadhouse you stop at, they look at you like you was a varmint and say, 'We don't serve colored.' I tell you I do not want no parts of the country in this country."

"You do not go to the country to drink," I said.

"What am I gonna do, hibernate?"

"You could lie in a hammock and read a book, then go in the house and eat chicken."

"I do not know anybody in the country around here, and you know these summer resort places up North don't admit colored. Besides, the last time I was laying out in a hammock reading the funnies in the country down in Virginia, it were in the cool of evening and, man, a snake as long as you are tall come whipping through the grass, grabbed a frog right in front of my eyes, and started to choking it down."

"What did you do?"

"Mighty near fell out of that hammock!" said Simple. "If

that snake had not been so near, I would've fell out. As it were, I stepped down quick on the other side and went to find myself a stone."

"Did you kill it?"

"My nerves were bad and my aim was off. I hit the frog instead of the snake. I knocked that frog right out of his mouth."

"What did the snake do?"

"Runned and hid his self in the grass. I was scared to go outdoors all the rest of the time I was in the country."

"You are that scared of a snake?" I said.

"As scared of a snake as a Russian was of a Nazi. I would go to as much trouble to kill one as Stalin did to kill Hitler. Besides, that poor little frog were not bothering that snake. Frogs eat mosquitoes and mosquitoes eat me. So I am for letting that frog live and not be et. But a snake would chaw on my leg as quick as he would a frog, so I am for letting a snake die. Anything that bites me must die—snakes, bedbugs, bees, mosquitoes, or bears. I don't even much like for a woman to bite me, though I would not go so far as to kill her. But of all the things that bites, two is worst—a mad dog and a snake. But I would take the dog. I never could understand how in the Bible Eve got near enough to a snake to take an apple."

"Snakes did not bite in those days," I said. "That was the Age of Innocence."

"It was only after Eve got hold of the apple that everything got wrong, huh? Snakes started to bite, women to fight, men to paying, and Christians to praying," said Simple. "It were awful after Eve approached that snake and accepted that apple! It takes a woman to do a fool thing like that."

"Adam ate it, too, didn't he?"

"A woman can make a fool out of a man," said Simple. "But don't let's start talking about women. We have talked about enough unpleasant things for one night. Will you kindly invite me into the bar to have a beer? This sidewalk is hot to my feet. And as a thank-you for a drink, the next time I write a poem, I will give you a copy. But it won't be about the country, neither about nature."

"As much beer as you drink, it will probably be about a bar,"

I said. "When are you going to wake up, fellow, get wise to yourself, settle down, marry Joyce, and stop gallivanting all over Harlem every night? You're old enough to know better."

"I might be old enough to know better, but I am not old enough to *do* better," said Simple. "Come on in the bar and I will say you a toast I made up the last time somebody told me just what you are saying now about doing better. . . . That's right, bartender, two beers for two steers. . . . Thank you! . . . Pay for them, chum! . . . Now, here goes. Listen fluently:

> *When I get to be ninety-one*
> *And my running days is done,*
> *Then I will do better.*
>
> *When I get to be ninety-two*
> *And just* CAN'T *do,*
> *I'll do better.*
>
> *When I get to be ninety-three*
> *If the womens don't love me,*
> *Then I must do better.*
>
> *When I get to be ninety-four*
> *And can't jive no more,*
> *I'll have to do better.*
>
> *When I get to be ninety-five,*
> *More dead than alive,*
> *It'll be necessary to do better.*
>
> *When I get to be ninety-six*
> *And don't know no more tricks,*
> *I reckon I'll do better.*
>
> *When I get to be ninety-seven*
> *And on my way to Heaven,*
> *I'll try and do better.*
>
> *When I get to be ninety-eight*
> *And see Saint Peter at the gate,*
> *I know I'll do better.*

When I get to be ninety-nine,
Remembering it were fine,
Then I'll do better.

But even when I'm a hundred and one,
If I'm still having fun,
I'll start all over again
Just like I begun—
Because what could be better?"

| Vacation

"WHAT's on the rail for the lizard this morning?" my friend Simple demanded about 1 A.M. at 125th and Lenox.

"Where have you been all week?" I countered, looking at the dark circles under his eyes.

"On my vacation *at last,*" said Simple.

"You look it! You appear utterly fatigued."

"A vacation will tire a man out worse than work," said Simple.

"Where did you go?"

"Saratoga—after the season was over and the rates is down."

"What did you do up there?"

"Got bug-eyed."

"You mean drank liquor?" I inquired.

"I did not drink water," said Simple.

"I thought people went to Saratoga Springs to drink water."

"Some do, some don't," said Simple, "depending on if you are thirsty or not. There is no water on Congress Street, nothing but bars—Jimmie's, Goldie's, Hilltop House. Man, I had myself a ball. I was wild and frantic as a Halloween pumpkin, drinking cool keggie and knocking myself out. I met some fine chicks, too! The first night I was there one big fat mellow dame, looking all sweet and sweetened, started making admiration over me. I would not tell you a word of lie, she wanted to latch on to me for life."

"Where was Joyce?"

"You know I did not take Joyce with me on no vacation," said Simple. "I left her in Harlem. Her vacation and mine does not come at the same time anyhow, and we do not go the same places. Joyce is a quiet girl. But this old girl I met in Saratoga—oh, boy! We was sitting at the bar. She started jitterbugging right on the stool, so I introduced myself. She said, 'Baby, play that piece again,' which I did. Then she said, 'Play "The Hucklebuck" about six times,' which I also did."

"So that's where your money went," I said, "right over the bar and down the juke box?"

"That's where it went," said Simple, "but it were worth it. This old gal looked like chocolate icing on a wagonwheel cake, partner. And I met another one looked like lemon meringue on a Sunday pie. Between the two of them I had a ball! But I come back to Harlem a week early because my money ran out. When I got home, first thing I did was go see Joyce.

"She said, 'Baby, how come you back so soon?'

"I said, 'Sugar, I wanted to see you'—and don't you know, Joyce believed me! Womens is simple.

"Joyce said, 'You sure do look tired.'

"I said, 'It's from just a-wearying for you, honey. I can't stay away from you a week at a time no more without it worries me.'

"Joyce said, 'I thought you would come back here looking all spruce and spry from drinking that sulphur water, baby.'

"But I told her, 'That water did not agree with me. Neither did that Saratoga food. Honey, you know the best thing about a vacation is coming home. When are you going to make some biscuits?'

"Man, don't you know Joyce went right out in the kitchen and made me some bread! I was hongry, too. Funny how fast your money can run out on a vacation."

"Especially when you're spending it on *two* women," I said. "You have got to learn to change your character and budget *both* your money and your pleasure."

"God gave me this character," said Simple. "In His own good time He will change it. You know that old saying:

A bobtail dog
Can't walk a log.
Neither can a elephant
Hop like a frog.

My character is *my* character! It cannot change."

"It's certainly true that nobody can make a silk purse out of a sow's ear," I said.

"Who wants to?" asked Simple.

| Letting Off Steam

"WINTER time in Harlem sure is a blip," Simple complained. "I have already drunk four beers and one whiskey and I am not warm yet."

"Your blood must be thin," I said.

"Thin, nothing! It's just cold out there. I do not like cold; never did, and never will, no place, no time."

"Well, what are you doing out in this weather if you're so cold-natured? Why didn't you stay home?"

"Man, this bar is the warmest place I know. At least they keep the steam up here."

"You mean to tell me you haven't got any steam in your room?"

"There's a radiator in my room," said Simple, "but my land-lady don't send up no steam. I beat on the radiator pipes to let her know I was home—and freezing."

"What happened?"

"Nothing. She just beat back on the pipes at me! I tell you, winter is a worriation."

"I don't like the cold, either," I said. "But mortal man can do very little about the weather. Of course, one could be rich and go to Florida."

"You couldn't give me Florida and all that Jim Crow on a sil-ver platter! But if these womens keep after me, I am liable to have to go somewhere."

"What's the matter now?" I asked.

"My wife writ me from Baltimore that if I don't buy her that divorce she's been wanting for seven years, she is going to get herself a new fur coat and charge it to me. She says I better pay for it or else! And Joyce has been hinting around lately that she needs a silver fox—and she ain't even married to me yet. Here I am going around wearing my prewar Chesterfield and can't get a new coat for myself. I ain't even got no rubbers for this snow."

"You love Joyce, don't you? So I know you wouldn't want to see her freeze."

"Freeze, nothing," said Simple. "If Joyce would put on some long underwear and drop them skirts down some more and wrap up her neck, she would be warm without a fur coat. Also, if she would stop wearing open-worked shoes. Women don't wear enough clothes."

"Do you want your best girl to look like somebody's grandma?"

"I don't want her to catch pneumonia," said Simple, "but I *ain't* gonna buy her no fur coat."

"A fur coat would have made a nice gift for Christmas. By the way, what did you give Joyce?"

"A genuine pressure-cooker-roasting-oven to cook chickens, since I like them. It cost me fifteen dollars, too. But when I was back in the kitchen Christmas Eve mixing drinks she came in and gave me one of them cold-roll-your-eyes looks and said real sweet-like, 'It's just what I wanted—except that I've got too many cooking utensils now to be just rooming—and that cute little fur jacket I showed you last week would've looked so nice on me.'"

"What did Joyce give you for Christmas?" I asked.

"A carton of *her* favorite brand of cigarettes. Ain't that just like a woman? Then she comes wanting a fur coat."

"Well, even dogs have fur coats. I see in the papers where a downtown store is advertising fur wrappers especially for dogs, priced up to Two Thousand Dollars. If someone would pay that much for a fur coat for a dog, it looks as though you might consider one for Joyce."

"Man, the rich peoples that buy them expensive dog-jackets

have paid Two Thousand Bucks for their dog in the first place. To have a fur coat like that, the dog is bound to be a thorough-bred-pedigreedy-canine dog. They ain't buying fur wrap-arounds for no mutt. They got their investment to protect. But Joyce ain't cost me nothing. Money couldn't buy that girl. I met her on a Negro Actors' Guild public boat ride when the moon were shining over Bear Mountain. She just floated into my life—free. And took up with me for the sake of love."

"So you would value a dog more than the woman who is your friend?"

"I do not have a dog, and if I did, as sure as my name is Jess Semple, I would not buy it no fur coat—a dog has its own fur. And unless Joyce raises herself some foxes, she will not get any, neither. I won't buy a human nor a dog a fur coat this winter."

"Why don't you just say you *can't* buy a fur coat?"

"You have hit the nail on the head. I have just cash enough for *one* more beer. You have that glass on me."

"No, thanks."

"Then I will have a *bottle* on you," said Simple, "before I go out in the cold. The Lord should have fixed it so humans can grow fur in the winter time—instead of buying it. . . . Hey, Bud, a bottle of Bud!"

| Jealousy

"THAT Joyce," said Simple, "is not a drinking woman—for which I love her. But if she wasn't my girl friend, I swear she would make me madder than she do sometimes."

"What's come off between you and Joyce now?" I asked.

"She has upset me," said Simple.

"How?"

"One night last week when we come out of the subway, it was sleeting too hard to walk and we could not get a cab for love nor money. So Joyce condescends to stop in the Whistle and

Rest with me and have a beer. If I had known what was in there, I would of kept on to Paddy's, where they don't have nothing but a juke box."

"What was in there?"

"A trio," said Simple. "They was humming and strumming up a breeze with the bass just a-thumping, piano trilling, and electric guitar vibrating with every string overcharged. They was playing off-bop. Now, I do not care much for music, and Joyce does not care much for beer. So after I had done had from four to six and she had had two, I said, 'Let's go.' Joyce said, 'No, baby! I want to stay awhile more.'

"Now that were the first time I have ever heard Joyce say she wants to set in a bar.

"I said, 'What ails you?'

"Joyce said, 'I *love* his piano playing.'

"I said, 'You sure it ain't the piano *player* you love?' He were a slickheaded cat that looked like a shmoo and had a part in his teeth.

"Joyce said, 'Don't insinuate.'

"I said, 'Before you sin, *you* better wait. It looks like to me that piano player is eying you mighty hard. He'd best keep his eyes on them keys, else I will close one and black the other, also be-bop his chops.'

"Joyce says, 'Huh! It is about time you got a little jealous of me, Jess. Sometimes I think you take me for granted. But I *do* like that man's music.'

" 'Are you sure it's his music you like?' I says. 'As flirtatious as you is this evening, your middle name ought to be Frisky.'

" 'Don't put me in no class with Zarita,' says Joyce right out of the clear skies. 'I am no bar-stool hussy'—which kinder took me back because I did not know Joyce had any information about Zarita. A man can't do nothing even once without Harlem and his brother knowing it. Somebody has been talking, or else Joyce is getting too well acquainted with some of my friends —like you."

"I never mention your personal affairs to anyone," I said, "least of all to Joyce, whom I scarcely know except through your introduction."

"Well, anyhow," said Simple, "I did not wish to argue. I says to her, 'I ignore that remark.'

"Joyce says, 'I ignore you.' And turned her back to me and cupped her ear to the music.

" 'Don't rile me, woman,' I says. 'Come out of here and lemme take you home. You know we have to work in the morning.'

" 'Work does not cross your mind,' says Joyce, turning around, 'when you're setting up drinking beer all by yourself—so you say—at Paddy's. I do not see why you have to mention work to *me* when I am enjoying *myself*. The way that man plays "Stardust" sends me. I swear it do. Sends me. Sends me!'

" 'Be yourself, Joyce,' I said. 'Put your coat around your shoulders. Are you high? We are going home.'

"I took Joyce out of there. And by Saturday, to tell the truth, I had forgot all about it. Come the week end, I says, 'Let's walk a little, honey. Which movie do you want to see?'

"Joyce says, 'I do not want to see a picture, daddy. They are all alike. Let's go to the Whistle and Rest Bar.'

" 'O.K.,' I said, because I knowed every Friday they change the music behind that bar. They had done switched to a great big old corn-fed blues man who looked like Ingagi, hollered like a mountain-jack, and almost tore a guitar apart. He were singing:

> *Where you goin', Mr. Spider,*
> *Walking up the wall?*
> *Spider said, I'm goin'*
> *To get my ashes hauled.*

The joint were jumping—rocking, rolling, whooping, hollering, and stomping. It was a far cry from 'Stardust' to that spider walking up the wall.

"When I took Joyce in and she did not see her light-dark shmoo with the conked crown curved over the piano smearing riffs, she said, 'Is this the same place we was at last time?'

"I said, 'Sure, baby! What's the matter? Don't you like blues?'

"Joyce said, 'You know I never did like blues. I am from the North.'

" 'North what?' I said. 'Carolina?'

" 'I thought this was a refined cocktail lounge,' says Joyce,
turning up her nose. 'But I see I was in error. It's a low dive.
Let's go on downtown and catch John Garfield after all.'

" 'No, no, no. No *after all* for me,' I said. 'Here we are—and
here we stay right in this bar till *I* get ready to go. . . . Waiter,
a beer! . . . Anyhow, I do not see why *you* would want to see
John Garfield. Garfield does not conk his hair. Neither is he
light black. Neither does he play "Stardust." '

" 'You are acting just like a Negro,' says Joyce."

" 'It's my Indian blood,' I admitted."

| Banquet in Honor

"WELL, sir, I went to a banquet the other night," said Simple,
"and I have never seen nothing like it. The chicken was good,
but the best thing of all was the speech."

"That's unusual," I said. "Banquet speeches are seldom good."

"This one were a killer," said Simple. "In fact, it almost killed
the folks who gave the function."

"Who gave it?"

"Some women's club that a big fat lady what goes to Joyce's
dancing class belongs to. Her name is Mrs. Sadie Maxwell-
Reeves and she lives so high up on Sugar Hill that people in
her neighborhood don't even have roomers. They keep the
whole house for themselves. Well, this Mrs. Maxwell-Reeves
sold Joyce a deuce of Three-Dollar ducats to this banquet her
club was throwing for an old gentleman who is famous around
Harlem for being an intellect for years, also very smart as well
as honest, and a kind of all-around artist-writer-speaker and
what-not. His picture's in the *Amsterdam News* this week. I
cannot recall his name, but I never will forget his speech."

"Tell me about it, man, and do not keep me in suspense," I
said.

"Well, Joyce says the reason that club gave the banquet is

because the poor old soul is so old he is about on his last legs and, although he is great, nobody has paid him much mind in Harlem before. So this club thought instead of having a dance this year they would show some intelligence and honor him. They did. But he bit their hand, although he ate their chicken."

"I beg you, get to the point, please."

"It seems like this old man has always played the race game straight and has never writ no Amos and Andy books nor no songs like 'That's Why Darkies Are Born' nor painted no kinky-headed pictures as long as he has been an artist—for which I give him credit. But it also seems like he did not make any money because the white folks wouldn't buy his stuff and the Negroes didn't pay him no mind because he wasn't already famous.

"Anyhow, they say he will be greater when he's dead than he is alive—and he's mighty near dead now. Poor old soul! The club give that banquet to catch some of his glory before he passes on. He gloried them, all right! In the first place, he ate like a horse. I was setting just the third table from him and I could see. Mrs. Maxwell-Reeves sort of likes Joyce because Joyce helps her with her high kicks, so she give us a good table up near the speaking. She knows Joyce is a fiend for culture, too. Facts, some womens—including Joyce—are about culture like I am about beer—they love it.

"Well, when we got almost through with the dessert, which was ice cream, the toastmistress hit on a cup with a spoon and the program was off. Some great big dame with a high voice and her hands clasped on her bosoms—which were fine—sung 'O Carry Me Homey.' "

" 'O Caro Nome,' " I said.

"Yes," said Simple. "Anyhow, hard as I try, daddy-o, I really do not like concert singers. They are always singing in some foreign language. I leaned over the table and asked Joyce what the song meant, but she snaps, 'It is not important what it means. Just listen to that high C above E'. I listened fluently, but it was Dutch to me.

"I said, 'Joyce, what is she saying?'

"Joyce said, 'Please don't show your ignorance here.'

"I said, 'I am trying to hide it. But what in God's name is she singing about?'

"Joyce said, 'It's in Italian. Shsss-ss-s! For my sake, kindly act like you've got some culture, even if you ain't.'

"I said, 'I don't see why culture can't be in English.'

"Joyce said, 'Don't embarrass me. You ought to be ashamed.'

"I said, 'I am not ashamed, neither am I Italian, and I do not understand their language.' We would have had a quarrel right then and there had not that woman got through and set down. Then a man from the Urban League, a lady from the Daughter Elks, and a gentleman librarian all got up and paid tributes to the guest of honor. And he bowed and smiled and frowned and et because he could not eat fast, his teeth being about gone, so he still had a chicken wing in his hand when the program started. Finally came the great moment.

" 'Shsss-ss-s-ssh!' says Joyce.

" 'I ain't said a word,' I said, 'except that *I sure wish I could smoke in here*.'

" 'Hush,' says Joyce, 'this is a cultural event and no smoking is allowed. We are going to hear the guest of honor.'

"You should have seen Mrs. Sadie Maxwell-Reeves. She rose to her full heights. She is built like a pyramid upside down anyhow. But her head was all done fresh and shining with a hair-rocker roached up high in front, and a advertised-in-*Ebony* snood down the back, also a small bunch of green feathers behind her ear and genuine diamonds on her hand. Man, she had bosom-glasses that pulled out and snapped back when she read her notes. But she did not need to read no notes, she were so full of her subject.

"If words was flowers and he was dead, that old man could not have had more boquets put on him if he'd had a funeral at Delaney's where big shots get laid out. Roses, jonquils, pea-lilies, forget-me-nots, pansies, dogwoods, African daisies, also hydrangeas fell all over his head out of that lady toastmistress's mouth. He were sprayed with the perfume of eloquence. He were welcomed and rewelcomed to that Three-Dollar Banquet and given the red plush carpet. Before that lady got through, I clean forgot I wanted to smoke. I were spellbound, smothered in it myself.

"Then she said, 'It is my pride, friends, my pleasure, nay, my honor—without further words, allow me to present this distinguished guest, our honoreeeee—the Honorable Dr. So-and-So-and-So.' I did not hear his name for the applause.

"Well, sir! That old man got up and he did not smile. It looked like he cast a wicked eye right on me, and he did like a snake charmer to Joyce, because nobody could move our heads. He did not even clear his throat before he said, 'You think you are honoring me, ladies and gentlemen of the Athenyannie Arts Club, when you invited me here tonight? You are *not* honoring me a damn bit! I said, not a bit.'

"You could have heard a pin drop. Mens glued to their seats. Joyce, too.

"'The way you could have honored me if you had wanted to, ladies and gentlemen, all these years, would have been to buy a piece of my music and play it, or a book of mine and read it, but you didn't. Else you could have booed off the screen a few of them Uncle Toms thereon and told the manager of the Hamilton you'd never come back to see another picture in his theater until he put a story of mine in it, or some other decent hardworking Negro. But you didn't do no such a thing. You didn't even buy one of my watercolors. You let me starve until I am mighty nigh blue-black in the face—and not a one of you from Sugar Hill to Central Park ever offered me a pig's foot. Then when *The New York Times* said I was a genius last month, here you come now giving a banquet for me when I'm old enough to fall over in my grave—if I was able to walk to the edge of it—which I'm not.

"'Now, to tell you the truth, I don't want no damned banquet. I don't want no honoring where *you* eat as much as me, and enjoy yourselves more, besides making some money for your treasury. If you want to honor me, give some young boy or girl who's coming along trying to create arts and write and compose and sing and act and paint and dance and make something out of the beauties of the Negro race—give that child some help. Buy what they're making! Support what they're do-

ing! Put out some cash—but don't come giving me, who's old
enough to die and too near blind to create anything any more
anyhow, a great big banquet that *you* eat up in honor of your
own stomachs as much as in honor of me—who's toothless
and can't eat. You hear me, I ain't honored!'

"That's what that old man said, and sat down. You could have
heard a pin drop if ary one had dropped, but nary one dropped.
Well, then Mrs. Maxwell-Reeves got up and tried to calm the
waters. But she made matters worse, and that feather behind
her ear was shaking like a leaf. She pulled at her glasses but she
could not get them on.

"She said, "Doctor, we know you are a great man, but, to tell
the truth, we have been kinder vague about just what you have
done.'

"The old man said, 'I ain't done nothing but eat at banquets
all my life, and I am great just because I am honored by you tonight. Is that clear?'

"The lady said, 'That's beautiful and so gracious. Thanks. It
sounds so much like Father Divine.'

"The old man said, 'Father Divine is a genius at saying the
unsayable. That is why he is great and because he also gives
free potatoes with his gospel—and potatoes are just as important
to the spirit as words. In fact, more so. I know.'

" 'Do you really think so, Doctor?'

" 'Indeed, or I wouldn't have come here at all tonight. I ate
in spite of the occasion. I still need a potato and some meat—
not honor.'

" 'We are proud to give you both,' said Mrs. Sadie Maxwell-
Reeves.

" 'Compliment returned,' said the old man. 'The tickets you
sold to this affair on the strength of *my* name are feeding us all.'

"Mrs. Sadie Maxwell-Reeves came near blushing, but she
couldn't quite make it, being brownskin. I don't know what I
did, but everybody turned and looked at me.

"I said, 'Joyce, I got to go have a smoke.'

"Joyce said, 'This is so embarrassing! You laughing out loud!
Oh!'

"I said, 'It's the best Six Dollars' worth of banquet I ever had

(Because I paid for them tickets although Joyce bought them.)
I said, 'If you ever want to take me to another banquet in honor,
I will go, though I don't reckon there will be another one this
good.'

" 'You have a low sense of humor, Mr. Semple,' said Joyce,
all formal and everything like she does when she's mad. 'Shut
up so I can hear the benediction.'

"Reverend Patterson Smythe prayed. Then it were over. I
beat it on out of there and had my smoke whilst I was waiting
for Joyce, because she looked mad. On the way home I stopped
at the Wonder Bar and had two drinks, but Joyce would not
even come in the back room. She waited in the cab. She said I
were not the least bit cultural. Still and yet, I thought that old
man made sense. I told Joyce, just like he said, 'It is more important to eat than to be honored, ain't it?'

"Joyce said, 'Yes, but when you are doing both at the same
time, you can at least be polite. I mean not only the Doctor,
but *you*. It's an honor to be invited to things like that. And Mrs.
Maxwell-Reeves did not invite you there to laugh.'

"I said, 'I didn't know I was laughing.'

" 'Everybody else knew it,' she said when we got to her door.
'You was heard all over the hall. I was embarrassed not only for
you, *but for myself*. I would like you to know that I am not built
like you. I cannot just drink and forget.'

" 'No matter how many drinks I drink,' I said, 'I will not forget this.' Then I laughed again—which were my error! I did
not even get a good-night kiss—Joyce slammed the vestibule
door dead in my face. So I went home to my Third Floor Rear
—*and laughed some more*. If I wasn't honored, I sure was tick-
led, and, at least, I ain't stingy like them Sugar-Hillers. They
wouldn't buy none of his art when he could still enjoy the bene-
fits. But me, I'd buy that old man a beer *any time*."

| A Veteran Falls

"It's a sad and sorry thing to see how some of these fellows come back from the war all wounded and crippled up, ain't it?" said Simple. "Last Saturday night I was climbing that 145th Street hill from Eighth Avenue when it was half raining, half sleeting, and cold. I was just thinking about turning into a bar to have me a drink, when I saw a long tall one-legged soldier coming down the hill on crutches, just swinging it, man, like he was in a hurry on one leg.

"He *was* in a hurry because two dopey dames was behind him trying to keep up with him, and it looked like he was disgusted with both of them. Then something kind of sad happened, man. Right in front of the bar under all them neon lights, one of his crutches skidded on the wet sidewalk and that veteran slipped and fell down. His one good leg went out from under him and he went flat on the pavement.

"But this were the other part—both of them women rushed to pick him up. You could see how that soldier was embarrassed, trying to ignore them homely dames, and here he had done fell down. The tall woman bent over and took him by the arm to pull him up from the sidewalk.

"But the little woman hollered, 'Don't you pick him up, Cassie! I'll pick him up, myself. He's mine! He was trying to jump salty with me tonight—but he's mine right on.'

" 'I will *so* pick him up,' yelled the tall woman. 'He's an old flame and I mean from way back! I will pick him up!'

" 'Charlie's more to me than he is to you,' said the little woman, tugging on his other arm. 'I'll pick him up myself.'

"Both of them was pulling and hauling at that one-legged soldier, and the boy was cussing like mad. When he got to his feet, he shook 'em both loose. I handed him his crutches my own self while them women was yapping at each other. The back of his uniform was all muddy and wet and his pants leg folded back over his stump was wet, too. I reckon he must have been on leave from a hospital because you could tell that leg hurt him. He tried to make out like it wasn't nothing happened. 'What's all this fuss these damn women are making? I just fell down, that's all!'

" 'Any man can fall,' I said. But I could see he was trembling and he couldn't help it. He put his hands over the stump of that leg.

"The little woman was standing at the curb yelling, 'Cab! Cab! Cab!' and taking time to turn around to see what the other woman was doing. 'Cassie, you leave that man be, I tell you! . . . Cab! Cab! Cab!'

"But you know on a rainy night how hard it is to get a cab. Meantime, the other woman had run one hand down his shirt front and was trying to give him a kiss. But he pushed her away. So she went to the curb and started yelling cab, too. Then in all that cold old drizzly rain them women started yapping at each other all over again. Man, a woman is something!

" 'I'll get a cab,' the tall one yells.

" 'I'll get it and pay for it, too,' hollered the little one. 'I know Charlie snuck off from me to go see you today. But I'm the one he comes to first—like this afternoon—first—soon as he gets in town.'

" 'That's what you think,' says the tall woman. 'Wheeeeeooo! Cab!'

" 'I'm the one he gets a dollar from when he needs it most,' yaps the little chick. 'Long as I'm working, Charlie'll eat! I'll get this cab and pay for it. Do you hear me, Cassie?'

"Some old agitating Negro standing in the doorway of the bar yells, 'One of you women better hurry up and get that taxi or won't neither one of you-all have no man. He'll be gone.'

"The soldier-boy did start to walk, but that leg—he must of hurt them nerve ends when he fell. I imagine it was like a aching tooth and he couldn't keep from grabbing it. Leaning on them crutches trying to keep his hands from going to that sawed-off leg, but he couldn't keep from grabbing it. He just stood still. I didn't know what to say to him, so I thought I would take

my handkerchief and wipe some of the wet off the back of his coat.

"But he said, 'Get away, man!'

"It was old Dad Martin what owns that little hamburger stand that did the best thing. Dad come out and said, 'Son, anybody could fall down on this wet night. Is you hurt?'

" 'Naw, Dad, I just slipped, that's all.'

" 'I mean, did it hurt your feelings?' Dad said.

" 'No,' said the soldier.

" 'Then everything's all right,' the old man said.

"Just then Cassie hollered, 'Baby, here's the cab! Come on!'

"The little woman beat Cassie to him, though. 'Here's our taxi, honey! Come on, Charlie, we got a cab.'

" 'You better set between them two women else they liable to tear each other's eyes out,' yells that agitating old Negro in the bar door.

" 'Everything's under control,' said the soldier, 'don't worry.'

"He pulled his own self up in that cab. But the women jumped in after him and there he was between them when the taxi pulled off in the rain—and they was still fussing over who he belonged to. It was funny—still and yet it wasn't funny either.

"You can laugh at a man when he falls if he's got two legs, but I couldn't laugh at him. Couldn't nobody laugh at that soldier like they would laugh at you and me if we fell down trying to ignore a couple of women. That's why it was kinder hard for that boy to take. I aimed to order a beer when I got in the bar but my mouth said, 'A double whiskey!' It damn sure did, after that boy fell down."

| High Bed

"I TOLD you you should take care of yourself," I said to Simple as I sat down beside his bed. "Running around half high in all this cold weather. If you had taken care of yourself, and not gotten all run down, you would not be here now in this hospital with pneumonia."

"If I had taken care of myself," said Simple, "I would not have these pretty nurses taking care of me."

"Everything has its compensations, I admit. But look at the big hospital bill you will have when you get out."

"Just let me draw two or three weeks' pay or hit one number, and I will settle it," said Simple. "But what worries me is when am I going to get out?"

"You should have worried about that before you got in," I said. "And you will never get out if you do not observe the rules and stop telling folks to bring you beer and pigs' feet and things you are not supposed to have."

"You didn't bring me that Three Feathers I told you to bring," said Simple. "And the nurse would not let me finish that little old sausage Zarita brought in her pocketbook yesterday. She said it would be a bad example for the rest of the patients in this ward. So I have not broken any rules. But if you gimme a cigarette, I sure will smoke it."

"I will not give you a cigarette," I said.

"O.K.," said Simple. "You will want me to do something for you someday."

"You have everything you need right here in this hospital," I said. "You know if you really needed something you are supposed to have, I would bring it."

"They feed me pretty good in here," said Simple. "Only one thing I do not like—they won't let you take your own bath."

"And what is wrong about that?"

"Well, the morning nurse, she comes in before day A.M. and grabs you by the head. When she gets through scrubbing your ears they feel just like they have been shucked. Ain't nobody washed my ears so hard since I got out from under my mother."

"Sleepy-headed as you are, I guess she is just trying to wake you up."

"And, man," said Simple, "when she washes your stomach, it tickles. I told her I was ticklish and not to touch me nowhere near my ribs, nor my navel."

"I do not see why a big husky fellow like you should be ticklish."

"I do not mind when she rubs my back, though. That alcohol sure smells fine."

"Reminds you of something to drink, I presume?"

"It do feel sort of cool and good like the last drop of a gin rickey. But I don't want to think of gin rickey now, pal."

"I shouldn't think you would," I said. "That is why you are here—becoming intoxicated and forgetting your overcoat."

"That is not true," said Simple. "I got mad. Joyce made me so mad I walked out of the house at one A.M. without my coat and the wind was frantic that night. Zero! But being drunk had nothing to do with it. A woman aggravates a man, drunk or sober. But Joyce is sorry now that she ever mentioned Zarita. She come here yesterday and told me so. She is sorry she done caused me to get pneumonia. She knows Zarita ain't nothing to me even if she did accidentally see me talking to her through the vestibule. But I do not want to discuss how come I am in this hospital. I *am* here. I *am* sick. And I cannot get out of this bed. Why do you reckon they make these hospital beds so high?"

"To keep people from getting out easily," I said.

"Well, they are so high that if a man ever *fell* out, he would break his neck. I am even afraid to turn over in this bed. I naturally sleeps restless, but this bed is so high I am scared to sleep restless, so I lay here stiff as a board and don't close my eyes. I mean I am really stiff when morning comes! This would be a right nice bed if it was not so narrow and so hard and so high."

"Everything must be wrong with that. bed," I said, "to hear you tell it."

"I don't see why they don't make hospital beds more comfortable. In a place where people have to *stay* in bed, they ought to have a feather mattress like Aunt Lucy used to have."

"If hospital beds were that comfortable," I said, "folks might never want to go home."

"I would, because I don't like even a pretty nurse to be washing my ears. That is one reason I was glad when I growed up, so I could wash my own ears, and comb my own head."

"Has any nurse here tried to comb your hair?" I inquired.

"These nurses are not crazy," said Simple. "My head is tender! Man, nobody here better not try to pull a comb through my hair but me. If they do, I will get up out of this bed—no matter how high it is—and carry my bohunkus on home."

"Calm down," I said. "You'll run your temperature up. Nobody is going to comb your hair, man."

"You can certainly think of some unpleasant subjects," said Simple. "Even if I was dying, I would comb my own head— and better not nobody else touch it! But say, boy, if you want to do me a favor, when you come back bring me a stocking-cap to make my hair lay down. That is one thing these white folks do not have in this hospital. I wonder if it is against the rules to wear a nylon stocking-cap in this here high bed? If it ain't you tell Joyce to send me one."

"Very well."

"Also a small drink, because you know it's a long time between drinks in a hospital. And sometimes I don't have nothing to do but lay here and think. The other day I got to thinking about the Age of the Air when rocket planes get to be common."

"What did you think about it?"

"About how women will have a hard time keeping up with their husbands then," said Simple.

"How's that?"

"Mens will have girl friends all over the world, not just around the corner where a wife can find out—and sue for divorce. Why, when rocket planes get to be as cheap as Fords, I'm liable to go calling in Cairo any week end."

"Joyce would be right behind you," I said.

"I expect so. Not even in a rocket plane could I keep Joyce from knowing my whereabouts. But you know what I am talking about is true, and in the future it is going to be even better. In 1975, when a man can get in a rocket plane and shoot through the stratosphere a thousand miles a minute—when he can get to London sooner than I can get from Harlem to Times Square—you know, and I know, a guy will meet some woman he likes halfway across the earth in Australia and any night after dinner he will shoot over there to see her while he tells his wife he's going out to play pool. He can be back by bedtime."

"Your imagination is certainly far-fetched," I said.

"No place will be far-fetched when them rocket planes gets perfected," said Simple. "If I can afford it, I sure will own one myself. Then, in my rocket I will rock! You won't see me hanging around no Harlem bars no more. Saturday nights I will rock on down to Rio and drink coconut milk and gin with them Brazilian chicks whilst dancing a samba. Sunday morning I will zoom on over to Africa and knock out some palm wine before I come back to Seventh Avenue around noon to eat some of Joyce's chicken and dumplings.

"Joyce will say, 'Jess, where you been this morning with your hair blowed back so slick?'

"I will say, 'Nowheres, baby, but just out for a little ride in the clouds to clean the cobwebs out of my brain. I drunk a little too much in Hong Kong last night. And don't you know, after them Chinese bars closed the sky was so crowded, it took me nearly ten minutes to fly back to Harlem to get an aspirin. So this morning, baby, I didn't fly nowheres but straight up in them nice cool clouds for a breath of fresh air, then right back home to you.' "

"What are you going to say if Joyce smells that African palm wine on your breath?" I asked.

"How do you know anybody can smell palm wine?" said Simple. "Maybe by that time somebody will have invented something to take the scent out of *all* lickers anyhow. Besides, I won't be drinking enough to get drunk. I'd be very careful with my rocket plane so as not to run into some planet, neither no star. I will keep a clear head in the air."

"That is more than you keep on earth, except when you're in the hospital."

"There you go low-rating me," sighed Simple. "But listen, daddy-o, such another scrambling of races as there is going to be when they gets that rocket plane perfected! Why, when a man can shoot from Athens, Georgia, to Athens, Greece, in less than an hour, you know there is going to be intermarriage. I am liable to marry a Greek myself."

"Are there any colored Greeks?"

"I would not be prejudiced toward color," said Simple, rising on his pillow, "and if I did not like the licker they drink in Greece, I would fly to Nagasaki and drink saki. Or I might come back to Harlem and have a beer with you."

"If you're doing all that flying around, what makes you think I would remain here in Harlem? I might be out in my rocket, too."

"Great stuff, daddy-o! We might bump into each other over London—who knows? Because I sure would be rocking through the sky. Why, man, I would rock so far away from this color line in the U.S.A., till it wouldn't be funny. I might even build me a garage on Mars and a mansion on Venus. On summer nights I would scoot down the Milky Way just to cool myself off. I would not have no old-time jet-propelled plane either. My plane would run on atom power. This earth I would not bother with no more. No, buddy-o! The sky would be my roadway and the stars my stopping place. Man, if I had a rocket plane, I would rock off into space and be solid gone. Gone. Real gone! I mean *gone!*"

"I think you are gone now," I said. "Out of your head."

"Not quite," said Simple.

Final Fear

THE next time I visited Simple, I found him convalescent, slightly ashy and a bit thinner, sitting up in bed, but low in spirits. He was gazing sadly at the inscription on a comic book, *"Lovingly yours, Joyce."*

"She has just been here," he said, "and I feel like I am going to have a relapse."

"If that's the way visitors affect you, then I will depart."

"Not all visitors," said Simple, "just Joyce. I love that girl."

"Then why does a visit from her get you down?"

"A woman brought me into this world," said Simple, "and I do believe women will take me out. They is the fault of my being in this hospital with pneumonia because my doctor told me the mind is worse than my body and from the looks of my chest, I must of been worrying."

"So you too have one of those fashionable psychosomatic illnesses," I said.

"No, it's Zarita and Isabel," said Simple, "plus Joyce. That wife of mine called me up New Year's Eve just when I was starting out to have some fun—long-distance, *collect,* from Baltimore—just to tell me that since another year was starting, she was tired of being tied to me and not being *with* me. She told me again either to come back to her or else get her a divorce. I said which would she rather have after all these years, me or the divorce.

"She said, 'Divorce!'

"I said, 'How much do a divorce cost nowadays?'

"She said, 'Three Hundred Dollars.'

"That is what I am feeling bad about, buddy-o. If I had not paid Five Dollars to marry that woman in the past, I would not have to pay Three Hundred now to get loose."

"Maybe it would be cheaper to go back to her."

"My nerves is wrecked," said Simple. "That woman is incontemptible. She has caused me mental anguish, also a headache. I will not go back. Besides, Joyce has been too good to me for me to cut out now. You see them flowers she brought to this hospital, also these two comic books and four packs of chewing gum. But Joyce is also a headache."

"You are just weak from your recent illness," I said.

"You mean Joyce is weak for me," corrected Simple. "Sitting right here on this bed today, she told me she is not built of bricks. Joyce says she's got a heart, also a soul, and is respectable. Joyce swears she is getting tired of me coming to her house so regular and everybody asking when is we gonna marry. She says I've been setting in her parlor too late for her respectability.

"I said, 'One o'clock ain't late.'

"She said, 'No, but two and three o'clock is, and you sure can't stay till four.'

"I said, 'Baby, it ain't what you do, it's how you do it.' But she disagreed.

"She said, 'No, it ain't what you do—it's what folks *think* you do. When folks see you coming out of my place at two-three-four o'clock in the morning, you know what they think—even if it ain't so. I have been knowing you too long not to be married to you. It were not just day before yesterday that we met,' Joyce says."

"Then a divorce would be good for both of you," I interjected. "You could get all those day-before-yesterdays straightened out."

"Days is like stair-steps," said Simple. "If you stumbled on the first day yesterday, you liable to be still falling tomorrow. I have stumbled."

"Anyhow," I said, "it is better to fall up than to fall down. You can get things straightened out when you get well."

"No matter what a man does, sick or well, something is always liable to happen," said Simple, "especially if you are colored."

"Race has nothing to do with it," I said. "In this uncertain world, something unpleasant can happen to anybody, colored or white, regardless of race."

"Um-hum," said Simple. "You can be robbed and mugged in the night—even choked."

"That's right," I said, "or you can get poisoned from drinking King Kong after hours."

"Sure can," said Simple. "Or you *can* go crazy from worriation."

"Or lose your job."

"Else your money on the horses."

"Or on numbers."

"Or policy."

"Or on Chinese lottery, if you live on the Coast."

"Or poker or blackjack or pokino or tonk. And you ain't mentioned Georgia skin," said Simple.

"I can't play skin," I said.

"It's a rugged card game," said Simple. "If I had never learnt it, I might be rich today. But skin's a mere skimption compared to some of the things that can happen to a man. For instant, if you was a porter, your train could wreck. If you was in the Merchant Marines, your boat could sink. Or if you're a aviator, you're liable to run into the Empire State Building or Abyssinia Baptist Church and bust up your plane. It is awful, man, what can happen to you in this life!"

"You talk as though you've had a hard time," I said. "Have any of those things ever happened to you?"

"What're you talking about?" cried Simple, sitting bolt upright in bed. "Not only am I half dead right now from pneumonia, but everything else *has* happened to me! I have been cut, shot, stabbed, run over, hit by a car, and tromped by a horse. I have also been robbed, fooled, deceived, two-timed, double-crossed, dealt seconds, and mighty near blackmailed—but I am still here!"

"You're a tough man," I said.

"I have been fired, laid off, and last week given an indefinite vacation, also Jim Crowed, segregated, barred out, insulted, eliminated, called black, yellow, and red, locked in, locked out, locked up, also left holding the bag. I have been caught in the rain, caught in raids, caught short with my rent, and caught with another man's wife. In my time I have been caught—but I am still here!"

"You have suffered," I said.

"Suffered!" cried Simple. "My mama should have named me Job instead of Jess Semple. I have been underfed, underpaid, undernourished, and everything but *undertaken*. I been bit by dogs, cats, mice, rats, poll parrots, fleas, chiggers, bedbugs, granddaddies, mosquitoes, and a gold-toothed woman."

"Great day in the morning!"

"That ain't all," said Simple. "In this life I been abused, confused, misused, accused, false-arrested, tried, sentenced, paroled, blackjacked, beat, third-degreed and near about lynched!"

"Anyhow your health has been good—up to now," I said.

"Good health nothing," objected Simple, waving his hands, kicking off the cover, and swinging his feet out of bed. "I done had everything from flat feet to a flat head. Why, man, I was born with the measles! Since then I had smallpox, chickenpox, whooping cough, croup, appendicitis, athlete's foot, tonsillitis, arthritis, backache, mumps, and a strain—but I am still here. Daddy-o, I'm still here!"

"Having survived all that, what are you afraid of, now that you are almost over pneumonia?"

"I'm afraid," said Simple, "I will die before my time."

There Ought to be a Law

"I HAVE been up North a long time, but it looks like I just cannot learn to like white folks."

"I don't care to hear you say that," I said, "because there are a lot of good white people in this world."

"Not enough of them," said Simple, waving his evening paper. "If there was, they would make this American country good. But just look at what this paper is full of."

"You cannot dislike *all* white people for what the bad ones do," I said. "And I'm certain you don't dislike them all because once you told me yourself that you wouldn't wish any harm to befall Mrs. Roosevelt."

"Mrs. Roosevelt is different," said Simple.

"There now! You see, you are talking just as some white people talk about the Negroes they *happen* to like. They are always 'different.' That is a provincial way to think. You need to get around more."

"You mean among white folks?" asked Simple. "How can I make friends with white folks when they got Jim Crow all over the place?"

"Then you need to open your mind."

"I have near about *lost* my mind worrying with them," said Simple. "In fact, they have hurt my soul."

"You certainly feel bad tonight," I said. "Maybe you need a drink."

"Nothing in a bottle will help my soul," said Simple, "but I will take a drink."

"Maybe it will help your mind," I said. "Beer?"

"Yes."

"Glass or bottle?"

"A bottle because it contains two glasses," said Simple, spreading his paper out on the bar. "Look here at these headlines, man, where Congress is busy passing laws. While they're making all these laws, it looks like to me they ought to make one setting up a few Game Preserves for Negroes."

"What ever gave you that fantastic idea?" I asked.

"A movie short I saw the other night," said Simple, "about how the government is protecting wild life, preserving fish and game, and setting aside big tracts of land where nobody can fish, shoot, hunt, nor harm a single living creature with furs, fins, or feathers. But it did not show a thing about Negroes."

"I thought you said the picture was about 'wild life.' Negroes are not wild."

"No," said Simple, "but we need protection. This film showed how they put aside a thousand acres out West where the buffaloes roam and nobody can shoot a single one of them. If they do, they get in jail. It also showed some big National Park with government airplanes dropping food down to the deers when they got snowed under and had nothing to eat. The government protects and takes care of buffaloes and deers—which is more than the government does for me or my kinfolks down South. Last month they lynched a man in Georgia and just today I see where the Klan has whipped a Negro within a inch of his life in Alabama. And right up North here in New York a actor is suing a apartment house that won't even let a Negro go up on the elevator to see his producer. That is what I mean by Game Preserves for Negroes—Congress ought to set aside some place where we can go and nobody can jump on us and beat us, neither lynch us nor Jim Crow us every day. Colored folks rate as much protection as a buffalo, or a deer."

"You have a point there," I said.

"This here movie showed great big beautiful lakes with signs up all around:

NO FISHING—STATE GAME PRESERVE

But it did not show a single place with a sign up:

NO LYNCHING

It also showed flocks of wild ducks settling down in a nice green meadow behind a government sign that said:

NO HUNTING

It were nice and peaceful for them fish and ducks. There ought to be some place where it is nice and peaceful for me, too, even if I am not a fish or a duck.

"They showed one scene with two great big old long-horn elks locking horns on a Game Preserve somewhere out in Wyoming, fighting like mad. Nobody bothered them elks or tried to stop them from fighting. But just let me get in a little old fist fight here in this bar, they will lock me up and the Desk Sergeant will say, 'What are you colored boys doing, disturbing the peace?' Then they will give me thirty days and fine me twice as much as they would a white man for doing the same thing. There ought to be some place where I can fight in peace and not get fined them high fines."

"You disgust me," I said. "I thought you were talking about a place where you could be quiet and compose your mind. Instead, you are talking about fighting."

"I would like a place where I could do both," said Simple. "If the government can set aside some spot for a elk *to be a elk* without being bothered, or a fish *to be a fish* without getting hooked, or a buffalo *to be a buffalo* without being shot down, there ought to be some place in this American country where a Negro can be a Negro without being Jim Crowed. There ought to be a law. The next time I see my congressman, I am going to tell him to introduce a bill for Game Preserves for Negroes."

"The Southerners would filibuster it to death," I said.

"If we are such a problem to them Southerners," said Simple, "I should think they would want some place to preserve us out of their sight. But then, of course, you have to take into consideration that if the Negroes was taken out of the South, who would they lynch? What would they do for sport? A Game Preserve is for to keep people from bothering anything that is living.

"When that movie finished, it were sunset in Virginia and it showed a little deer and its mama laying down to sleep. Didn't nobody say, 'Get up, deer, you can't sleep here,' like they would to me if I was to go to the White Sulphur Springs Hotel."

" 'The foxes have holes, and the birds of the air have nests; but the Son of man hath not where to lay his head.' "

"That is why I want a Game Preserve for Negroes," said Simple.

| Income Tax

On April fourteenth, just the day before his taxes came due, Simple was sitting in a booth across from the bar, figuring, and each time he figured he put his pencil in his mouth.

"Joyce's Fifty-Nine-Dollar birthday wrist watch on time, plus Two Dollars and Seventy-Five Cents cab fare to the Bronx for that wedding reception to which we was late, minus Twenty-Nine Dollars and Eleven Cents old-age dependency insurance, plus miscellaneous Five Hundred and Seventy-Nine Dollars and Twenty-Two Cents, minus One Dollar and Fifteen Cents work-clothes deduction—man! I ain't *never* gonna get it straight."

"What's all this high finance," I said, "concerning birthday watches and nondeductible cab fare?"

"Income tax," said Simple. "I deducts all."

"Pshaw! Just think of the movie stars and Wall Street people who really have to worry about income tax," I said.

"I don't care nothing about them folks," answered Simple. "All I know is that tomorrow the man is *demanding*—not asking—for money that I not only don't have—but ain't even seen."

"The Bureau of Internal Revenue seldom makes mistakes, Jess. If it does, they've got people to check and recheck, and if they miscalculate even as little as two cents, you'll eventually get it back."

"I just like to check for myself," said Simple. "So I been figuring on this thing for three days and it still don't come out right. Instead of them owing me, looks like I owe them something which I don't know where I'm going to get."

"Why didn't you just take your figures to a public accountant and let him figure it out for you?"

"Man, I took 'em to one of them noteriety republicans once and he charged me so much I got discouraged."

"Maybe next year things will be different, old man. According to the papers, Congress is considering a bill to reduce taxes."

"By the time Congress convenes, I'll be without means," said Simple. "Besides, I don't get enough for my taxes. I wants to vote down South. It's hell to pay taxes when I can't even vote down home."

" 'Taxation without representation is tyranny,' so the books say."

"Sure is!" said Simple. "I don't see why Negroes down South should pay taxes a-tall. You know Buddy Jones' brother, what was wounded in the 92nd in Italy, don't you? Well, he was telling me about how bad them rednecks treated him when he was in the army in Mississippi. He said he don't never want to see no parts of the South again. He were born and raised in Yonkers and not used to such stuff. Now his nerves is shattered. He can't even stand a Southern accent no more."

"Jim Crow shock," I said. "I guess it can be as bad as shell shock."

"It can be worse," said Simple. "Jim Crow happens to men every day down South, whereas a man's not in a battle every day. Buddy's brother has been out of the army three years and he's still sore about Mississippi."

"What happened to him down there?"

"I will tell it to you like it was told to me," said Simple. "You know Buddy's brother is a taxicab driver, don't you? Well, the other day he was telling me he was driving his cab downtown on Broadway last week when a white man hailed him, got in, and then said in one of them slow Dixie drawls, "Bouy, tek me ovah to Fefty-ninth Street and Fefth Avahnue.'

"Buddy's brother told him, 'I ain't gonna take you nowhere. Get outta my cab—and quick!'

"The white man didn't know what was the matter so he says, 'Why?'

"Buddy's brother said, 'Because I don't like Southerners, that's why! You treated me so mean when I was in the army down South that I don't never want to see none of you-all no more. And I *sure* don't like to hear you talk. It goes all through me. I spent eighteen months in hell in Mississippi.'

"The white man got red in the face, also mad, and called a cop to make Buddy's brother drive him where he wanted to go. The cop was one of New York's finest, a great big Irishman. The copper listened to the man, then he listened to Buddy's brother. Setting right there in his taxi at 48th and Broadway, Buddy's brother told that cop all about Mississippi, how he was Jim Crowed on the train on the way down going to drill for Uncle Sam, how he was Jim Crowed in camp, also how whenever he had a furlough, him and his colored buddies had to wait and *wait* and WAIT at the camp gate for a bus to get to town because they filled the buses up with white soldiers and the colored soldiers just had to stand behind and wait. Sometimes on payday if there were a big crowd of white soldiers, the colored G.I.'s would never get to town at all.

" 'Officer, I'm telling you,' Buddy's brother said, 'that Mississippi is something! Down South they don't have no nice polices like you. Down South all them white cops want to do is beat a Negro's head, cuss you, and call you names. They do not protect Americans if they are black. They lynched a man five miles down the road from our camp one night and left him hanging there for three days as a warning, so they said, to us Northern Negroes to know how to act in the South, particularly if from New York.'

"Meanwhile the Southern white man who was trying to get the cop to make Buddy's brother drive him over to Fifth Avenue was getting redder and redder. He said, 'You New York Negras need to learn how to act.'

" 'Shut up!' says the cop. 'This man is talking.'

"Buddy's brother talked on. 'Officer,' he says, 'it were so bad in that army camp that I will tell you a story of something that happened to me. They had us colored troops quartered way

down at one end of the camp, six miles back from the gate, up against the levee. One day they sent me to do some yard work up in the white part of the camp. My bladder was always weak, so I had to go to the latrine no sooner than I got there. Everything is separated in Mississippi, even latrines, with signs up WHITE and COLORED. But there wasn't any COLORED latrine anywhere around, so I started to go in one marked WHITE.

" 'A cracker M.P. yelled at me, *"Halt!"*

" 'When I didn't halt—because I couldn't—he drew his gun on me and cocked it. He threatened to shoot me if I went in that WHITE latrine.

" 'Well, he made me so mad, I walked all the way back to my barracks and got a gun myself. I came back and I walked up to that Southern M.P. I said, *"Neither you nor me will never see no Germans nor no Japs if you try to stop me from going in this latrine this morning."*

" 'That white M.P. didn't try to stop me. He just turned pale, and I went in. But by that time, officer, I was so mad I decided to set down and stay awhile. So I did. With my gun on my lap, I just sat—and every time a Southerner came in, I cocked the trigger. Ain't nobody said a word. They just looked at me and walked out. I stayed there as long as I wanted to—black as I am —in that WHITE latrine. Down in Mississippi a colored soldier has to have a gun even to go to the toilet! So, officer, that is why I do not want to ride this man—because he is one of them that wouldn't even let me go in their latrines down South, do you understand?'

" 'Understand?' says the cop. 'Of course, I understand. Be jeezus! It's like that exactly that the damned English did the Irish. Faith, you do not have to haul him. . . . Stranger, get yerself another cab. Scram, now! Quick—before I run you in.'

"That white man hauled tail! And Buddy's brother drove off saluting that cop—and blowing his horn for New York City. But me, if I'd of been there," said Simple, "I would of asked that officer just one thing about Ireland. I would have said, 'Well, before you-all got free—kicked around as you was—did you still have to pay taxes to the British?' "

"I can answer that for you," I said. "Of course, the Irish had to pay taxes. All colonial peoples have to pay taxes to their rulers."

"How do you know?" asked Simple. "You ain't Irish."

"No," I said, "but I read books."

"You don't learn everything in books," said Simple.

"It wouldn't hurt you to read one once in a while," I said.

"Not to change the subject, but I need a beer to help me figure up this income tax," said Simple. "Bartender, a couple of beers on my friend here—who reads books."

"I do not like your tone of voice," I said. "I will not pay for beer to entertain a man who has nothing but contempt for the written word."

"Buddy-o, daddy-o, pal, I do not want to argue with you this evening because I haven't got time. You are colored just like me, so set down and help me figure up my taxes for these white folks. What did you say that book says about taxation?"

"Without representation, it's tyranny."

"If you don't know how to add, subtract, multiply, erase, deduct, steal, stash, save, conceal, and long-divide, it is worse than that," said Simple. "Taxes is *hell!* Buddy-o, here's our beer."

"It seems to me you should understand mathematics," I said. "You've been to school."

"I didn't learn much," said Simple, "which is why I have to run my feet off all day long and work hard. What your head don't *under*stand, your feet have to stand."

"Well, you certainly have opinions about everything under the sun," I said. "You ought to have a newspaper since you have so much to say."

"I can talk," said Simple, "but I can't write."

"Then you ought to be an orator."

"Uh-um, I'm scared of the public. My place is at the bar."

"Of Justice?"

"Justice don't run no bar."

| No Alternative

"MAN, you don't know how I have suffered these last few weeks," Simple groaned into an empty glass. "Joyce's birthday, the Urban League ball we had to go to, income tax, hospital bill, and so forth—"

"What's 'and so forth'?" I asked.

"My landlady," said Simple. "That woman has no respect for her roomers a-tall. In fact, she cares less for her roomers than she does for her dog."

"What kind of dog has she got?"

"A little old houndish kind of dog," said Simple. "But is she crazy about that hound! She will put a roomer out—dead out in the street—when he does not pay his rent, but she does not put out that dog, not even when it chews up her favorite Teddy bear which her second husband give her for her birthday. That dog is her heart. She would feed that dog before she would feed me. When I went down in the kitchen last week to give her my room rent, I saw her hand Trixie a whole chicken leg—and she did not offer me a bite."

"Were you hungry?" I asked.

"I could have used a drumstick," said Simple. "It would have meant more to me than it did to that little fice."

"I gather you do not like dogs."

"I love dogs," said Simple. "When my landlady was laid up with arthritis and scared to get her feet wet, I even took that little old she-hound of hers out two or three times to the park to do its duty—although I would not be seen with no dog like that if it belonged to me. All I got was, 'Thank you, you certainly nice, Mr. Semple.' She used my real last name, all formal and everything. 'You certainly nice, yes, indeed.' But did I get a extra towel when I asked for it? I did not. All I got was, 'Laundries is high and towels is scarce.' Yet I seen her dry that dog on a nice big white bath towel, the likes of which she never give a roomer yet. I don't think that is right, to care less about roomers than you do about a dog, do you?"

"Ties between a dog and its master are often greater than human ties."

"Ties, nothing," said Simple. "That lazy little old mutt don't bring her in a thing, not even a bone. I bring in Ten Dollars rent each and every week—even if it is a little late."

"You got behind though, didn't you, when you weren't working?"

"I *tried* to get behind," said Simple, "but she did not let me get far. I told her they was changing from a ball-bearing plant to a screw factory and it might even take three months. But she said it better not take *three weeks*—do, and she would get eviction orders and evict me. So I had to go to the post office and draw out my little money and lay it on the line. That very evening she says, 'Oh, this poor dog ain't been out of the house in five days, bad as my knees ache.' So me, like a chump, I take it out to the park."

"Why doesn't her husband take care of it?" I asked.

"He runs on the road," said Simple. "When he gets through taking care of white folks, he does not feel like taking care of dogs. Harlem is no place for dogs—people do not have time to look after them."

"True," I said, "but Harlemites love dogs, and there are a great many here."

"Almost as many as there are roomers," agreed Simple. "But it is not good for the dogs, because people work all day and leave the dog by itself. A dog gets lonesome just like a human. He wants to associate with other dogs, but when they take him out, the poor dog is on a leash and cannot run around. They won't even let him rub noses with another dog, or pick out his own tree. Now, that is not good for a dog. For instant, take Trixie, my landlady's hound. Spring is coming. I asked her one day last week had Trixie ever been married.

"My landlady says, 'You mean mated?'

"I says, 'Yes, I was just trying to be polite.'

"She says, 'No, indeed! Trixie is a virgin.'

"Now, ain't that awful! That poor dog never had a chance in

life, which worried me. So I said, 'Next time I take Trixie to the park, I will see that she meets some gentleman dogs.'

"But, man, don't you know that woman hollered like she had been shot. She says, 'No, indeed, you won't! I do not want Trixie all crossed up with no low-breeded curs.'

"I says, 'You must be prejudiced, madam. Is Trixie got a pedigree?'

"My landlady says, 'She is pure Spotted Dutch Brindle.'

"Before I thought, I said, 'Pure mutt.'

"My landlady jumped salty, I mean salty! She reined in Trixie and yelled, 'You will apologize to this dog, Mr. Semple, else leave my house.' "

"Did you apologize to that dog?"

"I had no alternity. Hard as rooms is to find these days, I do not know which is worse, to be a roomer or a dog."

| Springtime

"I wish that spring would come more often now that it is here," said Simple.

"How could it come more often?"

"It could if God had made it that-a-way," said Simple. "I also wish it would last longer."

"It looks as if you would prefer spring all the year around."

"Just most of the year," said Simple. "As it is now, summer comes too soon and winter lasts too long. I do not like real hot weather, neither cold. I like spring."

"Spring is too changeable for me—sometimes hot, sometimes cold."

"I am not talking about that kind of spring," said Simple. "I mean June-time spring when it is just nice and mellow—like a cool drink."

"Of what?"

"Anything," said Simple. "Anything that is strong as the sun

THE BEST OF SIMPLE

and cool as the moon. But I am not talking about drinking now. I am talking about spring. Oh, it is wonderful! It is the time when flowers come out of their buds, birds come out of their nests, bees come out of their hives, Negroes come out of their furnished rooms, and butterflies out of their cocoons."

"Also snakes come out of their holes."

"They is little young snakes," said Simple, "else big old sleepy snakes that ain't woke up good yet till the sun strikes them. That is why I do not like summer, because the sun is so hot it makes even a cold snake mad. Spring is my season. Summer was made to give you a taste of what hell is like. Fall was made for the clothing-store people to coin money because every human has to buy a overcoat, muffler, heavy socks, and gloves. Winter was made for landladies to charge high rents and keep cold radiators and make a fortune off of poor tenants. But spring! Throw your overcoat on the pawnshop counter, tell the landlady to kiss your foot, open your windows, let the fresh air in. Me, myself, I love spring!

"Why, if I was down home now, daddy-o, I would get out my fishing pole and take me a good old Virginia ham sandwich and go set on the banks of the river all day and just dream and fish and fish and dream. I might have me a big old quart bottle of beer tied on a string down in the water to keep cool, and I would just fish and dream and dream and fish."

"You would not have any job?" I asked.

"I would respect work just like I respected my mother and not hit her a lick. I would be far away from all this six A.M. alarm-clock business, crowded subways, gulping down my coffee to get to the man's job in time, and working all day shut up inside where you can't even smell the spring—and me still smelling ether and worried about my winter hospital bill. If I was down home, buddy-o, I would pull off my shoes and let my toes air and just set on the riverbank and dream and fish and fish and dream, and I would not worry about no job."

"Why didn't you stay down home when you were there?"

"You know why I didn't stay," said Simple. "I did not like them white folks and they did not like me. Maybe if it wasn't for white folks, I would've stayed down South where spring comes earlier than it do up here. White folks is the cause of a lot of inconveniences in my life."

"They've even driven you away from an early spring."

"It do not come as early in Harlem as it does down South," said Simple, "but it comes. And there ain't no white folks living can keep spring from coming. It comes to Harlem the same as it does downtown, too. Nobody can keep spring out of Harlem. I stuck my head out the window this morning and spring kissed me bang in the face. Sunshine patted me all over the head. Some little old birds was flying and playing on the garbage cans down in the alley, and one of them flew up to the Third Floor Rear and looked at me and cheeped, 'Good morning!'

"I said, 'Bird, howdy-do!'

"Just then I heard my next-door roomer come out of the bathroom so I had to pull my head in from that window and rush to get to the toilet to wash my face before somebody else got there because I did not want to be late to work this morning since today is payday. New York is just rush, rush, rush! But, oh, brother, if I were down home."

"I know—you would just fish and dream and dream and fish."

"And dream and fish and fish and dream!" said Simple. "If spring was to last forever, as sure as my name is Jess, I would just fish and dream."

| Last Whipping

WHEN I went by his house one Sunday morning to pick up my Kodak that he had borrowed, Simple was standing in the middle of the floor in his shirttail imitating a minister winding up his Sunday morning sermon, gestures and all.

He intoned, " 'Well, I looked and I saw a great beast! And that great beast had its jaws open ready to clamp down on my mortal soul. But I knowed if it was to clamp, ah, my soul would escape and go to glory. Amen! So I was not afraid. My body was afraid, a-a-ah, but my soul was not afraid. My soul said whatsoever you may do to my behind, a-a-ah, beast, you *cannot* harm my soul. Amen! No, Christians! That beast *cannot* tear your immortal soul. That devil in the form of a crocodile, the form of a alligator with a leather hide that slippeth and slideth through the bayous swamp—that alligator *cannot* tear your soul!' "

"You really give a good imitation of a preacher," I said. "But come on and get dressed and let's go, since you say you left my Kodak at Joyce's. I didn't stop by here to hear you preach."

"I am saying that to say this," said Simple, "because that is the place in the sermon where my old Aunt Lucy jumped up shouting and leapt clean across the pulpit rail and started to preaching herself, right along with the minister.

"She hollered, 'No-ooo-oo-o! Hallelujah, no! It cannot tear your soul. Sometimes the devil comes in human form,' yelled Aunt Lucy, 'sometimes it be's born right into your own family. Sometimes the devil be's your own flesh and kin—and he try your soul—but your soul he cannot tear! Sometimes you be's forced to tear his hide *before* he tears your soul. Amen!'

"Now, Aunt Lucy were talking about *me* that morning when she said 'devil.' That is what I started to tell you."

"Talking about you, why?" I asked.

"Because I had been up to some devilment, and she had done said she was gonna whip me come Monday. Aunt Lucy were so Christian she did not believe in whipping nobody on a Sunday."

"What had you done?"

"Oh, I had just taken one of her best laying hens and give it to a girl who didn't even belong to our church; to roast for her Sunday school picnic, because this old girl said she was aiming to picnic *me*—except that she didn't have nothing good to eat to put in her basket. I was trying to jive this old gal, you know —I was young—so I just took one of Aunt Lucy's hens and give her."

"Why didn't you pick out a pullet that wasn't laying?"

"That hen was the biggest, fattest chicken in the pen—and I wanted that girl to have plenty to pull out of her basket at that picnic so folks would make a great big admiration over her and me."

"How did your Aunt Lucy find out about the hen?"

"Man, you know womenfolks can't keep no secret! That girl told another girl, the other girl told her cousin, the cousin told her mama, her mama told Aunt Lucy—and Aunt Lucy woke me up Sunday morning with a switch in her hand."

"Weren't you too old to be whipped by then?"

"Of course, I was too old to whip—sixteen going on seventeen, big as a ox. But Aunt Lucy did not figure I was grown yet. And she took her duty hard—because she always said the last thing my mother told her when she died was to raise me right."

"What did you do when you saw the switch?"

"Oh, I got all mannish, man. I said, 'Aunt Lucy, you ain't gonna whip me no more. I's a man—and you ain't gonna whip me.'

"Aunt Lucy said, 'Yes, I is, too, Jess. I will whip you until you gets grown enough to know how to act like a man—not just *look* like one. You know you had no business snatching my hen right off her nest and giving it to that low-life hussy what had no better sense than to take it, knowing you ain't got nowhere to get no hen except out of *my* henhouse. Were this not Sunday, I would whale you in a inch of your life before you could get out of that bed.'"

"Aunt Lucy was angry," I commented.

"She was," said Simple. "And big as I was, I was scared. But I was meaning not to let her whip me, even if I had to snatch that sapling out of her hand."

"So what happened on Monday morning?"

"Aunt Lucy waited until I got up, dressed, and washed my face. Then she called me. 'Jess!' I knowed it were whipping time. Just when I was aiming to snatch that switch out of her hand, I seed that Aunt Lucy was crying when she told me to come there. I said 'Aunt Lucy, what you crying for?'

"She said, 'I am crying 'cause here you is a man, and don't know how to act right yet, and I done did my best to raise you so you would grow up good. I done wore out so many switches on your back, still you tries my soul. But it ain't *my* soul I'm

thinking of, son, it's yourn. Jess, I wants you to carry yourself right and 'sociate with peoples what's decent and be a good boy. You understand me? I's getting too old to be using my strength like this. Here!' she hollered, 'bend over and lemme whip you one more time!' "

"Did she whip you?"

"She whipped me—because I bent," said Simple. "When I seen her crying, I would have let her kill me before I raised my hand. When she got through, I said, 'Aunt Lucy, you ain't gonna have to whip me no more. I ain't gonna give you no cause. I do not mind to be beat. But I do not *never* want to see you cry no more—so I am going to do my best to do right from now on and not try your soul. And I am sorry about that hen.'

"And you know, man, from that day to this, I have tried to behave myself. Aunt Lucy is gone to glory this morning, but if she is looking down, she knows that is true. That was my last whipping. But it wasn't the whipping that taught me what I needed to know. It was because she cried—and cried. When peoples care for you and cry for you, they can straighten out your soul. Ain't that right, boy?"

"Yes," I said, "that's right."

| Seeing Double

"I wonder why it is we have two of one thing, and only one of others."

"For instance?"

"We have two lungs," said Simple, "but only one heart. Two eyes, but only one mouth. Two——"

"Feet, but only one body," I said.

"I was not going to say *feet*," said Simple. "But since you have taken the words out of my mouth, go ahead."

"Human beings have two shoulders but only one neck."

"And two ears but only one head," said Simpl .

"What on earth would you want with two heads?"

"I could sleep with one and stay awake with the other," explained Simple. "Just like I got two nostrils, I would also like to have two mouths, then I could eat with one mouth while I am talking with the other. Joyce always starts an argument while we are eating, anyhow. That Joyce can talk and eat all at once."

"Suppose Joyce had two mouths, too," I said. "She could double-talk you."

"I would not keep company with a woman that had two mouths," said Simple. "But I would like to have two myself."

"If you had two mouths, you would have to have two noses also," I said, "and it would not make much sense to have two noses, would it?"

"No," said Simple, "I reckon it wouldn't. Neither would I like to have two chins to have to shave. A chin is no use for a thing. But there is one thing I sure would like to have two of. Since I have—"

"Since you have two eyes, I know you would like to have two faces—one in front and one behind—so you could look at all those pretty women on the street both going and coming."

"That would be idealistic," said Simple, "but that is *not* what I was going to say. You always cut me off. So you go ahead and talk."

"I know you wish you had two stomachs," I said, "so you could eat more of Joyce's good cooking."

"No, I do *not* wish I had two stomachs," said Simple. "I can put away enough food in one belly to mighty near wreck my pocketbook—with prices as high as a cat's back in a dogfight. So I do not need two stomachs. Neither do I need two navels on the stomach I got. What use are they? But there is one thing I sure wish I had two of."

"Two gullets?" I asked.

"Two gullets is *not* what I wish I had at all," said Simple. "Let me talk! *I wish I had two brains.*"

"Two brains! Why?"

"So I could think with one, and let the other one rest, man, that's why. I am tired of trying to figure out how to get ahead in this world. If I had two brains, I could think with one brain while the other brain was asleep. I could plan with one while the other brain was drunk. I could think about the Dodgers with one, and my future with the other. As it is now, there is too much in this world for one brain to take care of alone. I have thought so much with my one brain that it is about wore out. In fact, I need a rest right now. So let's drink up and talk about something pleasant. Two beers are on me tonight. Draw up to the bar."

"I was just at the bar," I said, "and Tony has nothing but bottles tonight, no draft."

"Then, daddy-o, they're on *you*," said Simple. "I only got two dimes—and one of them is a Roosevelt dime I do not wish to spend. Had I been thinking, I would have remembered that Roosevelt dime. When I get my other brain, it will keep track of all such details."

| Simple on Military Integration

"Now, the way I understand it," said Simple one Monday evening when the bar was nearly empty and the juke box silent, "it's been written down a long time ago that all men are borned equal and everybody is entitled to life and liberty while pursuing happiness. It's in the Constitution, also Declaration of Independence, so I do not see why it has to be resolved all over again."

"Who is resolving it all over?" I asked.

"Some white church convention—I read in the papers where they have resolved all that over and the Golden Rule, too, also that Negroes should be treated right. It looks like to me white folks better stop resolving and get to *doing*. They have resolved enough. *Resolving ain't solving.*"

"What do you propose that they do?"

"The white race has got a double duty to us," said Simple. "They ought to start treating us right. They also ought to make up for how bad they have treated us in the past."

"You can't blame anybody for history," I said.

"No," said Simple, "but you can blame folks if they don't do something about history! History was yesterday, times gone. Yes. But now that colored folks are willing to let bygones be bygones, this ain't no time to be Jim Crowing nobody. This is a new day."

"Maybe that is why they are resolving to do better," I said.

"I keep telling you, it has come time to stop *resolving!*" said Simple. "They have been *resolving* for two hundred years. I do not see how come they need to *resolve* any more. I say, they need to *solve.*"

"How?"

"By treating us like humans," said Simple, "that's how!"

"They don't treat each other like human beings," I said, "so how do you expect them to treat you that way?"

"White folks do not Jim Crow each other," said Simple, "neither in past have a segregated army—except for me."

"No, maybe not," I said, "but they blasted each other down with V-bombs during the war."

"To be shot down is bad for the body," said Simple, "but to be Jim Crowed is worse for the spirit. Besides, speaking of war, in the next war I want to see Negroes pinning medals on white men."

"Medals? What have medals to do with anything?"

"A lot," said Simple, "because every time I saw a picture in the colored papers of colored soldiers receiving medals in the last war, a white officer was always doing the pinning. I have not yet seen a picture in *no* papers of a *colored* officer pinning a medal on a white soldier. Do you reckon I will ever see such a picture?"

"I don't know anything about the army's system of pinning on medals," I said.

"I'll bet there isn't a white soldier living who ever got a medal from a colored officer," said Simple.

"Maybe not, but I don't get your point. If a soldier is brave enough to get a medal, what does it matter who pins it on?"

"It may not matter to the soldiers," said Simple, "but it matters to *me.* I have never yet seen no *colored* general pinning a medal on a *white* private. That is what I want to see."

"Colored generals did not command white soldiers in the last war," I said, "which is no doubt why they didn't pin medals on them."

"I want to see colored generals commanding white soldiers, then," said Simple.

"You may want to see it, but how can you see it when it just does not take place?"

"In the next war it must and should take place," said Simple, "because if these white folks are gonna have another war, they better give us some generals. I know if I was in the army, I would like to command white troops. In fact, I would like to be in charge of a regiment from Mississippi."

"Are you sober?" I asked.

"I haven't had but one drink today."

"Then why on earth would you want to be in charge of a white regiment from Mississippi?"

"They had white officers from Mississippi in charge of Negroes—so why shouldn't I be in charge of whites? Huh? I would really make 'em toe the line! I know some of them Southerners had rather die than to *left face* for a colored man, buddy-o. But they would *left face* for me."

"What would you do if they wouldn't *left face*?"

"Court-martial them," said Simple. "After they had set in the stockade for six months, I would bring them Mississippi white boys out, and I would say once more, '*Left face!*' I bet they would *left face* then! Else I'd court-martial them again."

"You have a very good imagination," I said, "also a sadistic one."

"I can see myself now in World War III," said Simple, "leading my Mississippi troops into action. I would do like all the other generals do, and stand way back on a hill somewheres and look through my spyglasses and say, 'Charge on! Mens, charge on!' Then I would watch them Dixiecrat boys go—like true sons of the old South, mowing down the enemy.

"When my young white lieutenants from Vicksburg jeeped back to Headquarters to deliver their reports in person to me, they would say, 'General Captain, sir, we have taken two more enemy positions.'

"I would say, 'Mens, return to your companies—and tell 'em to *charge on!*'

"Next day, when I caught up to 'em, I would pin medals on their chests for bravery. Then I would have my picture taken in front of all my fine white troops—*me*—the first black American general to pin medals on white soldiers from Mississippi. It would be in every paper in the world—the great news event of World War III."

"It would certainly be news," I said.

"Doggone if it wouldn't," said Simple. "It would really be news! You see what I mean by *solving*—not just resolving. I will've done solved."

| Blue Evening

WHEN I walked into the bar and saw him on the corner stool alone, I could tell something was wrong.

"Another hangover?"

"Nothing that simple. This is something I thought never would happen to me."

"What?" I asked.

"That a woman could put *me* down. In the past, I have always left womens. No woman never left me. Now Joyce has quit."

"I don't believe it," I said. "You've been going together for two or three years, and getting along fine. What happened? That little matter of the divorce from your wife, the fur coat, or what?"

"Zarita," said Simple.

"Zarita! She's nothing to you."

"I know it," said Simple. "She never was nothing to me but a now-and-then. But Zarita has ruint my life. You don't know how it feels, buddy, when somebody has gone that you never had before. I never had a woman like Joyce. I *loved* that girl. Nobody never cared for me like Joyce did."

"Have a drink," I said, "on me."

"This is one time I do not want a drink. I feel too bad."

"Then it *is* serious," I said.

"It's what the blues is made out of," said Simple. " 'Love, oh, love, oh, careless love!' Buddy, I were careless."

"What happened, old man?"

"Zarita," said Simple. "I told that woman never to come around to my room without letting me know in advance. Joyce is too much of a lady to be always running up to my place, which is why I love her. Only time Joyce might ring my bell is when she can't get me on the phone due to my landlady is evil and sometimes will not even deliver a message. Then maybe Joyce might ring my bell, but she never comes upstairs, less it is to hang me some new spring curtains she made herself or change my dresser scarf. What's come up now is Zarita's fault, plus my landlady's. Them two womens is against me. That word *Town & Country* uses for female dogs just about fits them."

"I understand. They are not genteel characters. But what exactly took place?"

"It hurts me to think of it, let alone to talk about it. But I will tell you. Zarita not only came around to my room the other night, but she brought her whole birthday party *unannounced, uninvited,* and *unwanted*. I didn't even know it were her birthday. I had just come in from work, et a little supper at the Barbecue Shack, and was preparing to take a nap to maybe go out later and drop by to see were Joyce in the mood, when my doorbell rung like mad nine times—which is the ring for my Third Floor Rear. It were about nine P.M. I go running downstairs in my shirttail, and sixty-eleven Negroes, male and female, come pouring in the door led by Zarita herself, whooping and hollering and high, yelling they come to help me celebrate her birthday, waving three or four bottles of licker and gin.

"Zarita say, 'Honey, I forgot to tell you I'm twenty-some-odd years old today. Whoopeee-eee-e! We started celebrating this morning and we still going strong. Come on up, folks! Let's play his combination. This man has got some *fine* records!'

"I didn't have a chance to say nothing. They just poured up the steps with me trailing behind, and my landlady looking cross-eyed out of her door, and Zarita talking so loud you could hear her in Buffalo. Next thing I knowed, Louis Jordan was turned up full-blast and somebody had even put a loud needle in the victrola. Them Negroes took possession. Well, you know I always tries to be a gentleman, even to Zarita, so I did not ask them out. I just poured myself a half glass of gin—which I do not ordinarily partake. Then I hollered, 'Happy birthday,' too.

"Well, the rest of the roomers heard the function and started coming in my room. Boyd next door brought his girl friend over, and before you knowed it, the ball was on. The joint jumped! To tell the truth, I even enjoyed myself.

"By and by, Zarita said, 'Honey, send out and get some more to drink.'

" 'Send who?' I said. 'We ain't got no messenger boy.'

"She said, 'Just gimme the money, then, and I will send that old down-home shmoo who has been trying to make love to me since four o'clock this afternoon. That man ain't nothing to me but a errand boy.'

"So we sent the old dope after a gallon of beer and pretzels. Soon as he left out the door Zarita grabbed me close as paper on the wall and started to dance. She danced so frantic, I could not keep up with her, so I turned her loose and let her go for herself. She had a great big old pocketbook on her arm and it were just a-swinging. Everybody else stopped dancing to watch Zarita, who always did want to be a show girl. She were really kicking up her heels then and throwing her hips from North to South. All of a sudden she flung up her arms and hollered, 'Yip-peee-ee-ee-e!' whilst her pocketbook went flying through the air. When it hit the ceiling it busted wide open. Man, everything she had in it strewed out all over my floor as it come down. " 'Lord have mercy!' Zarita said. 'Stop the music! Don't nobody move a inch. You might step on some of my personal belongings.'

"Just about then the downstairs doorbell rung nine times—my ring. I said, 'Somebody go down and let that guy in with the beer, while we pick up Zarita's stuff.'

"Zarita said, 'You help me, baby. The rest of you-all just stay where you are. I ain't acquainted with some of you folks and I don't want to lose nothing valuable.'

"Well, you know how many things a woman carries in her pocketbook. Zarita had lost them all, flung from one wall to the other of my room—compact busted open, powder spilt, mirror, key ring with seven keys, lipstick, handkerchief, deck of cards, black lace gloves, bottle opener, cigarette case, chewing gum, bromo-quinine box, small change, fountain pen, sun glasses, big old silver Bow-Dollar for luck, address books, fingernail file, three blue poker chips, matches, flask, also a shoehorn. Her perfume bottle broke against the radiator so my room smelt like womens, licker, mens, and a Night in Paris.

"Zarita was down on her hands and knees scrambling around for things, so I got down on my hands and knees, too.

" 'Baby,' she says to me, 'I believes my lipstick has rolled under your bed.'

"We both crawled under the bed to see. While we was under there, Zarita kissed me. She crawled out with the shoehorn and I crawled out with her lipstick—some of it on the side of my mouth. Just as I got up, there stood Joyce in my door with a package in her hand.

"Have you ever seen a man as dark as me turn red? I turned red, daddy-o! I opened my mouth to say 'Howdy-do?' but not a sound come out. Joyce had on her gold earrings and I could see they were shaking. But she did not raise her voice. She were too hurt.

"Zarita said, 'Why, Joyce, tip on in and enjoin my birthday. We don't mind. Just excuse my stuff flying all over the room. Me and Mr. Semple is having a ball.'

"Joyce looked at the black lace gloves, playing cards strewed all over the place, cigarette case, compact, poker chips, address book, powder, Bow-Dollar, and nail file on the floor with all them strange Negroes setting on the bed, in the window sill, on the dresser, everywhere but on the ceiling, and lipstick on my cheek. She did not say a word. She just turned her head away and looked like tears was aching to come to her eyes.

"I says, 'Joyce, baby, listen,' I says, 'I want a word with you.'

"She said, 'I come around here to bring you your yellow

rayon-silk shirt I ironed special for you for Sunday. Since your landlady said you was at home, she told me to bring it on upstairs myself. Here it is. I did not know you had company.'

"Just then that old down-home Negro come up with the beer yelling, 'Gangway! The stuff is here. Make room!' and he almost run over Joyce.

"Joyce says, 'Excuse me for being in your guests' way.'

"She turned to go. In facts, she went. I followed her down the steps but she did not turn her head. That loud-mouthed Zarita put the needle on Louis Jordan's bodacious 'Let the Good Times Roll,' and the ball were on again. When I got to the bottom of the steps, my landlady was standing like a marble statue.

"Landlady says, 'No decent woman approves of this.' Which is when Joyce started crying.

"Boy! My heart was broke because I hates to be misunderstood. I said, 'Joyce, I did not invite them parties here.'

"Joyce says, 'You don't need to explain to me, Jess Semple, getting all formal and everything. She says, 'Now I have seen that woman with my own eyes in *your* bedroom with her stuff spread out every which-a-where just like she was home. And people I know from their looks could not be *your* friends because I never met any of them before—so they must be hers. Maybe Zarita lives with you. No wonder you giving a birthday party to which I am not invited. Good night, I am gone out of your life from now on. Enjoy yourself. Good night!'

"If she had fussed and raised her voice, I would not have felt so bad. But the sweet way she said, 'Enjoy yourself,' all ladylike and sad and quiet, as if she was left out of things, cut me to my soul. Joyce ought to know I would not leave her out of nothing.

"I would of followed her in the street, but she said, 'Don't you come behind me!'

"The way she said it, I knowed she meant it. So I did not go. When I turned back, there was my landlady. All I said to that old battle-ax was, 'Go to hell!' I were so mad at that woman for sending Joyce upstairs.

"She started yelling as I went on up the steps, but I didn't hear a word she said. I knowed she was telling me to find another room. But I did not care. All I wanted was to lay eyes on

Zarita, stop them damn records from playing, and get them low-down dirty no-gooders out of my room. Which I did before you could say 'Jackie Robinson.' But after they left, I could not sleep. It were a blue evening.

"Some of Zarita's stuff was still on the floor next day when I went to work, so I gathered it up and brought it down here to the bartender and left it for her. I do not want to see Zarita no more again. The smell of that Night in Paris water is still in my room. I'll smell it till the day I die. But I don't care if I die right now. I don't know what to say to Joyce. A man should not fool around a bad woman *no kind of way* when he's got a good woman to love. They say, 'You never miss the water till the well runs dry.' Boy, you don't know how I miss Joyce these last few days."

"Haven't you tried to see her?" I asked.

"Tried?" said Simple. "I phoned her seventeen times. She will not answer the phone. I rung her bell. Nobody will let me in. I sent her six telegrams, but she do not reply. If I could write my thoughts, I would write her a letter, but I am no good at putting words on paper much. The way I feel now, nobody could put my feelings down nohow. I got the blues for true. I can't be satisfied. This morning I had the blues so bad, I wished that I had died. These is my bitter days. What shall I do?"

"I don't know."

"You never know anything important," said Simple. "All you know is to argue about race problems. Tonight I would not care if all the race problems in the world was to descend right on New York. I would not care if Rankin himself would be elected Mayor and the Ku Klux Klan took over the City Council. I would not care if Mississippi moved to Times Square. But nobody better not harm Joyce, I'm telling you, even if she has walked out of my life. That woman *is* my life, so nobody better not touch a hair of her head. Buddy-o, wait for me here whilst I walks by her house to see if there's a light in her window. I just want to know if she got home from work safe tonight."

"She's been getting home safely by herself all these years," I said. "Why are you so worried tonight?"

"Please don't start no whys and wherefores."

"I sympathize with you—still, there are always ameliorating circumstances."

"I don't know what that word means," said Simple, "but all that rates with me now is what to say to that girl—if I ever get a chance to say anything. If she does not come to the door when I ring this time, if I see a light I am going to holler."

"Since she lives on the third floor, you can hardly play Romeo and climb up," I said. "Still, I don't believe Joyce would relish having her name called aloud in the street."

"If she don't let me through the door, I will have to call her," said Simple. "I can explain by saying that I have lost my mind, that she has driv me crazy. And I will stand in front of her house all night if she don't answer."

"The law would probably remove you," I said.

"They would have to use force to do it," said Simple. "I wouldn't care if the polices broke my head, anyhow. Joyce done broke my heart."

"You've got it bad," I said.

"Worse than bad," moaned Simple. "Here, take this quarter and buy yourself a beer whilst you wait till I come back."

"I have some affairs of my own to attend to," I protested, "so I can't wait all night."

"I thought you was my ace-boy," he said as he turned away. "But everybody lets you down when trouble comes. If you can't wait, then don't. To hell with you! Don't!"

I started to say I would wait. But Simple was gone.

A Letter from Baltimore

As I walked into Paddy's, there stood Simple grinning from ear to ear. He greeted me like a long-lost brother, pulling me toward the bar as he announced, "This evening the beers are on me and I have the where-with-all to pay for two rounds and a half, so pick up and drink down."

"What, may I ask, is the occasion for this sudden conviviality? Tonight is not Saturday."

"No," said Simple, "but it is a new day right on, a new week, and a new year. They say a man's life changes every seven years. I am in the change. Here, read this letter that I found laying on the radiator in the hall this evening when I come in that I know my landlady tried to peer through the envelope. It's from my wife, Isabel."

"I have no desire to pry into your personal correspondence," I said.

"Read it, man, read it," urged Simple. "Desire or not, read it. I want to hear it in words *out loud* what Mrs. Semple says— because I cannot believe my eyes. Unfold it, go ahead."

"She writes a nice clear hand," I said, "big round letters. You can tell this woman is a positive character. I see she's still in Baltimore, too. Well, here goes:

Dear Mr. Semple:

Jess, at last I have found a man who loves me enough to pay for my divorce, which is more than you was ever willing to do and you are my husband. Now, listen, this man is a mail clerk that owns two houses, one of which he has got rented and the other one he needs somebody to take care of it. His first wife being dead so he wants me for his second. He knows I have been married once before and am still married in name only to you as you have not been willing to pay for the legal paper which grants freedom from our entanglement. This man is willing to pay for it, but he says I will have to file the claim. He says he will get a lawyer to furnish me grounds I have to swear on and that you also have to swear on unless you want to contest. I do not want no contest, you hear me? All I want is my divorce, since I have found a nice man, willing to marry me and pay for it, too. I am writing to find out if you will please not make no contest out of this because he has never done nothing to you, only do you a favor by bearing the expenses of the grounds that rightly belong to a husband. Let me hear from you this evening as he has already passed the point where he could wait.

Once sincerely yours but not now,
ISABEL

"I suppose you would have no intention of cross-filing," I said.

"I would not cross that wife of mine no kind of way," said Simple, "with a file nor otherwise. My last contest with that woman was such that the police had to protect me. So that man can have her. He can have her! I do not even want a copy of the diploma."

"A divorce paper does not look like a diploma," I said.

"I knew a woman once who framed her divorce and hung it on the wall," said Simple. "But if my wife serves *me* with one, I will throw it out."

"That would render it invalid," I said, "also null and void. You will have to sign all the papers and mail them back to Baltimore so the proceedings can go through."

"Just so they get out of my sight," said Simple. "Joyce would not want no other woman's divorce papers hanging around. If she did, Joyce could have bought them papers herself by now. I gave her the opportunity."

"I am always puzzled as to why you have been so unwilling to pay for your own divorce," I said.

"I told Isabel when we busted up that she had shared my bed, she had shared my board, my licker, and my Murray's, but that I did not intend to share another thing with her from that day to this, not even a divorce. That is why I would not pay for it. Let that other man pay for it and they can share it together."

"But it will free you to marry Joyce," I said.

"Joyce will be free to marry me, you mean."

"Joyce is not being divorced from anyone. You are the one who is being divorced."

"Which means I will no longer be free, then," said Simple. "I will be married again before the gold seal is hardly out from under the stamper."

"That will be good for you. Perhaps you will settle down, stay home, stop running around nights."

"I will," said Simple, "because I will have a home to stay at. I will not have to live in bars to keep from looking at my landlady in the face."

"Maybe married you can save a little money and get somewhere in the world."

"Them would be my best intentions," said Simple. "Facts is, I always did have ambitions. When I were a little boy in Virginia, my grandma told me to hitch my wagon to a star."

"Did you try?"

"I did," said Simple, "but it must have been a dog-star."

"Well, now things will be different. Joyce is a good girl. You love her and she loves you, so this time you should make a go of it. And I will dance at your wedding."

"You will be my best man," said Simple.

"Well, of course, I'd be delighted—but—but maybe you'd like a relative or some other more intimate friend for your best man. After all, Joyce doesn't know me very well."

"*I* know you," said Simple, "which is enough. As many beers as you have bought me right here at this bar, and as often as you lent me a buck when I was trying to make the week, you deserve to be my best man. So no arguments! Now that my luck is turned, daddy-o, you'll be there at the finish."

"Thanks, old man," I said. "Certainly you seem to be coming out ahead at last—a *free* divorce from a wife you don't like, no contest, no expenses, and, all but for the formalities, a new wife you love."

"*I am* coming out ahead for once," said Simple, "which just goes to prove what's in that little old toast I learned from my Uncle Tige. Listen fluently:

> *When you look at this life you'll find*
> *It ain't nothing but a race.*
> *If you can't be the winning horse,*
> *Son, at least try to place.*

"I believe I have placed—so let's drink to it."

"You have won," I said.

"Providing that Negro in Baltimore keeps his promise to my wife. If he don't, as sure as my name is Simple, I will go down there and beat his head."

"Do you mean to say you'd lay hands on your first wife's second husband?"

"Listen! I married Isabel for better or for worse. She couldn't do no better than to get a free divorce," said Simple. "That man made my wife a promise. *He better not betray her.* If he does, he'll have me to contend with because I dare him to stand in *my* way. I'll fix him! Just like that toast says:

> *If they box you on the curve, boy,*
> *Jockey your way to the rail,*
> *And when you get on the inside track—*
> *Sail! . . . Sail! . . . Sail!*
> *In a race, daddy-o,*
> *One thing you will find—*
> *There ain't NO way to be out in front*
> *Without showing your tail*
> *To the horse behind."*

"One regrets," I said, "that, after all, life is a conflict."

"I leave them regrets to you," said Simple.

| Seven Rings

EARLY blue evening. The street lights had just come on, large watery moonstones up and down the curbs. April. The days were stretching leisurely. This particular evening had become too old to eat dinner and too young to do much of anything else. It was unseasonably warm. Tasting spring, Harlem relaxed. Windows, stoops, and streets full of people not doing anything much. In spite of his landlady's request *not* to sit on the steps in front of her house, Simple was sitting there. Harlem has few porches. In his youth in Virginia, Simple had been accustomed to sitting on porches. His youth was some thirty-odd years gone, but the habit remained. The lights looked pretty in the smoke-blue evening of sudden spring. But did Simple see the lights?

Who knows? He didn't see me as I came down the street. His legs were stretched out over three steps and he leaned back staring at nothing.

"Good evening," I said, "if you're not too tired to open your mouth."

"Tired, nothing. Man, I'm natural-born disgusted," said Simple. "My divorce didn't come through."

"What?"

"That fool man that promised to marry my wife and pay for our divorce, too, did not pay her lawyer to clinch the proceedings," said Simple, "and until he does, the judge will not hand down no decree. Divorces and money is all mixed up in Baltimore. In fact, I believe divorces costs more there than they do here in New York. The last time I asked about a divorce in Harlem, the man told me Three Hundred Dollars. My wife writ me that her present boy friend is paying Four Hundred for hers —and she ain't got it yet—which is hindering me, because I am due to marry Joyce. If it had not been that I showed Joyce Isabel's last letter, I do believe Joyce would have thought I am standing her up. But you know as nice as Joyce is to me, I would almost marry that girl without a divorce."

"Joyce would hardly want to marry a man who is already married," I said.

"No, but she wants me so bad that if I was to press her, she might even lend me the money to pay for the rest of my wife's divorce. Joyce swore she would never outright pay for no other woman's divorce, but a loan is a different thing."

"Why don't you accept the loan?"

"Because I do not want the shadow of nothing having to do with Isabel hanging over me and Joyce. I swore and be damned I wouldn't pay for no divorce for Isabel. Neither will I let Joyce pay for it. If that man in Baltimore who wants to marry Isabel can't even pay for a little old decree for her, he ain't much good. And he is bugging me!"

"I thought you told me the man is a widower who owns two houses and is a very solid citizen."

"That's the jive Isabel wrote. But Isabel might just be trying to shame me by comparison, because I never owned nothing.

All I do know is, I wish the man would hurry up and pay that lawyer so me and Joyce can complete our arrangements. Isabel had no business getting my expectations up like this.

" 'I have got all my trousseau clothes,' Isabel wrote me, 'and everything but the decree'—which is where I reckon the man's money went. Isabel done made him buy her a whole lot of clothes. Then she writ on, 'If you was any kind of a husband, Jess Semple, you would help me to get this decree. You ought to want a divorce as much as I do. The least you could do is to assist my husband-to-be pay for your wife-that-was to get rid of you.' "

"What did you answer to that?"

"Nothing," said Simple. "The only answer would be money —and money I do not have. They say silence is golden—which is all the gold she can get out of me. Are you walking toward the corner?"

"Yes."

"I will keep you company as far as the bar. Maybe a little further. Maybe I will take a walk, too."

He rose, sighed, stretched, and, as we filed through the crowded block, for no good reason whatsoever started singing:

> Two things, Miss Martin,
> I cannot stand,
> A bow-legged woman
> And a cock-eyed man.

"Kindly lower your voice," I requested.

> Two things, Miss Martin,
> I adore,
> One is some loving—
> And the other is
> Some more!

"Cease your rowdyism," I said. "People will conclude you're drunk."

Two things, Miss Martin,
That bug a man . . .

Cars sped by. The city hummed like a mechanical beehive. Beneath the street lights among the crowded stoops, the broken end of the song got lost in the early blue. With his mouth open Simple stopped indecisively at the corner to look slowly up and down the street.

"Which way are you going?" I asked.

"Come with me," said Simple, "and I will show you where I am going—to Joyce's."

"There is no point in my going with you to see Joyce. She's not *my* girl."

"You can keep the ball rolling," said Simple. "With me, Joyce is kind of silent these days. But if you are there, she will act like we got company—then *I* can talk, too. Otherwise, she will just *um-hum* when I say something and let it go at that. There is nothing worse than a woman that will not talk. You get so used to women rattling away that when they keep quiet you are scared they will explode. Are you coming with me or not?"

"If I am going to be in an explosion, I'll go. I'd like to see Joyce give you a good dressing down. Here you are, a man in your prime—and can't pay for one divorce. Why, some men at your age are already paying three alimonies."

"White men," said Simple. "The most alimonies I ever knowed a Negro to pay was *one*—and he didn't keep that up to date. What I like about Joyce is she would never alimony me. Joyce works and makes her own money and does not want anything out of me but love."

We stopped in front of the neat brownstone house around the corner from Seventh Avenue where Joyce roomed. He rang seven times.

"Joyce knows my ring," said Simple.

Nobody came to the door. He rang again, counting out loud from one to seven.

"Maybe Joyce is in the bathroom."

No answer.

"I wonder should I ring for her big old fat landlady?"

"You have walked way over here," I said, "so you might as well find out if she's home or not."

Simple rang one long ring and two short, the landlady's private signal. Presently the floor boards creaked. The inner door opened. An enormous figure filled the vestibule. Then the outer glass door cracked just a crack.

The landlady said, "I knowed it was you all the time. Joyce is not here. She went to a movie."

"You don't know which one?"

"Joyce does not tell me her business. There's a draft in this door, Mr. Semple. Excuse me."

The door closed.

"Um-huh! You see," said Simple. "Joyce has done made that woman mad at me, too. Done told her something. Her landlady is most in generally more pleasanter than mine, but you see how she acts tonight. When a woman is mad at a man, she always wants every other woman to be mad at him, too. Well, daddy-o, let's go have a beer. We done took our walk."

So we went and had a beer. Simple drank in silence, but not for long. As he ordered a second round, he said dolefully, "These are dark days for me, man. Joyce is as touchous as a mother hen done lost her chicks. She knows she has not lost me—she just has to wait a little longer. But she acts like I have put her down. That girl is bent, bound and determined to marry me. She has asked me seven times already.

" 'I'm tired of not seeing hair nor hide of neither ring, license, orange blossoms, or veil,' Joyce told me last week. 'I try to keep my head up and my back straight—but how straight can a girl's back be without breaking? You know I don't believe in no common-law stuff. But in the framework of marriage, that's different. Jess Semple, my patience is about done wore out with you.'

"I said, 'Joyce, don't render me liable to commit bigamy.'

"Whereupon, she stuck her hands on her hips and yelled, 'Bigamy? Every time I mention marriage to you, *bigamy* is the first thing that jumps into your mind. I'm warning you, Jess Semple, for the last time, if you don't hurry up and think of something more respectable to commit besides bigamy. you're going to see mighty little of me. I have never known any one Negro so long without having some kind of action out of him.'

"I said, 'Baby, you talk like you have been married before.'

"Joyce said, 'No, I have not been married before. But I have been proposed to. You have not even yet, in going on several years, formally proposed to me, let alone writing my father for my hand.'

"I said, 'I did not know I had to write your father for your hand. This is the first time you mentioned that, honey. I thought this here living-together business, when it does come off, would be just between us.'

"She says, 'I do not like that *living-together* phrase, Jess Semple. We will be legally married as soon as you get legally divorced—and there will be no *living together* to it. Also, you will write my father.'

" 'Joyce, you know I cannot write good,' I said.

" 'Then I can dictate for you, and tell you what to say.'

"I said, 'I know what to say. But I still do not understand how a girl as big and old as you are has to have somebody ask her father if she can get married.'

" 'Marriage involves changing *my* name to *your* name, that is why,' says Joyce. 'Since I bear my father's name—although he is only my step-father—you have to ask him can you change it. Then I will cease to be *Miss* Lane and become *Mrs.* Semple— as soon as that woman in Baltimore lets loose of your name. Do you reckon she will ever do so?'

" 'The wheels of justice grind slow. But, Joyce, you know I mean well. I would have taken your hand long ago, had it not been for bigamy.'

" 'I thought your first wife's name was Isabel, not *Bigamy*.'

" 'Don't be funny,' I says. 'You know what I mean. I do not want to get in jail and leave you in disgrace. I love you, woman! I want all to be well with us, also between us. I will even write your old man tomorrow, if you say so.'

" 'My *father*,' says Joyce, 'not my *old man*. I never did like crude-talking people. I bet no child of mine better not call you *old man*, nor me *old lady*. Any child of mine will be brought up after me, not after you.'

" 'That's good,' I said. 'One thing, Joyce, for which I admires you is your culture. Was your old man cultured? I mean, your *father?*'

" 'He is a bricklayer,' said Joyce, 'but my mother was a Daughter of the Eastern Star, also a graduate of Fessenden Academy. She always worked around fine white folks. She never did work for no poor white trash. In fact, she wouldn't. Poor folks have nothing to give nobody—least of all culture. I come by mine honestly.'

" 'Well, you will have to tell me what to ask your father because I am not used to writing no man for a woman's hand.'

" 'When the time comes, I will put you straight,' said Joyce. 'But do not let it be too long. After all, I am only human and June don't come but once a year.'

" 'Meaning what?'

" 'Meaning I might meet some other man before next year,' said Joyce.

"That is what hurt me about our conversation, daddy-o. Pulling all them technicalities on me, then talking about *she might meet some other man.* Joyce better not meet no other man. She better not! Do, and I will marry her right now this June, in spite of my first wife, bigamy, or her old man—I mean, her father. Don't Joyce know I am not to be trifled with? I am Jesse B. Semple."

| What Can a Man Say?

SWEEP, rain, over the Harlem rooftops. Sweep into the windows of folks at work, not at home to close the windows. Wet the beds in side bedrooms almost as narrow as the bed against the window. Sweep, rain! Have fun with the brownstone fronts of rooming houses full of people boxed in *this* room, *that* room, seven rings, two rings, five, nine.

"Who are they ringing for? It ain't me, is it? Did you count how many rings?"

Turn into a spring equinox, rain, and blow curtains from Blumstein's until they flop limp-wet. Dampen drapes. Soak shades until they won't pull up or down. Make folks mad who come home from work and find everything all wet.

" 'It was so hot this morning any fool might have knowed it was going to rain. What did you leave the windows open for? It ain't summer yet. You just don't think,' says my big old landlady to me.

"Yet and still, it ain't my fault," said Simple, "she's got arthritis-rheumatis so bad she can't get up the steps to shut the windows when it starts raining. Now she comes blaming me for letting *my* things get all wet! I come home from work tonight and find a puddle of water in the middle of the floor. Mattress soaked where I pushed the bed up against the window on account of the heat. The Bible my grandma gave me with my birth date writ in it looking like somebody run it through the laundry-mat. Ink all blurred. Nobody'll ever know when I was borned.

"Old landlady says, 'Ain't you got a birth certificate?'

"I says, 'No'm.'

"She says, 'Why, even my dog has got one on his pedigree.'

"I says, 'I am not a dog, so I has no pedigree. And everything I own has got wet upstairs today, madam.'

" 'I *tells* you roomers to pull down your windows when you leave the house. I cannot be running up and down steps looking after you-all. That is not my responsibility. You due to protect my house. Who's gonna pay for my rug when it molds and mildews that this rain done wet up in your room? Who's gonna buy me a new mattress for your Third Floor Rear when that one wets out? Mr. Semple, *I could charge you* with destroying my property. Don't come down here telling me about your things got all wet today. If you had a wife to stay home and shut the windows, instead of running around with them gals from the corner bar—that Zarita, for instance, passing here yesterday with her head looking like a hurrah's nest, switching worse than a dog. Trixie has got more respect for herself than that bar-butterfly with that red streak in the front of her hair.'

" 'Madam, you are talking about my friends. I will thank you to hush. As much as I have walked your dog for you, is that the thanks I get?'

" 'My dog is at least a lady. Ain't you, Trixie?'

" 'That dog makes me sick. I cannot stand such talk. I am going upstairs and hang my bed clothes up to dry.'

" 'Bring your dirty sheets down here and I'll give you some fresh ones—*this once*. Your week's almost up anyhow.'

" 'Three flights up—three flights down—three flights back up again! Thank you. Don't do me no favors. Do, and you'll want me to be walking that lady hound of yours around again. Madam, I am not a dog walker. And I reckon my sheets will dry out by the time I get ready to go to bed.'

" 'Which is three, four A.M. Every night the Lord sends I hear you coming in staggle-legged.'

" 'Don't you never sleep?'

" 'With roomers in the house, how can I? No telling what you-all might do. I'm responsible.'

" 'Well, I wish you'd be responsible for folks' things getting all wet when a thunderstorm comes up and a man is at work. That is more important than hearing who comes in when.'

" 'I know what my responsibilities is. You don't need to tell me. And if you just must keep on chewing the rag, complaining and arguing, you move.'

" 'I have been here seven years, madam, but you liable to find me gone *soon*. Then who will walk your dog for you? Don't none of your other roomers do it. Neither your husband. Madam, you will miss me when I move. Won't she, Trixie?'

" 'Don't try to get on the good side of me through Trixie.'

" 'Madam, have you got a good side?'

" 'Mr. Semple, I am hurted by that last remark. I tries to treat everybody nice. I do! And I am hurted. As often as I let you slip a week, sometimes two, on your rent. Nice as I been to you compared to most landladies, I tell you, I am hurted. You can just move, if you want to. Move.'

" 'Madam, I do not wish to move. And I did not mean what I said. You got three or four good sides. I expect more. If it wasn't so damp right now I would walk Trixie for you.'

" 'Trixie! Trixie! Trixie! Do you think that nobody else lives downstairs here in this Dutch basement but Trixie? Ain't you got no regard for me?'

"'Madam, does you want me to walk *you*?'

"'I likes to go out once in a while myself. And you ain't never so much as invited me to Paddy's for a beer in all these years you been living in my house.'

"'But you got a husband, madam.'

"'It were my understanding that *you* also had a wife when you moved in here. But that does not, and has not, stopped you from running with every woman that wears a skirt—and some in pedal-pushers.'

"'But, madam, you always said you did not drink.'

"'What I say and what I do are two different things.'

"'Do you want me to bring you back a can of beer when I go out?'

"'Oh, no! Don't worry about *me*, Mr. Semple. Just bring Trixie some dog food—since you are so concerned about her. And excuse me, I am going to fix my husband's dinner. I don't need a thing. Excuse me.'

"'You are excused,' I said, to which she did not answer. Wrong again! What can a man say to a woman that is not wrong, be they landladies, wives, or Joyce?"

| Empty Room

ONE night Paddy's bar for once was strangely quiet. I soon learned why. Watermelon Joe was going around taking up a collection to bury a fellow who had just died that day, a boy everybody around that corner knew. The bartender said the fellow had been in Paddy's drinking just a few nights before, now he was gone. The juke box was not playing as continuously that evening because most of the men had given their last spare change to help put their late bar-buddy away. Everybody was a little sad.

"Zarita has just been in here, cried, and gone," Simple said.

"I expect she knew that boy better than she makes out—Zarita being a woman. We all knew him pretty well. Just to think, here today, gone tonight! I can't quite get it. You know, pal, I have not been around people dying very much."

"Neither have I," I said.

"But once in Baltimore, in the first house where I roomed, a man died quick like that. It was before me and Isabel got married so I was living alone, being just a young man. I did not know this fellow who died very well, but he roomed next to me on the same floor, three rings. Sometimes I would hear him stumbling around in his room, humming and singing to himself:

> *I got the Dallas blues*
> *And the Fort Worth*
> *Heart's disease . . .*

"Once in a while we shared a quart of beer together and talked about the weather. But I never went nowhere with the man and he never went nowhere with me, and I only ran into him once on the street, so I did not know him very well. But when he died I missed him. Just like sometimes when somebody dies in the papers that you did not know, President Roosevelt, or a movie star. You never did know them to speak to them a-tall, but you miss them right on.

"Well, when this same-floor roomer of mine died, I were asleep. The next morning, they told me he was dead. It was hard to believe because I had just seen the guy the night before in the hallway going to the bathroom to soak his corns.

"He told me, 'My feet's been giving me hell today.'

"I said, 'Not you, but me. I do believe black feet hurt worse than white.'

"We laughed. He said, 'Dark men, dark feet, dark days.'

"That were the last thing that man said to me. Next morning he were gone.

"Where do people go when they are gone? And why? One day, here, the next day, gone. They could not find no address for that man's people for nobody to claim the funeral. Maybe none of his kinfolks had the money to pay for it. And he did not have no insurance. Anyhow, he went unclaimed. The city came and took him away, Baltimore City, which is a prejudiced town, so I do not know what they do with colored folks who have died, maybe give them to the medical students, because even when you are alive they do not treat you very well. Anyhow, the city taken that man. I did not see him come down the hall no more that day, nor never.

"I have not seen nobody die in their presence, so I do not know how that roomer went except that he went in the night when he were alone by hisself. I would not want to go like that. I would want somebody with me. I want some woman to hold my hand, some slim tall sweet old gal like Joyce to say, 'Baby, don't go! I do not *know* what I can do without you.'

"I would want somebody to miss me—even *before* I am gone. I want somebody to cry real loud, scream and let the neighbors know I am no longer here. I want my passing to be a main event, 'Dear Jesus, Jesse B. is gone! The one I love is gone! Why did you take him this evening, Lord?'

"In fact, if there are more than one woman crying over me, I will be glad. If there are three or four, or seven, I would not care. Let the world, the rest of the womens in it, and everybody know that I have been here and gone, been in this world, and passed through, and left a mighty mourning. I want some woman to yell, 'Why? Why did you take him, Lord?'

"When I go, I would not like to die like that fellow in Baltimore with nobody to claim his body, nobody to lay out Five Hundred Dollars for a funeral, nobody to come and cry. Only a lonesome few roomers knowed when he were taken down the steps with his room door left open—and it were empty in there. Empty, empty, and quiet.

"No, I would not want to be carried out that way, feet first. I would really like to walk down the steps, out to my own funeral —if I had to go at all. Anyhow, after I'm gone, I would like there to be such another weeping and wailing as you never heard. Not quiet like it were that day in Baltimore.

"Not having been around people very much who are dying, I did not know until then how it felt to see somebody walking down the hall tonight, then not see them in the morning because they are gone. *Gone* with a big letter, *gone* with a capital G. I mean *solid and really* not-here-no-more—gone. Silent, with nobody to scream. Nobody like Zarita around to make a big noise, nor Joyce to cry sweet and polite. Nobody to yell, 'He's gone.' His name I can't recall. But maybe why I remember that man in Baltimore so well is because there was no human to cry, 'Gone! He's gone!'

"The landlord said to his wife the next day, 'Put that sign— ROOM FOR RENT—back in the window. But don't let nobody have that room unless they pay a full week in advance.'

"That's all anybody said after that roomer were gone. But one night somebody come and rung his bell, three rings. He were not there."

| Picture for Her Dresser

IT WAS a warm evening not yet dark when I stopped by Simple's. His landlady had the front door open airing the house, so I did not need to ring. I walked upstairs and knocked on his door. He was sitting on the bed, cutting his toenails, listening to a radio show, and frowning.

"Do you hear that?" he asked. "It's not about me, neither about you. All these plays, dramas, skits, sketches, and soap operas all day long and practically nothing about Negroes. You would think no Negroes lived in America except Amos and Andy. White folks have all kinds of plays on the radio about themselves, also on TV. But what have we got about us? Just now and then a song to sing. Am I right?"

"Just about right," I said.

"Come on, let's go take a walk." He put on his shoes first, his pants, then his shirt. "Is it cool enough for a coat?"

"You'd better wear one," I said. "It's not summer yet, and evening's coming on. You probably won't get back until midnight."

"Joyce is gone to a club meeting, so I won't be going to see her," he said. "She's expecting her sister-members to elect her a delegate to the regional which meets in Boston sometime soon. If they don't, she'll be a disappointed soul. She used to skip meetings, but that regional is why she goes regular now. Let's me and you stroll up Seventh Avenue to 145th, then curve toward Sugar Hill where the barmaids are beautiful and barflies are belles. I have not been on Sugar Hill in a coon's age."

It was dusk-dark when we reached the pavement. Taxis and pleasure cars sped by. The Avenue was alive with promenaders. On the way up the street we passed a photographer's shop with a big sign glowing in the window:

HARLEM DE-LUXE PHOTOGRAPHY STUDIO
IF YOU ARE NOT GOOD-LOOKING
WE WILL MAKE YOU SO
ENTER

"The last time I come by here," said Simple, "before my lady friend started acting like an iceberg, Joyce told me, 'Jess, why don't you go in and get your picture posed? I always did want a nice photograph of you to set on my dresser.'

"I said, 'Joyce, I don't want to take no picture.' But you know how womens is! So I went in.

"They got another big sign up on the wall inside that says:

RETOUCHING DONE

" 'I don't want them to *touch* me, let alone *retouch*,' I told Joyce.

"Joyce said, 'Be sweet, please, I do not wish no evil-looking Negro on my dresser.' So I submitted.

"Another sign states:

COLORED TO ORDER—EXPERT TINTING

"I asked, 'Joyce, what color do you want me to be?'

"Joyce said, 'A little lighter than natural. I will request the man how much he charges to make you chocolate.'

"About that time a long tall bushy-headed joker in a smock came dancing out of a booth and said, 'Next.'

"That were me next. There was a kind of sick green light blazing inside the booth. That light not only hurt my eyes, but turned my stomach before I even set down.

"The man said, 'Pay in advance.'

"My week's beer money went to turn me into chocolate to set on Joyce's dresser—providing I did not melt before I got out of there, it were so hot.

"The man said, 'Naturally, you want a retouching job?'

"I said, 'You know I *don't* want to look like I am.'

" 'That will be one Dollar extra,' he stated. 'Would you also wish to be tinted?'

" 'Gimme the works,' I said.

" 'We will add Three,' he additioned. 'And if you want more than one print, that will be Two Dollars each, after the negative.'

" 'One is enough,' I said. 'I would not want myself setting around on my *own* dresser. Just one print for the lady, that's all.'

" 'How about your mother?' asked the man. 'Or your sister down home?'

" 'Skip down home,' I said.

" 'Very well,' said the man. 'Now, look pleasant, please! You have observed the sign yonder which is the rule of the company:

IF YOU MOVE,
YOU LOSE.
IF YOU SHAKE—
NO RE-TAKE!

So kindly hold your position.'

" 'As much of my money as you've got,' I said, 'I will not bat a eye.'

" 'Tilt your head to one side and watch the birdie. Don't look like you have just et nails. . . . Smile! . . . Smile! . . . Smile! . . . Brightly, now! That's right!'

" 'I cannot grin all night,' I said. 'Neither can I set like a piece of iron much longer. If you don't take me as I am, *damn!*'

" 'No profanity in here, please,' says the man. 'Just hold it while I focus.'

"I held.

"He focused.

"I sweated.

"He focused.

"I said, 'Can't you see me?'

"He said, 'Shussh-ss-s! Now, a great big smile! . . . Hold it!'

"F—L—A—S—H!

"I were blind for the next ten minutes. Seven Dollars and a Half's worth of me to set on Joyce's dresser! When I go to get that picture out next week it better be good—also have a frame! As touchous as Joyce is these days, I want her to like that picture."

By that time we had reached the Woodside. The corner of 141st and Seventh was jumping. King Cole was coming cool off the juke box inside the bar.

"Daddy-o, let's turn in here and get a beer," said Simple. "I never was much on climbing hills and if I go any further, I'll have too far to walk back. Besides, I got to wake myself up in the morning. My Big Ben won't alarm, my wrist watch is broke, and my landlady is evil. She says I don't pay her to climb three flights of steps to wake me up—so I have got nobody to wake me in the morning. That is one reason why I wish I was married, so I would not have to worry about getting to work on time. Also I would have somebody to cook my breakfast. I am tired of coffee, crullers, coffee and crullers, which is all I can afford. Besides, I hate an alarm clock. . . . Two beers, bartender! . . . I like to be woke up gentle, some woman's hand shaking saying, 'Jess, honey, ain't you gonna make your shift?'

"And if I was to say, 'No,' she would say, 'Then all right, baby. You been working too hard lately anyhow. Sleep on. We will get up about noon and go to the show.'

"That is the kind of woman I would like to have. Most womens is different. Most womens say, 'You better get up from there, Jess Semple, and go to work.' But even that would be better than a *brr-rrr-rr-r!* alarm clock every morning in your ears. I rather be woke up by a human than a clock."

"So you would make your wife get up before you, *just to wake you up*, would you?"

"Which is a woman's duty," said Simple. "He that earns the bread should be woke up, petted, fed, and got off to work in time. Then his wife can always go back to bed and get her beauty sleep—providing she is not working herself."

"No doubt a woman of yours would have to work."

"Only until we got a toe-holt," said Simple, "then Joyce could stay home and take care of the children."

"I haven't heard you speak of children before," I said. "You'll be too far along in age to start raising a family if you don't soon get married."

"You don't have to marry to have a family," said Simple.

"You wouldn't care to father children out of wedlock, surely?"

"A man slips up sometimes. But I don't need to worry about that. Joyce is a respectable woman—which is why I respects her. But she says as soon as we are wedlocked she wants a son that looks like me—which will be just as soon as that Negro in Baltimore pays for Isabel's divorce. So far that igaroot has only made one payment."

"I thought that man loved your wife so much he was willing to pay for the *whole* divorce. What happened?"

"I reckon inflation got him," said Simple. "Some things makes me sad to speak of. It takes three payments to get a decree. He made the down payment. Isabel writ that if I would make one, she would make one, then everybody could marry again. But I cannot meet a payment now with food up, rent up, phones up, cigarettes up, Lifebuoy up—everything up but my salary. Isabel wrote that divorces are liable to go up if I don't hurry up and pay up. I got a worried mind. Let's order one more beer—then I won't sleep restless. Have you got some change for this round?"

"I paid the last time."

"Except that *that* were not the last time. This round will be the last time. Just like a divorce in three installments, the last time is not the *last* time—if you still have to pay another time. Kindly order two beers."

"What do you take me for, a chump?"
"No, pal—a friend."

| Cocktail Sip

ALONG about nine o'clock Sunday evening, Simple emerged grinning from the dusky backroom of Paddy's Bar to spy me at the front. I was surprised to see him so early and so hilarious. He was half high.

"Mulberries, sweet, my Lord," he cried, "also the lips of a woman!"

"You sound like an Elizabethan," I said. "What's up?"

"Lizzie who?" asked Simple.

"Poets of long ago I studied in school.'

"It must have been long ago, because you have been out of school a long time."

"I still remember some of their poems, though. For instance:

> Drink to me only with thine eyes,
> And I will pledge with mine,
> Or leave a kiss but in the cup,
> And I'll not ask for wine."

Meanwhile, Simple was beckoning the bartender, and the juke box was blaring.

I said, "Are you listening?"

"I'm listening fluently," he protested. "But I would like some beer. Besides, these kisses I'm talking about were not in no cup."

"You're probably in your cups," I said.

"I am not," said Simple. "I am half sober. See this lipstick on my handkerchief? I just got through wiping my mouth."

"Whom, may I ask, were you kissing?"

"Zarita—in the phone booth."

"Are you running with that light-o'-love again?"

"Only occasionally," said Simple. "This evening is one of the occasions."

"If Joyce catches you, you will run *from* Zarita, not with her."

"I hope Joyce don't catch me," said Simple. "Sometimes a man likes a woman with experience."

"Then you ought to like Zarita a lot."

"I do and I don't. Zarita is strictly a after-hours gal—great when the hour is late, the wine is fine, and mellow whiskey has made you frisky."

I quoted over the juke-box blare:

> *"The thirst that from the soul doth rise*
> *Doth ask a drink divine. . . ."*

"Zarita will drink anything," said Simple. "She is like me in that respect, from beer to champagne. But this Sunday, we been to a Five O'clock Cocktail Sip where they empty all the different left-over bottles on the bar into the shaker, shake it up, put in a cherry—and call it a Special. We had several Specials.

"I did not know I was going to meet Zarita there, but I did. She were unescorted, so we sipped together. Then we danced together. Then we sat together. Then I went by her house. Then she came by my house. After which, we both came here to cool. I still had to kiss her one more time in the phone booth before she shoved off. She spends every Sunday night with her foster-mama, so she has to go now. In fact, I think she already went out the side door because she does not like Buster to see her in here with me. Old funny-looking Buster standing over there thinks he likes her."

"It's a good thing you are not jealous," I said.

"I have an open mind about Zarita. I am only jealous of Joyce. I may not see Zarita again for a month. But somehow or other, her kisses make me think of mulberries—that sloe gin they colored them cocktails, I reckon."

"It's a wonder you are not rocking and reeling."

"Rocky, but not really. I feel like hey! hey! hey! Come on, have a beer!"

"On you?"

"On me," said Simple. "My generosity has come down on me! I am glad I run into you while I still have some change left. I spent Three Dollars and a Half at the Cocktail Sip, threw a Dollar to the shake dancer when the floor show come on, tipped the waiter Fifty Cents, checked out my hat—then borrowed Five Dollars from Zarita that she said Buster gave her—so it all come out even. Zarita is a good old girl. She will give you the shirt off her back, also take yours off your back. But in due time, we more than gets it back, both of us. So nobody's worried. What did you say about that kiss in the cup?"

> *"Leave but a kiss within the cup*
> *And I'll not look for wine. . . ."*

"I sure won't," said Simple. "Won't and don't! But lately there ain't been nary kiss in *my cup*."

"You mean where you ring seven bells?"

"That's right," said Simple. "Joyce is still acting like she just met me—like I was a total stranger with no divorce—which maybe is why I fell into Zarita's arms today, which were wide open. You don't need a decree to relax with Zarita. You know, I usually spends Sundays with Joyce. But she said she were going to Jersey to see her godchild this afternoon. I wonder if she went? I did not ring seven to find out. Sometimes if her landlady catches me when Joyce ain't home, she just wants to talk and talk and talk, and I did not feel like talking to that woman today. So when I passed by the Heat Wave and saw that sign up —COCKTAIL SIP—I went in."

"And what did you find but sin—in the form of Zarita. 'When the cat's away, the mouse will play.'"

"Did Lizzie Beasley say that, too?"

"That's not Elizabethan, that's doggerel," I stated, "simple but true."

"Do you think I'm simple? If I wasn't drunk, I would feel bad. But I do not feel bad. I feel like if Joyce had rather go see some godchild than to see me, okay. Let the good times roll! They have rolled this evening! Look, am I wrong?"

"I am neither Judge Rivers nor Judge Delany, so I will not pass judgment on you," I said.

"I had rather go up before them than to go up before a lady judge. If my case ever got in front of any lady judge, I bet she would make me pay for Isabel's divorce. Lady judges is tight, tight, tight. But let us not mention judges this evening, partner. As long as I know what I am doing, I will never appear before one."

"You had better stop mixing your drinks then. You've been drinking cocktails, now you are drinking beer—so after a while you will not be clear as to what you are doing. Have you had your dinner yet?"

"You know I don't like restaurant cooking. And Joyce—let's not talk about her—no invite there this Sunday. I believe I will go home to bed right now, up to my Third Floor Rear. I told Zarita I might wait till she comes back, but I changed my mind. Them Specials is wearing off. Tell her I have went. If she's got any more kisses for me, tell her to leave 'em in a cup."

| Apple Strudel

"I DO believe if I was a woman I would be a nervous wretch," said Simple. "They are always worrying about dusting something, cleaning up something, or washing something, especially in the spring. Now, you take Joyce, every time I go by her place, either she, or her landlady one, is bulldozing the house—sweeping or mopping or dusting or washing out curtains, or ironing slip-covers. I swear there is many a thing to keep clean in a house. But a man do not worry about it as much as a woman."

"That's true," I said. "Still, a man has to worry about a few things, mostly personal. They take up enough time."

"Right," said Simple. "If you got any clothes at all, you have to keep them pressed. And laundry! I don't know which is worse, to have too little shirts or too many. If you only got three, you rotate them. If you got a dozen, it costs you more than you make to get them washed. And shoes, one pair ain't so bad to keep shined. You can do it yourself. But if you got three or four pair, skippy! Shining them is a nuisance. And paying good money to have them shined is more so, especially when the shine boy's hand is out for a tip each and every time."

"Well, anything one owns demands care," I said. "Did you ever read Thoreau's *Walden* when you were in school?"

"I never got that far."

"Thoreau says that his few belongings took up so much of his time when he was living in the woods trying to write and think, that he started to simplify life by eliminating things. He said to himself, 'More than one chair just means another one to dust,' so he threw out his chairs. 'Shelves are things on which one accumulates more *things*,' so he threw them out. Then he said, 'I can sleep on the floor,' so he discarded his bed. After a while his house was bare. But he didn't have to worry about a thing."

"He really cleaned house," said Simple. "But there ain't a Negro living would throw out his bed. A Negro might throw out his rug if it was summertime. He might throw out his chairs if they broke down. But bed, uh-uh, no, never would a Negro throw out his bed. It is too useful—even if it do have to be made up every morning and the sheets changed every week. Beds and Negroes go together."

"You certainly are race-conscious," I said. "Negroes, Negroes, Negroes! Everything in terms of race. Can't you think just once without thinking in terms of color?"

"I *am* colored," said Simple. "That man you was talking about were white. He could afford to throw out things. White folks have got plenty of things. Almost all we got is problems, especially the race problem. Everybody's talking about it. The white folks down where I work is always discussing this race problem. I tell them that white folks can measure their race problem by how far they have come. But Negroes measure ours by how far we have got to go.

"Them white folks are always telling me, 'Isn't it wonderful the progress that's been made amongst your people. Look at Dr. Bunche!'

"All I say is, 'Look at me.'

"That jars them because I don't look nothing like Dr. Bunche.

"Then they say, "Well, take Marian Anderson.'

"I say, 'Take Zarita,' which shakes them, because when I get through describing all the furnished-room gals in Harlem that never heard of Marian Anderson they change the subject.

"Sometimes they say, for example, 'Years ago, Mr. Semple, Negroes could not stay at the Waldorf-Astoria.'

"I say, 'Mr. Semple can't stay there right now—because Mr. Semple ain't able.'

"They say, 'But in your case it's money, not race.'

"I say, 'Yes, but if I were not of the colored race, smart as I am, I would have money.'

"That shakes them again so they switch around to something else. 'Look at Dawson and Powell, those fine men you colored folks have in Congress.'

" 'Yes,' I say, 'just two in Washington all by their lonesome. As many Negroes as there are in the U.S.A. there ought to be *two dozen* colored Congressmen. But half the Negroes in the South is scared to vote.'

" 'The Supreme Court says Negroes have the right to vote.'

" 'Can a Negro take time off from work to go running to the Supreme Court every time the Klan keeps him from voting? We can't enforce no laws by ourselves.'

" 'You are most pessimistic about things,' says the white folks.

" 'You would be, too, if you was black,' I say.

"They mean well, them white folks I work with, but they just don't know. One white fellow last week says, 'Here. I was telling my wife about you and she baked some apple strudel and sent you one for a present for you and your girl.'

"I said, 'Thank you,' because I knew he meant well. He would also like to do well. Still and yet, he is one of the very ones who will argue with me most about how the Negro problem is improving, beat me down that things is getting *so* much better, how we got so many white friends in America. Just because he gives me an apple strudel, does he think I can give everybody in Harlem a slice?

"I wish I could. To tell the truth, I really wish we could."

| Bop

SOMEBODY upstairs in Simple's house had the combination turned up loud with an old Dizzy Gillespie record spinning like mad filling the Sabbath with Bop as I passed.

"Set down here on the stoop with me and listen to the music," said Simple.

"I've heard your landlady doesn't like tenants sitting on her stoop," I said.

"Pay it no mind," said Simple. "Ool-ya-koo," he sang. "Hey Ba-Ba-Re-Bop! Be-Bop! Mop!"

"All that nonsense singing reminds me of Cab Calloway back in the old *scat* days," I said, "around 1930 when he was chanting, 'Hi-de-*hie*-de-ho! Hee-de-*hee*-de-hee!'"

"Not at all," said Simple, "absolutely not at all."

"Re-Bop certainly sounds like scat to me," I insisted.

"No," said Simple, "Daddy-o, you are wrong. Besides, it was not *Re*-Bop. It is *Be*-Bop."

"What's the difference," I asked, "between *Re* and *Be?*"

"A lot," said Simple. "Re-Bop was an imitation like most of the white boys play. Be-Bop is the real thing like the colored boys play."

"You bring race into everything," I said, "even music."

"It is in everything," said Simple.

"Anyway, Be-Bop is passé, gone, finished."

"It may be gone, but its riffs remain behind," said Simple. "Be-Bop music was certainly colored folks' music—which is why white folks found it so hard to imitate. But there are some few white boys that latched onto it right well. And no wonder, because they sat and listened to Dizzy, Thelonius, Tad Dameron, Charlie Parker, also Mary Lou, all night long every time they got a chance, and bought their records by the dozens to copy their riffs. The ones that sing tried to make up new Be-Bop words, but them white folks don't know what they are singing about, even yet."

"It all sounds like pure nonsense syllables to me."

"Nonsense, nothing!" cried Simple. "Bop makes plenty of sense."

"What kind of sense?"

"You must not know where Bop comes from," said Simple, astonished at my ignorance.

"I do not know," I said. "Where?"

"From the police," said Simple.

"What do you mean, from the police?"

"From the police beating Negroes' heads," said Simple. "Every time a cop hits a Negro with his billy club, that old club says, 'BOP! BOP! . . . BE-BOP! . . . MOP! . . . BOP!'

"That Negro hollers, 'Ooool-ya-koo! Ou-o-o!'

"Old Cop just keeps on, 'MOP! MOP! . . . BE-BOP! . . . MOP!' That's where Be-Bop came from, beaten right out of some Negro's head into them horns and saxophones and piano keys that plays it. Do you call that nonsense?"

"If it's true, I do not," I said.

"That's why so many white folks don't dig Bop," said Simple. "White folks do not get their heads beat *just for being white*. But me—a cop is liable to grab me almost any time and beat my head—*just* for being colored.

"In some parts of this American country as soon as the polices see me, they say, 'Boy, what are you doing in this neighborhood?'

"I say, 'Coming from work, sir.'

"They say, 'Where do you work?'

"Then I have to go into my whole pedigree because I am a black man in a white neighborhood. And if my answers do not satisfy them, BOP! MOP! . . . BE-BOP! . . . MOP! If they do not hit me, they have already hurt my soul. *A dark man shall see dark days.* Bop comes out of them dark days. That's why real Bop is mad, wild, frantic, crazy—and not to be dug unless you've seen dark days, too. Folks who ain't suffered much cannot play Bop, neither appreciate it. They think Bop is nonsense—like you. They think it's just *crazy* crazy. They do not know Bop is also MAD crazy, SAD crazy, FRANTIC WILD CRAZY—beat out of somebody's head! That's what Bop is. Them young colored kids who started it, they know what Bop is."

"Your explanation depresses me," I said.

"Your nonsense depresses me," said Simple.

| Formals and Funerals

SUDDENLY spring had turned off cold again. The day after Easter it was drizzling rain. Easter Monday night I was standing under the Theresa Hotel's protecting canopy watching the cars cutting and curving around each corner at 125th and Seventh. Simple was walking against the wind with his head down, his coat collar up, and his hat dripping.

"Where are you going this cold night with the rain raining and the elements blowing?" I asked.

"Hi, there!" he said. "I am ankling to the flower shop to buy a corsage. Come on with me."

"In this rain! Are you simple?"

"Somewhatly," he said, "but I got to do it."

"So you and Joyce are going out sporting this evening, I divine."

"You know it's not me and no other woman," said Simple. "I *certainly* would not spend Ten Dollars for a corsarge for nobody else, even if she is paying half of it herself."

"You mean to say Joyce has to go halfers on her own corsage," I asked, "when *you* are taking her out?"

"She is liable to have to go *more* than half before this evening is done," said Simple. "We are going to a formal, the Beaux Noirs Annual Easter Monday Dance. Do you know what a formal is? It is a function where you have to wear a tux with a shirt that buttons only with studs and a tie that is a bow. Joyce has got herself an evening gown that is cut so low it looks like she is trying to show how little she can wear and not catch pneumo-

nia. If you are anybody in society at all at a formal you have to
have a box to retire to between dances. Me and Joyce is sharing
our box with another couple, which makes us only have to pay
half, which is Twelve Dollars, the box costing Twenty-Four to
seat eight. When you go to a formal it is necessary to invite
guests to set in your box, so we have invited two couples. Since
Joyce and me and the other couple are the hosts, we have to
furnish the licker. I got one bottle of White Mule and one bottle of White Horse. The Horse is for Joyce—since she says a
lady drinks nothing but Scotch at a public formal.

"I'm telling you, a formal is something! Right there, daddy-o,
I have done spent Twenty-Three Dollars and Eighty-Two
Cents, not counting renting the tux which also required a Ten
Dollar deposit in case I snag it or do not bring it back. Raining
and blowing like it is tonight, I got to take Joyce in a cab, which
is another Dollar and a Half. Fifty Cents for the checkroom
girl, tips for the waiter that brings the set-ups, another tip for
extra ice. Then after the dance, womens always have to eat even
if it is mighty nigh breakfast time, so you have to take them for
four A.M. barbecue at Ribs-In-The-Ruff, so they can gaze at
Sidney. Man, a formal costs almost as much as a funeral! Since
Joyce just *has* to go to a formal, what reason is it she shouldn't
pay half? It were not my idea in the first place."

"One doesn't take a woman out on her own money," I said.

"I do," said Simple, "when she insists on going some place I
can't afford. Why can't they have a formal without all this rig-
marole? I had rather die than put on a stud-buttoned shirt. And
I do not understand why it takes a formal for Joyce to wear a
dress cut so low everybody can see almost as much of her as I
could if I was married to her."

"Maybe that is why folks like formals," I said, "because
women reveal their hidden charms."

"Such charms should be reserved for husbands."

"You're as old-fashioned as a Sultan. In Turkey in the old
days Sultans made their wives put on veils when they went
out, and wrap up from top to toe."

"Here," said Simple, "women take off practically everything
when they go out. Joyce is liable to catch her death of cold unless

I buy her a *great big* corsarge to cover up her chest. How many dozen orchids do you reckon you get for Ten Dollars?"

"About one," I said. "Not one dozen, but *one orchid*."

"I am going to get her carnations," said Simple.

"If you do, Joyce will never speak to you again. An orchid is *the* flower for a formal."

"Are orchids made of gold?"

"Of course not."

"Neither am I," said Simple.

| Fancy Free

"BEFORE spring is over, if I can't get no spring clothes, at least I would like to have me a real good mess of greens."

Simple stood at the bar and uttered this statement as though it were of great importance. Then he shook his head with a gesture of despair.

"But there is no place in New York to pick greens. Maybe that is why womens do not cook them much in Big Cities. Not even a dandelion do I see growing in Morningside Park. If there was, it wouldn't stay there long because some Negro would pull it and eat it."

"Greens *are* good," I said.

"Don't talk!" cried Simple. "All boiled down with a side of pork, delicious! Greens make my mouth water. I have eaten so many in my life until I could write a book on greenology—and I still would like to eat that many more. What I wouldn't give right now for a good old iron pot full! Mustard greens, collard greens, turnip greens, dandelions, dock. Beet-tops, lamb's tongue, pepper grass, sheepcress, also poke. Good old mixed greens! Spinach or chard, refined greens! Any kind of fresh greens. I wonder why somebody don't open a restaurant for nothing but greens? I should think that would go right good up North."

"I hear you always talking about going into business," I said. "Why don't you open one?"

"Where would I get the greens?" asked Simple. "They don't grow around here. Wild mustard has never been known to be found sprouting on Lenox Avenue. And was I to see poke in New York, I would swear it were a miracle. Besides, even if they did grow here, who would pick 'em? That is woman's work, but I would not trust it to Joyce. She might not know greens from poison weeds, nor pepper grass from bridal mist. Joyce were not raised on dandelions like me. I don't expect she would be caught with a basket picking greens. Joyce is cultural."

"She likes greens, though, doesn't she?"

"Eats them like a horse," said Simple, "when somebody else serves them. The same by chitterlings. Joyce tried to tell me once she did not eat pig ruffles, would not cook them, couldn't bear to clean them, and *loathed* the smell. But when my cousin in the Bronx invited us to a chitterling supper, I could hardly get near the pot for Joyce. I do not believe people should try to pass."

"What do you mean, *pass?*"

"Pass for non-chitterling eaters if they are chitterling eaters," said Simple. "What I like, I like, and I do not care who knows it. I also like watermelon."

"Why not?" I asked.

"Some colored folks are ashamed to like watermelon. I told you about that woman who bought one in the store once and made the clerk wrap it up before she would carry it home. She didn't want nobody to see her with a watermelon. Me, I would carry a watermelon unwrapped any day any where. I would eat one before the Queen of England."

"A pretty picture you would make, eating a slice of watermelon before the queen."

"I would give the queen a slice—and I bet she would thank me for it, especially if it was one of them light green round striped melons with a deep red heart and coal-black seeds. Man, juicy! Oh, my soul! Sweet, yes! And good to a fare-thee-well! I wish I had a pot of greens right now, a pitcher of buttermilk, and a watermelon."

"You would have a stomach ache."

"It would be worth it! But let's talk no more about such things. I would settle for a cold bottle of beer on you here."

"I see no reason why I should buy you a bottle of beer."

"I am broke and I have dreamed you up a beautiful dream," said Simple. "You know you like them things, too. If I had not dreamed them up, you might not of thought of watermelon or greens tonight—greens, greens, greens!"

"Thinking of greens is not the same as eating them," I said.

"No," said Simple, "but at least we can share the thought. It was my thought. Don't you intend to share the beer? O.K. Draw two, bartender! Pay the man—and let us wash down those greens we have thought up. Pass the corn bread. I thank you, daddy-o! Now, hand me the vinegar, also the baby onions."

"You are certainly indulging in a flight of fancy! In fact, your imagination is running riot. Beer is not free."

"No, but fancy is, and if I had my way," said Simple, seizing his beer, "I would be a bird in a meadow full of greens right now!"

"Why a bird? Why not a horse, or a sheep?"

"A bird can fly high, see with a bird's eye, and dig all that is going on down on earth, especially what people are doing in the springtime."

"Birds are not customarily interested in the doings of human beings," I said, "except to the point of keeping out of their way."

"I would keep out of people's way," said Simple, "but also I would observe everything they do."

"Suppose they captured you and put you in a cage?"

"No, I would not be a pretty bird, the kind anybody would want in a cage. I would be just a plain old ugly bird that caws and nobody would want. That way I would be free. I would sail over towns and cities and look down and see what is going on. I would ride on tops of cars in Italian weddings, on top of hearses in Catholic funerals, I would light on the back of fish-tail Cadillacs in Harlem, and when I wanted to travel without straining myself, I would ride the baggage rack of a Greyhound bus to California.

"Before I left I would build me a nest on top of the Empire

State so that when I came home I could rest on top of the world. I would dig worms in Radio City's gardens and set underneath a White House bush when I visited Washington. I would wash my feet in every fountain from here to yonder, and eat greens in every meadow. Down South I would ignore FOR WHITE and FOR COLORED signs—I would drink water anywhere I wished. I would not be tied to no race, no place, nor fixed location.

"I would be the travelingest bird you ever met—because everywhere that Jackie went, I would go. Every time Robinson batted a ball over the fence, I would be setting on that fence. I would watch Joe Black daily, and caw like mad for Campanella. I would outfly the Dodgers from New York to St. Louis, and from Boston to Chicago. Everywhere they went, there would be old me. Ah, but I would fly! On summer evenings I would dip my wings in the sea at Southampton and in winter live on baby oranges in Florida—if I did not go further to the West Indies and get away from Jim Crow. In fact, come to think of it, I believe I would just fly *over* the South, stopping only long enough to spread my tail feathers and show my contempt.

"If I was a bird, daddy-o, I would sometimes fly so high I would not see this world at all. I would soar! Just soar way up into the blue where heaven is, and the smell of earth does not go, neither the noise of juke boxes nor radios, television or record shops. Up there, I would not hear anything but winds blowing. I would not see anything but space. I would not remember no little old taw-marble called the world rolling around somewhere with you on it and Joyce and my boss and my landlady and her hound-dog of a Trixie. There would not be no paydays up there, neither rent-days nor birthdays nor Sunday. There would not be nothing but blue sky—and wind—and space. So much space!

"But when I got real lonesome looking at space, I would head back towards earth. I would pierce old space with my beak and cleave the wind with my wings. Yes, I would! I would split the sky wide open to get back to earth. And when I come in sight of Lenox Avenue, man, I would caw once real loud. Everybody would look up and think it was a horn honking on the Chariot of God. But it wouldn't be nobody but me—coming back to Harlem.

"I would swoop down on Seventh Avenue at six P.M. in the evening like a bat out of hell, do two loop-the-loops over the Theresa, and land on 125th Street by the Chock-Full-O'-Nuts. Then I would change myself back into a human, take the bus to my corner, put my key in my old landlady's vestibule, go up to my Third Floor Rear, wash my face, change my clothes, lay my hair down, and go see Joyce, and tell her I am tired of eating raw greens—to cook me up some ham and collards. I could not stand to be no bird anyhow if Joyce were not with me. Also, I would miss my friends. I would see how lonesome it were all day long up there in the heavenly blue and I would come back to this earth and home. Two beers, bartender!"

| Midsummer Madness

PAVEMENT hot as a frying pan on Jennie Lou's griddle. Heat devils dancing in the air. Men in windows with no undershirts on—which is one thing ladies can't get by with if they lean out windows. Sunset. Stoops running over with people, curbs running over with kids. August in Harlem too hot to be August in hell. Beer is going up a nickel a glass, I hear, but I do not care. I would still be forced to say gimme a cool one.

"That bar's sign is lying—AIR COOLED—which is why I'd just as well stay out here on the sidewalk. Girl, where did you get them baby-doll clothes? Wheee-ee-oooo!" The woman did not stop, but you could tell by the way she walked that she heard him. Simple whistled. "Hey, Lawdy, Miss Claudy! Or might your name be Cleopatra?" No response. "Partner, she ig-ed me."

"She really ignored you," I said.

"Well, anyhow, every dog has its day—but the trouble is there are more dogs than there are days, more people than there are houses, more roomers than there are rooms, and more babies than there are cribs."

"You're speaking philosophically this evening."

"I'm making up proverbs. For instance: 'A man with no legs don't need shoes.' "

"Like most proverbs, that states the obvious."

"It came right out of my own head—even if I did hear it before," insisted Simple. "Also I got another one for you based on experience: 'Don't get a woman that *you* love. Get a woman that loves you!' "

"Meaning, I take it, that if a woman loves *you*, she will take care of you, and you won't have to take care of her."

"Something like that," said Simple, "because if you love a woman you are subject to lay down your all before her, empty your heart and your pockets, and then have nothing left. I bet if I had been born with a silver spoon in my mouth, some woman would of had my spoon before I got to the breakfast table. I always was weak for women. In fact, womens is the cause of my being broke tonight. After I buy Joyce her summer ice cream and Zarita her summer beer, I cannot hardly buy myself a drink by the middle of the week. At dinner time all I can do is walk in a restaurant and say, 'Gimme an order of water in a clean glass.' "

"I will repeat a proverb for *you*," I said. " 'It's a mighty poor chicken that can't scratch up his own food.' "

"I am a poor rooster," said Simple. "Womens have cleaned me to the bone. I may give out, but I'll never give up, though. Neither womens nor white folks are going to get Jesse B. down."

"Can't you ever keep race out of the conversation?" I said.

"I am race conscious," said Simple. "And I ain't ashamed of my race. I ain't like that woman that bought a watermelon and had it *wrapped* before she carried it out of the store. I am what I am. And what I say is: 'If you're corn bread, don't try to be an angel-food cake! That's a mistake. . . . Look at that chick! Look at that de-light under the light! So round, so firm, so fully packed! But don't you be looking, too, partner. You might strain your neckbone."

"You had better take your own advice," I said, "or you might get your head cut off. A woman with a shape like that is bound to have a boy friend."

"One more boy friend would do her no harm," said Simple,

"so it might as well be me. But you don't see me moving out of my tracks, do you? I have learned one thing just by observation: Midsummer madness brings winter sadness, so curb your badness. If you can't be good, be careful. In this hot weather with womens going around not only with bare back, but some of them with mighty near everything else bare, a man has got to watch his self. Look at them right here on the Avenue—play suits, sun suits, swim suits, practically no suits. I swear, if I didn't care for Joyce, I'd be turning my head every which-a-way, and looking every which-a-where. As it is, I done eye-balled a plenty. This is the hottest summer I ever seen—but the womens look cool. That is why a man has to be careful."

"Cool, too, you mean—controlled!"

"Also careful," said Simple. "I remember last summer seeing them boys around my stoop, also the mens on the corner jiving with them girls in the windows and the young mens in the candy store buying ice cream for jail bait and beating bongos under her be-bop windows. And along about the middle of the winter, or maybe it was spring, I heard a baby crying in the room underneath me, and another one gurgling in the third floor front. And this summer on the sidewalk I see *more* new baby carriages, and rattles being raised, and milk bottles being sucked. It is beautiful the way nature keeps right on producing Negroes. But the Welfare has done garnished some of these men's wages. And the lady from the Domestic Relations Court has been upstairs in the front room investigating twice as to where Carlyle has gone. When he do come home he will meet up with a summons."

"I take it Carlyle is a young man who does not yet realize the responsibilities of parenthood."

"Carlyle is old enough to know a baby has to eat. And I do not give him credit for cutting out and leaving that girl with that child—except that they had a fight, and Carlyle left her a note which was writ: 'Him who fights and runs away, lives to fight some other day.' The girl said Carlyle learned that in high school when he ought to have been learning how to get a good job that pays more than thirty-two dollars a week. When their baby was born, it was the coldest day in March. And my big old fat landlady, what always said she did not want no children in the house, were mad when the Visiting Health Nurse came downstairs and told her to send some heat up.

"She said, 'You just go back upstairs and tell that Carlyle to send me some money down. He is two weeks behind now on his rent. I told him not to be setting on my stoop with that girl last summer. Instead of making hay while the sun were shining, he were using his time otherwise. Just go back upstairs and tell him what I said.'

" 'All of which is no concern of mine,' says the Health Nurse. 'I am concerned with the welfare of mother and child. Your house is cold, except down here where you and your dog is at.'

" 'Just leave Trixie out of this,' says the landlady. 'Trixie is an old dog and has rheumatism. I love this dog better than I love myself, and I intends to keep her warm.'

" 'If you do not send some steam upstairs, I will advise your tenants to report you to the Board of Health,' says the Health Nurse.

"She were a real spunky little nurse. I love that nurse—because about every ten days she came by to see how them new babies was making out. And every time she came, that old landlady would steam up. So us roomers was warm some part of last winter, anyhow."

"Thanks especially to Carlyle and his midsummer madness," I said. "But where do you suppose the boy went when he left his wife?"

"To his mama's in the Bronx," said Simple. "He is just a young fellow what is not housebroke yet. I seen him last night on the corner of Lenox and 125th and he said he was coming back soon as he could find himself a good job. Fight or not fight, he says he loves that girl and is crazy about his baby, and all he wants is to find himself a Fifty or Sixty Dollar a week job so he can meet his responsibilities. I said, 'Boy, how much did you say you want to make a week?' And he repeated himself, 'Fifty to Sixty.'

"So I said, 'You must want your baby to be in high school before you returns.'

"Carlyle said, 'I'm a man now, so I want to get paid like a man.'

" 'You mean a white man,' I said.

" 'I mean a *grown* man,' says Carlyle.

"By that time the Bronx bus come along and he got on it, so I did not get a chance to tell that boy that I knowed what he meant, but I did not know how it could come true. . . . Man, look at that chick going yonder, stacked up like the Queen Mary! . . . Wheee-ee-ooo! Baby, if you must walk away, walk straight—and don't shake your tail-gate."

"Watch yourself! Have you no respect for women?"

"I have nothing but respect for a figure like that," said Simple. "Miss, your mama must of been sweet sixteen when she borned you. Sixteen divided by two, you come out a figure 8! Can I have a date? Hey, Lawdy, Miss Claudy! You must be deaf—you done left! I'm standing here by myself.

"Come on, boy, let's go on in the bar and put that door between me and temptation. If the air cooler is working, the treat's on me. Let's investigate. Anyhow, I always did say if you can't be good, be careful. If you can't be nice, take advice. If you don't think once, you can't think twice."

| Morals Is Her Middle Name

"IT TAKES a whole lot of *not* having what you want, to get what you want most," said Simple, cooling off at the bar.

"Meaning?" I asked.

"Meaning you have got to do without a lot of things you want in order to get the main thing you want."

"What do you want?"

"Joyce," said Simple, "to be my wife—*soon.*"

"And what is it that you will have to do without?"

"My beer and my sport," said Simple. "I am on an allotment, in other words, a budget. I have made up my mind to make that final payment on my first wife's divorce myself, so I can be free to marry my final wife. So now I do not buy but one glass of beer per day—which is my allotment. After hours I no longer sport around a-tall, neither gamble—which is my budget. I have opened a savings account and I put Ten to Fifteen Dollars in it each and every week. I soon will have that One Hundred and Thirty-Three Dollars which is the third payment on my divorce. Since my wife's husband-to-be made the first payment, and Isabel made the second, I have now made up my mind to make the third.

"I think it is no more than right," I said.

"It is *not* right," said Simple. "Isabel run me out of the house. If she wants a divorce, she should pay for it herself. But now that she has found a chump who will marry her, and pay a third of it, too, I figure it will speed things up if I meet that other third—since I want to marry Joyce before I get old as Methusaleh."

"All this time you've been standing Joyce off waiting for your divorce; you should consider yourself lucky. She certainly has more patience than most women."

"Joyce is a saint," said Simple. "She knows my heart is in the right place even if my pocketbook is empty. That girl knows I love her. But life ain't all that long, that a girl so good should be stood up indefinite. Joyce says if I don't marry her this year, skippy! She says she is tired of paying room rent by herself. Also if she stays *Miss* much longer, she will have missed the boat. Joyce says she is going to get on board some kind of boat this year even if it is a tug.

"I told her, 'Baby, don't put me in a class with no tug. I am a big-time excursion boat, myself. I hauls the finest only, that is why I am waiting now to take you on my deck.'

"'When will your decks be clear?' asks Joyce.

"'When I have saved One Hundred,' I said, 'which will be when I have done without *One Thousand* glasses of beer.'"

"You have counted carefully," I said.

"Which is why, daddy-o, I have give up drinking, also any other kind of sport which takes money. I even skipped seeing the Dodgers play this season, and only looked at Jackie on television, in order to prove to that woman that I will do a whole lot of not having what I want, to get what I want—which is her. Joyce is sweet, I mean! In my heart she is a queen! My desire, my fire, my honey—the only woman who ever made me save my money!"

"I am glad to see your mind made up," I said.

"A man has to make his mind up," said Simple, "to get a woman to make his bed down. You know, Joyce is not like a lot of these women around New York. She don't have no truck for trash that don't act right. Just this evening she was reading and it were a colored paper, and she asked me why it is that every time she looks in it they got on the society page the picture of some colored pimp or racketeer or low lady stuck up there as representative of society. That I do not understand myself."

"I understand it," I said. "The racketeer people and night-life folks are about the only ones in these days of high prices who have got the money to entertain lavishly."

"Well, money or not," said Simple, "Joyce says she do not see why they is got to be set up as examples for kids to imitate. She tried to make a issue out of it with me, even, when I told her that Sweet Beak Charlie was after all a nice guy, even if he did have an apartment on Sugar Hill, a house in Long Island, two Cadillacs, a wife and six other womens, and made his money out of numbers. Naturally, him and his wife is bound to go in society."

"They are way up there," I said.

"They are," said Simple, "but Joyce won't admit it, even if they do give cocktail parties all winter and garden parties all summer.

"Joyce yells, 'They ain't no society to me, them and nobody else like them! I know how too many of them got their money. and they did not get it right. They got it out of crooked dice, good-time houses, reefers, bootlegging, and not paying off when somebody hits for more than a quarter—like I did once— and haven't got my money till this day. I do not see how such people rate to be society, their pictures always stuck up on the Society Page of our papers.' "

"Joyce is a pretty strict moralist," I said.

"Morals is her middle name," said Simple. "But she says them other folks do not have neither morals or manners.

"I says, 'Well, at least, they have got money.'

" 'Money is not everything,' says Joyce.

" 'No,' I says, 'but it will do till everything comes along.'

"That makes Joyce mad all over again. 'Do?' she hollers. 'Do for what? Money cannot give back a prostitute her virginity! Neither can money give a P.I. back his good name, nor turn a dope pusher into a Christian. Any woman with money can buy a mink coat, but that does not make her a lady. Any hussy in society can hire a cater to cater a party and roast her a ham and grind it up and ruin it for appetizers when everybody has got an appetite already and would rather have ham sandwiches without calling them hore-do-beers on crackers. I would not care if I served chitterlings,' says Joyce; 'I would rather have my good name, even if I never get it in the papers.'

"Man, Joyce really raved—and she looked at me like as if I was in society. And I ain't never even been in jail—let alone society—but once."

"What were you in jail for?" I asked.

"Not for doing nothing wrong," said Simple. "I just happened to be present when they raided a house."

"What kind of a house?"

"A gambling house."

"Then you were contributing to crime," I said, "by supporting the place."

"I sure did support it," said Simple, "because they got all I had. But I did not run it. It belonged to Sweet Beak who's always got his wife's picture in the society columns nowadays for giving parties."

"Racketeers are not in the papers just for the parties they give," I said. "They often donate a lot of money to charity, or marry one actress after another, or open night clubs, or do something sensational. If good people want to be news, they have to do sensational things, too. Just being good is not enough—at least, not for the newspapers."

"It's not enough for making money either," said Simple.

| They Come and They Go

"Do you know what happened to me last night when I got home?" said Simple.

"How could I—when I haven't seen you since?"

"F. D. was setting in my room."

"Who in the world is F. D.?"

"Franklin D. Roosevelt Brown."

"I haven't the least idea whom you are talking about," I said.

"I am talking about the fact I never did think I would be being a father to a son who is not my son, but it looks like that is what is about to happen to me."

"A son?"

"Same as," said Simple. "I've been adopted."

"It's beyond my comprehension."

"Mine, too," said Simple. "But his name ought to make you remember what I told you once about my Cousin Mattie Mae's baby being born down in Virginia a long time ago when she were working for them rich white folks, and she named that baby Franklin D. Roosevelt Brown. Them rich old Southerners got mad when they heard it, and told Mattie Mae she better take that white name off that black child. Mattie Mae told them she'd quit first, which she did.

"Well, when I got home high last night at one-two A.M.—having fell off my budget—and come creeping up the steps not to disturb my old landlady, I saw a light under the crack of my door. I thought maybe Zarita had got in my room by mistake, since sometimes she do inveigle my landlady. But when I opened the door, I hollered out loud, also damn near turned pale. I had not expected to see no Negro setting on my bed. I thought he were a robber. Every hair on my head turned to wire. But it were not no robber. It were a boy.

"When he riz up grinning, instead of fighting, I yelled, 'If I knowed who you was I'd grab my pistol out of that drawer and shoot you before you could speak your name, but I do not want to kill nobody I don't know. Who *in the hell* is you?'

" 'F. D.'

" 'F. D. who?' I said, still shaking.

" 'Don't you remember me? I'm your Cousin Mattie Mae's boy, Franklin D. Roosevelt Brown. You saw me when I was five years old.'

" 'You sure ain't five now,' I said, 'and you done scared the hell out of me, setting on *my* chair in *my* room at this time of night, and I ain't seen you since you was a baby. You big as I am. How old are you?'

" 'Seventeen, going on eighteen,' he said.

" 'What are you doing out so late?'

" 'I'm not just out, Cousin Jess. I'm gone.'

" 'Gone! From where?'

" 'Home. I left.'

" 'Left what home? I ain't heard tell of you, nor Mattie Mae neither, in ten years. Where do you live, Brooklyn?'

" 'Virginia,' he said.

" 'Your mother sent you here?'

" 'My mama does not know I am gone,' he said. 'I ran away.'

" 'Well, how come you run *here*?'

" 'Because you're my favorite cousin. I got your address from Uncle George William. I've heard tell of you all my life, Cousin Jess. Folks at home're always talking about you. And I never will forget that hard big-league ball you bought me when I was five years old, and you came home on that visit. I broke my mama's lamp with it and got whipped within an inch of my life. But I never did blame you for it—like the rest of them did. I sure am glad to see you now, Cousin Jess. Howdy!'

" 'Set down,' I said. He set. 'On what did you come here— hitch-hike?'

" 'No, sir. Train. I didn't dream of getting to New York, Cousin Jess, wasn't even thinking of it. But I've been wanting to come, ever since my step-father raw-hided me. Then when Mama Mattie just keeps on telling me I'm just like my father, no-good, I was thinking of running away to Norfolk and joining the navy, till somebody told me I wasn't old enough without my parents' consent. Then I thought I'd run as far as Baltimore maybe before frost sets in. But all this was just kind of vague in my mind. Then, last night, I was hanging around the station watching the trains come in and the girls eating ice-cream cones when a colored man got off the streamliner from the North and he said to me, *Here, boy, here is a ticket for you. The rest of this here round-trip, I do not want it. Use it, sell it, tear it up, or give it away. I don't care.*

" 'I looked at it and saw that it was a ticket to New York—a great long yellow ticket. I said, *Aren't you going back up North?*

" 'The man said, *I been up North. They comes and they goes. You go.*

" 'He cut out and left me standing there on the train platform with the ticket in my hand. So when the night train came along in a few minutes heading North, I got on. Here I am.'

" 'Here you is, all right,' I said.

" 'I always did want to come North, Cousin Jess, so I come to you—'

" 'Don't get *me* confused with the North! I ain't the North.'

" 'And I always wanted to see New York and—'

" 'My room ain't New York. Out yonder is New York.'

" 'You are all the Harlem I knew to come to, so—'

" 'Excuse me from being Harlem, because I ain't. Where are you going to sleep? Also eat?' I said. 'How are you going to live?'

"Then that kid took his eyes off me for the first time. He looked down. In fact he looked like he were going to cry.

" 'O.K.,' he said, 'I guess I can't sleep here. And I'm not hungry. So so long, Cousin Jess.'

"He got up and reached for his hat which were on my dresser. In my mind I was going to say, 'Go on back home.'

"Instead I heard my mouth say, 'Hey, you, F.D.! Hang your clothes on the back of that chair. You can sleep over there next to the wall—I got to jump out early when the alarm goes off. I'm telling you, though, I'm a man that snores when I'm in my licker, so if you can sleep through—'

" 'If you don't mind a fellow that kicks in his sleep, Cousin Jess—'

" 'Did you bring your toothbrush?'

" 'No, sir, just the clothes on my back.'

" 'Well, you can get a toothbrush tomorrow.'

"So that's the way it were. My big old landlady let F. D. in to wait for me when I wasn't home. Now, what am I gonna do?"

"You say he's going on eighteen. He's practically a man, isn't he? So he'll know his way around soon."

"I don't know my way around yet," said Simple.

| A Million—And One

"WHEN I first come to Harlem, I remember, some of them folks that was here then are gone now. It's true, all right, as that man told F. D., 'They come and they go.' New York is too much for them. Some can't make the riffle, just can't stand the pace. Some go to Sea View, some to Lawnside Cemetery, some to Riker's Island, and some go back home. Some get off trains back down South where they come from—and stay. They *been* North, like that man said.

"If I had not told so many lies myself in my time, I would believe F. D. was lying. But I know that sometimes a lie is the truth. And some things that really happen are more like lies than some things that don't. F. D. couldn't make up nothing like his story about that ticket that would be *that* true. So I know it was true. That boy wanted to come to New York so bad he wished himself up on a ticket. Then he had sense enough to believe the ticket was real. It were real. And here he is!

"Do you think I will tell F. D. to go home? I would not!" said Simple. "I remember when I first come to Harlem, nobody had better not tell me to return back home. I do not know if I looked like that kid or not. But I can see F. D. now setting there last night on that chair with one million dreams in his eyes and a million more in his heart. Could I tell him to go home?"

"What kind of kid is F. D.?"

"About the darkest *young* boy I ever seen. And he has the whitest teeth which, when he smiles, lights up the room. He also looks like he has always just taken a bath, he is so clean. Fact is, I would say F. D. is a handsome black boy, but my judgment might be wrong. I want you and Joyce to meet him. He's a husky young cat, done picked so much tobacco he's built like a boxer. Also plays basketball, says his high-school team were the county champeens last spring. He's graduated and got a diploma, too. I know he's smart because the first thing he asked me for this morning when that alarm clock went off, was, 'Cousin Jess, you got any books I can read while you're at work?'

"You know, I couldn't find nothing but a comic book. But I borrowed a dollar from my landlady and told him, 'Go out and look at Harlem today—till I find my books. There ain't but about a million Negroes in Harlem. You will make One Million and *One*. Get acquainted with your brothers.'

"You mean you turned him loose on the town unaccompanied, just like that, and he's never been here before?"

"Could I stay off from work just to go sightseeing with F. D.?"

"I suppose not, but—"

"And do I know anybody else rich enough to be off from work in the daytime? I do not. That young boy did not want to be cooped up in that hot room in the warm summertime with nobody there. And it was a good thing I turned him loose this morning, too, because do you know what he did?"

"No."

"F. D. found himself a job the *first* day he was here. I'm telling you the Semple family is smart even on the Brown side."

"How did he accomplish that miraculous feat?"

"He asked a boy running for the subway if he knew where a job was. The boy said, 'I'm running to my job now. If you can keep up with me, there might me another one down where I am.'

"So F. D. run, too. He like to lost that boy in the subway rush, but he pushed and scrooged along with him, and ended up in the garment center. When that boy run in and grabbed a hand-truck loaded with ladies' garments, F. D. grabbed a hand-truck, too. So the man thought he was working there all the time and give him a invoice to deliver. When he come back, he give him another one. And they put F. D. down on the payroll as hired. That boy just went to work on his nerve."

"It runs in the family," I said. "That's the way you drink, on your nerve—and your friends."

"Come Saturday, I can borrow from F. D.," said Simple.

"Where is he now while you're supporting the bar?"

"I sent him to the movies. He is too young to invite in a bar. But if it was left up to me, I would rather have him in this nice noisy café which ain't no more immoral than them jitterbug candy stores where they sell reefers and write numbers for kids. More junkies hang around a candy store than in a bar, also dope pushers, which I hope F. D. do not meet. What am I going to do with that boy when he starts getting around? Harlem is a blip. He cannot just go to movies every night."

"What you are going to do about sending him back home or, at least, getting in touch with his parents, is the problem it seems to me you should be considering."

"I should?" asked Simple. "I took for granted F. D. were here to stay. I ain't none of his close relations that I have to correspond with his ma. And from what he told me tonight whilst we was eating in the Do-Right Lunch, in my opinion, he just as well not be with Mattie Mae. She's married again and got seven children by another man, not F. D.'s father. They got more mouths than they can feed now. Which is maybe why that boy is so smart. He's been working since he were eight-nine years old. So if he has to look out for his self anyhow, it might as well be in New York where the color line will not choke him to death. I ain't even thought about F. D. going back home."

"Don't you suppose his mother will worry about where he is?"

"I will tell F. D. to drop Mattie Mae a card tonight when I get in. I do not intend to stay out until A.M. and set a bad example for that boy. And he better be home when I get there."

"Do you intend to start bossing the boy around immediately?"

"I intend to start keeping him straight," said Simple. "I know some of the ropes in New York, and if I find him pulling on the wrong ones, I will pull him back."

"Do you intend to keep him with you in that small room of

yours?" I asked. "That will cramp your style slightly for entertaining, will it not?"

"Zarita better not light around that room while F. D. is there," said Simple. "I will ask Joyce to take him to church to meet some nice young girls what attends Christian Endeavor or B.Y.P.U. Since I am F. D.'s favorite cousin, he is going to meet some of Harlem's *favorite* people, you know, society, *up there*—the kind I do not know very well myself, but which Joyce knows. I will not let a fine boy like F. D. down. I might even try to meet a few undrinking folks myself—just to have somebody to introduce F. D. to. He ain't got around to the point of asking me yet where I go when I go out. But if he gets curious I'm liable to end up at Abyssinia's prayer meeting some night."

"For you," I said, "I think that would be carrying things a little far. That boy will like you just as well when he finds out your true character. With young people, just be yourself, and you'll get along. Kids don't like four-flushers, nor false fronts, you can be sure of that. Take my advice and just be yourself with F. D."

"There's something else you can give me tonight besides advice, daddy-o. Maybe you'll lend—"

"My good man, please don't start that again. Always borrowing—"

"You thought I was going to say money, didn't you? Uh-uh! Fooled you for once. I was going to say, lend me some extra books you got around your place for that boy to look at."

"Happy to, of course. When?"

"Right now, tonight," said Simple. "I don't want that boy to wake up nary another morning and I ain't got a single book in the house. He will think I am ignorant. Give me some books now."

"Suppose I am not going home now?"

"I very seldom ask of you a favor outside a bar."

"You have *never* asked me for one like this before. Come on, let's go get the books. The Lord must have sent that boy up North to bring a little culture into your life. Joyce has been trying all these years without success. Thank God for Franklin D Roosevelt Brown!"

"Mattie Mae had a point when she gave that boy that powerful name," said Simple. "It has done took effect on me. I might even read one of them books you are going to lend me. I got to have something to talk about with my cousin. He's educated. Virginia schools for colored ain't as bad as they used to be, so he has learned a lot more than I. Of course, I can talk with you because when you drink beer you come down to my level. But F. D. is too young to drink, so I got to come *up* to his. Am I right?"

"I think you are very right."

"Then pick me out a book I can read *now* this evening," said Simple.

"They say *Knowledge cannot be assimilated overnight*," I reminded him.

"I don't care what they say," said Simple. "It can be laying there ready to assimilate in the morning."

Two Loving Arms

"I AM glad F. D. got a job in that Jewish dress factory," said Simple, "because he will learn something. It is good to work around some other kinds of people than Gentiles. I thought all white folks was white folks until I come North to Maryland. I did not know some were Jews. In Virginia I do not recall that it made any difference. The better-class folks is more gentlemen down there than to use bad names about somebody's race. But in Baltimore at the shipyards where I worked, folks flung words round right freely about Jews and Negroes, too. But I would fling the dozens right back at them—and back up the dozens with my fists. You see this scar over my left eye? Well, the white man what give it to me got a worse scar over his right lip. I was the baddest Negro God's got when I were young.

"Anyhow, when I first got to Baltimore, before I worked in either the foundry or the shipyards, I worked in a Jewish dress store where colored people could not try on a dress. You know most downtown stores in Baltimore is like that. A colored

woman has to buy hats, dresses, and shoes by sight, without trying them on, if she buys them at all, less'n she shops in the colored neighborhood. Baltimore is worse than way down South
in some things.

"Anyway, Mr. Harris what owned this store was a right nice
man and he told me—it were not his fault Baltimore had them
kinds of customs because in the Old Country where he come
from there was no prejudices against colored folks, just against
Jews. He said some places was RESTRICTED to Jews in the Old
Country when he was a kid. That was the first time I knowed
this. We used to talk about race problems quite a heap, because
Mr. Harris were what he called a 'liberal,' which meant he voted
for Roosevelt three times.

"I used to love to hear them Jewish people-talk in their own
language to each other and with their hands, too. I got so I used
my hands a lot myself, throwing them up in the air, which is
maybe why Isabel thought sometimes I was going to hit her. I
never hit no woman—although I have sometimes been forced
to protect myself and push them *off of me*. The only woman I
sometimes wish I had hit now is Cherie—that girl that run
when Mabel looked her in the eyes in the beer booth. Cherie
were really no-good—like Zarita. Except that Zarita will drink
you up for fun, whereas Cherie drunk you up only for money.
But I did not know that then. I used to talk big around the store
about little slick Cherie and how glamorous she was. I never
did mention Mabel at work, only Cherie. I used to tell the nice
old head Jewish lady clerk about how swell she looked.

"That old lady must of knowed I was young and foolish because she would say to me, 'Swell—*smell!* Swell is what swell
does, not how swell she looks!'

" 'But this girl is beautiful!' I'd say.

" 'Beautiful, *snootiful,*' this old Jewish lady clerk said—which
was just about right. Cherie was snooty. As long as a man was
putting down cash, she was O.K. But don't pay, and she
snubbed you in public. When the contest come, she run off and
left me to face Mabel in that booth by myself. She rooked me,
then shook me. If I had not met Isabel, I would have been alone
again.

"Working in that dress shop, I used to hear the Jewish people talking all the time about Palestine, like the Irish talk about Ireland. I wondered how come Negroes don't talk much about Africa. But we don't. And practically nobody wants to go back there. I guess because it is so different and so dark and so far away. We been here in America longer than lots of other folks have, yet we can't even buy a pair of shoes in them downtown shops in Baltimore. That is Baltimore. That is one reason why when I got here to Harlem, I stayed."

"I see you stayed," I said. "Yet ever so often you speak of the South with longing. You're like those foreign people you spoke of—who come to America, but still remember home. You're a kind of displaced person yourself."

"I'd be a *displeased* person if I had to live down South again," said Simple. "Harlem has got everything I want from A to Z Here, like the song says, 'I have found my true love.' Them Baltimore womens was just preliminaries, my A-B-C's."

"You've certainly told me plenty about the A-B-C's of your love life in Baltimore," I said, "but not too much about your X-Y-Z's in Harlem."

"*J* is as far as I go nowadays," said Simple. "I stops with Joyce. I can't spell with letters no further down in the alphabet than A-B-C-D-E-F-G-H-I-J-O-Y-C-E."

"Zarita begins with a Z."

"Hers is one name I will never write on no paper. Yet and still, I likes Zarita. When you are happy, she is happy. Zarita likes to be happy with people."

"That's why they call women like her *playgirls*," I said.

"I reckon it is," said Simple. "And she can be a right good plaything. But don't get me wrong, bud, I don't love Zarita. She is always broke. And when I am hang-overed, Zarita is hang-overed. Zarita ain't good for but one thing, to have fun with. Cherie in Baltimore was like that, too, and being young, I made the mistake of loving her. Never no more! That is not really love."

"Just what do you call love, I'd like to know?"

"Love is—when you are broke and hungry, she says, 'I don't mind being hungry either.' When you are hang-overed, she says, 'I will put a cold towel on your head.' When you are happy, she will say, 'You make me happy, too.' Instead of, 'Why don't you get out of here and earn me some money?' Or, 'How come you didn't come home sober?' Or, 'I can't see nothing to be so happy about when I ain't got a rag to put on my back?' Do you see what I mean by *love*?"

"Long-suffering," I said.

"Exactly," said Simple. "Some women pretends they like to suffer, but when a man is really suffering, they ain't got no sympathy for him. Cherie runs. Isabel raised a flat-iron, even Joyce just turns cool. Don't womens know a man's got feelings, too, as well as they have? When you're broke you need company. When you got a hang-over, you need sympathy. And when you're happy, you need somebody to be happy along with you."

"You want an angel," I said, "not a woman."

"I wouldn't want to be bothered with all them wings an angel's got," said Simple. "Wings might fly up and hit me in the eye. Arms is all I need, just two pairs of arms."

"*One* pair, you mean, don't you?"

"Whatever two arms is called—just so they're loving," said Simple.

| All in the Family

"F. D. says he don't know which one is the biggest, my landlady or Joyce's. And don't you know both of them evil old landladies is just crazy about that boy!"

"So you took F. D. around to meet Joyce?"

"I did. And Joyce said, 'Jess, when we get married, we're going to adopt F. D.'

"I said, 'In another year F. D. will be big enough to adopt you. He's mighty near grown now.'

" 'We will need a big brother for our babies,' says Joyce. 'And F. D. is a fine boy. He likes culture.'

"Joyce were referring to the fact that he read one of them books you lent us. I ain't read mine yet. But F. D. has done read one and started on mine, too. So when he gets through and tells me what it's all about, I won't have to read mine. He is a very nice young boy, and polite to womens. Southern folks raises their kids better than Northerners, I do believe. F. D. has got manners—even if he is got the nerve to call me *coz* already—short for cousin. One thing, he is about the most pleasantest young fellow I been around, always talking and smiling that big old bright smile of his. I do not mind having him in my room at all. In facts, he is company for me. Also he has offered to pay half the rent.'

"Did you accept?"

"What do you mean, did I accept? F. D. has not been here hardly a week yet. He is a young boy just getting started in New York, and I am his kinfolks. You know I would not accept no rent from that boy. What good is relatives if they can't do a little something for you once in a while? None of mine never helped me since Aunt Lucy died. But if somebody had of helped me just a little bit when I were in my young manhood, I might of gotten somewhere further by now, not just laboring from hand to mouth. I am going to help this boy, and he is going to get somewhere. F. D. is already helping me."

"How do you mean, helping you?"

"With somebody around to talk to, I don't spend so much dough in bars any more, as early as Joyce goes to bed."

"You don't mean to tell me you keep that young man up all night long talking to you after you get home from your rounds?"

"I get home early now—to see if he has got home. I done commanded F. D. to be in the house by midnight. Just so he won't think I'm spying on him, I comes home about twelve-thirty or one. He's laying on his side of the bed reading a book. I do not want to put the light out while he's reading—also I am not sleepy so early—so I start talking to him. And we talks sometimes till two-three in the morning."

"It must run in the family," I said, "both of you are night-owls. What can you find to talk about with a youngster like F. D.?"

"Life," said Simple.

"That covers a very wide range of subjects," I said.

"F. D. ain't no baby. When you are going on eighteen now, it is just like going on twenty-eight when I were a child. Besides, he were raised by Mattie Mae, and even though she's my cousin, she never was known to be no lily."

"You don't need to tell everything you know about your Cousin Mattie Mae," I said.

"I say that to say this," said Simple, "Mattie were not bashful with nobody. So I know she did not raise F. D. on Sunday school cards alone. He knows the facts of life. You know what he asked me already? I were telling him about the reason I have started putting Five or Ten dollars in the leaves of the Bible every week is because I am preparing to pay for my divorce.

"F. D. says, 'Then you were married legally, and not common law?'

" 'I regrets it, but I were,' I said.

"F. D. said, 'But, coz, I always heard common law is better since it doesn't cost so much to get loose.'

"I did not think it would be good morals to agree with F. D., so I said, 'Boy, where did you hear that?'

" 'From mama,' said F. D.

" 'Mattie Mae said that?' I acted like I was surprised.

" 'Yes, but mama didn't really believe it herself, after she saw the results,' said F. D., 'because after my third brother and sister came, she told my step-father he had *better* marry her—or she would get out an injunction to keep him from rooming at our house. So they got married. Which was all right by me,' says F. D., 'except that he thought his fatherly duty was to tan *my* hide, which I never did like, not being his child. And you know I am too big to whip now. But look at these scars on my legs.'

"F. D. stretched one leg out from under the sheet and raised it up, then he pulled the other one out. Both of them were whelped up.

" 'Mama should not have let him whip me like this, should she? But she is crazy about that Negro.'

" 'I will whip you myself,' I said, 'if you talk to anybody else that way about your mama, F. D. After all she is *my* cousin.

'Course, you can talk to me—since it's all in the family. But let's keep it there.'

" 'Naturally,' says F. D."

| Kick for Punt

" 'Did you know who my father was, Cousin Jess?' F. D. asked me last night, 'because I never even as much as laid eyes on him.'

" 'I knowed the Negro,' I said. 'I met him once when I were home on a visit before I settled permanent in the North. He were a big black handsome man. Folks called him John Henry because he worked on the railroad and were just passing through with the construction.'

" 'I wonder where the construction gang went on to?' asked F. D.

" 'That, son, I do not know,' I said. I meant coz. But not being around that boy since he was five, he seemed more like a son to me than a cousin, even a third or fourth cousin. I always think of cousins as being around my age. Anyhow, I told him I did not know much more about his father than his mother did, except that he were a great one for bawling and brawling, laughing and joke-telling, drinking and not thinking. I wanted to say, 'F. D., I am surprised at you taking to books because all your father could read were the spots on the cards. But he really could play skin, blackjack, and poker. How I know is he beat me out of my fare back to Baltimore, then laughed, and took me out and bought me all I could drink.' But I did not tell that boy that about his father. I said, 'Coz, he were a right nice fellow, always smiling and good-natured just like you, so you come by it naturally. And if he had ever seen you, he would have been crazy about you because you were sure a lively boy-baby. It is too bad that construction gang moved on before you were born. They was working Northwards. I wouldn't be surprised if your daddy warn't somewhere in Harlem by now.'

" 'I wish I could find him,' said F. D. 'But he wouldn't know me and I wouldn't know him, we never having seen each other. But I wish I would find him.'

" 'Wishing that hard, I expect you will find him,' I said, 'just like you wished up a ticket to come to New York.'

" 'I wish I would,' he said, half asleep by that time, and he went on to sleep. So I turned out the light—but not before I jumped into my shirt and pants, and come on out here to the bar to grab myself a couple of more beers. You see I ain't got on nothing now but house shoes, don't you?"

"That boy is liable to wake up and wonder where in the hell you have gone," I said.

"If he do, it won't be the first time he has missed a relative in the middle of the night, I bet. I have been behaving myself right good since I had F. D. under my wing. At least I do come home, even if I might maybe sneak right out again soon as he goes to sleep."

"Why you think you have to deceive that boy about your night-prowl habits, I don't know," I said. "You do nothing vicious or wrong, and I am sure he's not the kind of boy who would look down on a man for imbibing a bit of beer, would he?"

"No, he would not," said Simple. "But I do not want him to think because I am out all night, he should maybe be out, too. So I come in—and come out again when he is unconscious. Just like it took Joyce two or three years to find out I did not go *right* home to bed when I used to leave her house. She knows it now, though."

"And she loves you right on. Just as this boy will still like you when he finds out you don't need more than three or four hours' sleep. He'll probably admire you just for that."

"Next week will be time enough for him to find out, though, won't it? This week lemme set a good example."

"Good examples are not set by deceit," I argued.

"Oh, but sometimes they are," said Simple. "A congressman is a good example until somebody catches him with a deep freeze. A minister is a good example until he gets caught with the deacon's wife. I am a good example as long as F. D. *thinks*

I am in my bed asleep. I don't have to always be there in person, do I?"

"Getting your proper rest would do you no harm, however."

"Vacation's coming up. I'll rest then. So don't worry about me."

"Last year you went to Saratoga, didn't you? Where are you going this time?"

"I know where I *ain't* going—and that is to the country. Yes, I know the poem says, 'Only God can make a tree.' But I sure am glad God let Edison make street lights, too, also electric signs. I like electric signs better than I do trees. And neon signs over a bar, man, I love! A bar can shelter me better than any tree. And a tall stool beats short grass any time. Grass is full of chiggers. It is too dark in the country at night, and sunrise comes too early. In the daytime you don't see nothing but animals. Horses, pigs, cows, sheep, birds, chickens. Not a one of them animals ever said one interesting word to me. Animals is no company. I like them in zoos better. Trees I like in parks, birds in somebody else's cages, chickens in frozen-food bins, and sunrise in bed. No, daddy-o, I will not go to the country this summer. I like lights too well."

"You see Tony flashing these lights off and on, don't you? He is about to close the bar. We'd better get out or there won't be any light—except daylight."

"Doggone if it ain't four A.M.," said Simple. "Yonder is dawn breaking. Dawn never was as pretty in the country as it is sneaking over Lenox Avenue. Lemme get on home and see is F. D. done kicked the pillow out from under his own head. That is the kickingest boy! Punt formation! He dreams he's playing football in his sleep—drop-kicks, place-kicks, punts, goals. Dream on, coz, but damn if I want to be the ball! If you kick me this morning, I sure will kick you back."

"You won't get much sleep anyhow, going to bed this late."

"Yes, I will, too," said Simple. "I sleep quick."

| Subway to Jamaica

"F. D. WERE not there when I got back home last night in spite of the fact that it were 12:30, past P.M., so I came back out. I did not see you, so I went back in—and I come back out again. I broke my money-savings rule not to drink more than one beer on myself so I can pay for that divorce. I bought four, also a drink of whiskey. I was worried about that boy being a new boy in the block and a stranger in town—some of them young hellions might of ganged him.

"I stood on the corner of Lenox Avenue and looked up and down. No F. D. I walked to Seventh Avenue and looked up and down. No F. D. All the movies was closed. Nothing but bars open, so I went in a bar I had never been in before.

"Then I said, 'To hell with F. D.! He's big as me, so I ain't responsible. I do not care where he's at. What right has he got to worry me like this? I ain't his daddy.'

"I returned back to my Third Floor Rear. He still were not there—going on four in the morning. So I took off my clothes and went to bed. I did not sleep.

"F. D. come in later than me by twice. But I give that boy credit he did not try to tiptoe. If he just had come in with his shoes in his hands sneaking up the steps, I would have riz up mad and caught him with, 'Where the damnation you been, arriving back this time of night?'

"But when F. D. come walking in loud like nothing had happened, creaking every step and hitting on his heels, I pretended to be asleep. F. D. set down on the bed to take his shoes off. I grunted and groaned, "Uh-er-ummm-uh! Man, why don't you turn on the light so you can see?'

" 'Cousin Jess, I've been having a ball,' he said. 'Listen! We've been to the Savoy. It's fine up there! Two bands and a rainbow chandelier that goes around. I'm learning the mambo. I had to take a girl all the way home to Brooklyn.'

"I could not help it but say, 'Late as it is, I thought maybe you had gone to Georgia.'

" 'No, I got on the wrong subway coming back and forgot to change. I went all the way to some place called Jamaica.'

" 'That happens to every Negro what ever comes to New York, at least once,' I said. 'I think they just made that Jamaica line to confuse Negroes, because everybody knows somebody that lives in Brooklyn, and the first time you start back to Harlem you *always* end up in Jamaica. Don't you have to work in the morning, F. D.?'

" 'Yes, sir.'

" 'Then fall on over in this bed and get your rest.'

" 'She's a sweet little number, coz.'

" 'Um-hummmm, well, tell me about her tomorrow.'

" 'Were you asleep, coz?'

"Yes, I were asleep—till you woke me up.'

" 'I got her phone number.'

" 'Um-hum! Well, I suppose you'll be running to Brooklyn every night now.'

" 'Not every night. I couldn't get a date in edgewise till Sunday. That girl is popular. Sunday we're going to Coney Island.'

" 'I want you to bring that girl up here and let me look her over before you-all get too thick. You hear me, F. D.?'

" 'Yes, sir, but I'll bet you're gonna like her, Cousin Jess. Her name is Gloria. She's eighteen and keen. Dresses crazy—had on a big wide leather belt with green shoe strings in the front and a little tiny waist about the size of this bed post. You gonna like her.'

" 'Turn over and go to sleep, boy. And next time, don't get mixed up on no subway to Jamaica. What you due to take is the *A Train* to Harlem. Otherwise, you will arrive at nowhere, square.'

" 'She don't think I'm a square, Cousin Jess.'

"I made out like I were snoring so that boy would stop talking. Next thing I knew, we was both asleep. F. D. must have been sleeping real good because in a few minutes he hauled off and kicked me, which woke me up. In another half-hour the alarm went off. So I didn't get much rest last night. But I'm glad the boy had fun, though. If you do not have a good time in your young years, you might not know how when you get old. And the sooner you find out what train to take to get to where you are going in this world, the better. The Jamaica train does *not* run to Harlem. It goes somewhere else."

| No Tea for the Fever

"Joyce says she rid back from Boston with Mrs. Sadie Maxwell-Reeves," said Simple. "Now you can hardly touch her with a ten-foot pole, she is so proud."

"You can't much blame her, can you?" I said. "Mrs. Reeves is one of Harlem's leading club ladies."

"*The* leading, according to Joyce, always giving banquets and teas and things. So cultured she wears her glasses on her bosom. I met her once. Well, anyhow, on the train she told Joyce, 'Darling, you are a clever woman, such as our race needs. Your club ought to make you a delegate to the National Convention next spring, not just to a Summer Regional.'

"So now you know there will be no getting along with Joyce come next winter. She will have me tromping through the cold selling more tickets to teas and forums and recitals than enough. The more tickets Joyce sells, the better club worker she is. She could pay her own fare to the National seven times over, were it meeting in California, if all the work it takes to sell them tickets was put into a *paying* job. Somehow or another Joyce has got the idea that a tea uplifts the race."

"You ought to be glad Joyce has some social and civic interests," I said. "You don't want just a stick-in-the-mud for a fiancée, do you?"

"I want somebody who is going to stick by me," said Simple, "which Joyce has been doing right well until lately. But, buddy, as the summer gets hotter, that girl is getting increasing cool. I told her last night, 'Baby, I done saved Fifty-Five Dollars toward paying for our—I mean *my*—divorce. So it won't be long now.'

"Joyce says, 'It's been too long already. You know I wanted to get married *last* June. All my friends are talking about how you been stringing me along. They think you don't take me serious.'

"'Look here,' I says to her, 'if I don't get the rest of that money together by Labor Day, baby, I am going to borrow it—some maybe from F. D. who is working like a man, and some from my best bar-buddy, who will do me a favor, I know. Meaning, of course, you."

"Meaning me!" I exclaimed. "You realize, I suppose, that I have obligations too, though I may not be so vocal about mine."

"I didn't know you're taking singing lessons," said Simple. "Are you a baritone—or a nary tone?"

"I can't carry a tune," I said, "so I'm not taking vocal lessons. But I do have other things to do with my money."

"Whatever you've got to do with your money, I know you'll lend me Twenty or Thirty if push comes to shove. I got to get together One Hundred and Thirty-Three Dollars and Thirty-three and One-Third Cents to make up my share of that Four Hundred Dollar divorce. I writ Isabel I would send it soon. I am getting tired of them proceedings dragging on forever. Nothing but money is holding things up. Joyce is getting ready to go on her vacation and I want to have them divorce papers to show her when she gets back."

"Where is Joyce going this year?" I asked.

"She will not tell me," said Simple. "Joyce is acting salty about almost everything this summer. But I expect she will go over to Jersey and spend it with her friends and her godchild. She is crazy about that little varmint. Joyce pretends like she wanted to spend her vacation with me—that is, had we been married. But she knows I don't get off at the same time she does. Her vacation comes in August, and mine is always in September.

"Sne says, 'Any man with any gumption could arrange it so he's off the same time as his wife,' she says, 'and if you don't, I will, if and when we are ever united. I will go down and see your boss myself.'

"I says, 'Joyce, it is not that I don't want to. It's just, what's the use? You have told me yourself morals is your middle name, and you would not go nowhere for no two weeks with a single man—nor a married one neither that you are not married to yourself. That is why I did not get my vacation changed.'

" 'You always got an explanation for everything,' says Joyce. 'If you are late getting to heaven, you will give Saint Peter some jive excuse. Well, I will go on my vacation alone, as usual. I had expected this vacation this year to be my second honeymoon—had we been married last spring. But I'm going to have a bang-up good trip anyhow. My vacation will not be no dud, with or without you, Jess Semple. My plans is laid.'

" 'Laid where?'

" 'You will find out in due time. I intends to relax and have myself a ball wherever I go. I have been working hard all winter and all summer. Now I am going to relax.'

"The way she said that word *relax*, daddy-o, I do not feel so good about. What do you reckons she means?"

"Probably just lying in a hammock and reading a book," I said. "You don't have to worry about Joyce."

"I may not have to, but I do," said Simple. "And this is one time I do not want her going off nowheres without me. To tell the truth, if I find out where she is going, I'm liable to take a week off from my work and relax with her."

"You might be unwelcome," I said, "since you say she's holding you at arm's length these days."

"My arm is as long as hers. I will reach out and snatch her bald-headed if she fools with me. She must not know who I am. I am Jesse B. Semple. I loves that girl, and I have come to the point where I will not take no tea for the fever. In fact, I will get rough."

"Do you intend to state all that to Joyce?"

"My statement is being considered," said Simple.

| Boys, Birds, and Bees

"Joyce is gone," said Simple.

"Where?"

"That is just it. I do not know where. She must of left right from work yesterday, which were Friday, because when I rung them seven bells last night, her big old fat landlady waddled to the door and hollered, 'Joyce is gone.'

" 'Gone where?' I says.

" 'You ought to know. You closer than her shadow.'

" 'Madam, I am asking you a question.'

" 'You know her vacation has started. She told me to tell you she would be away for a fortnight, whatever that is.'

" 'A fourth-night?'

" 'Them is her words, not mine, so figure it out for yourself.'

"And she waddled on back through them double doors. What is a fourth-night?"

"Two weeks," I said.

"Well, why didn't Joyce say so? That girl is been around that Maxwell-Reeves woman too much. She's talking in tongues. Two weeks! Well, she can stay gone *two years* for all I care. Facts is, Joyce can *stay* gone. She do not need to come back to me."

"Consider well what you are saying, old boy."

"Don't worry about what I am saying. When she returns, I will close my door against her. I'm a good mind to go home right now and get that money out of that sock I been saving and blow it all in, every damn penny."

"Before I let you do that," I said, "I'll treat you to a whole bottle of beer myself. Bartender, set 'em up! And you, I do not want to hear you talking like that just because Joyce is a little piqued."

"I wish I could peek on her wherever she is at now. Relaxing! I would unlax her."

"Let that girl relax alone and get herself together, calm her nerves, think things over, and come back refreshed. You'll be so glad to see her you won't know what to do."

"She better let me know where she's at by Monday morning," said Simple. "If she do not drop me a line at once *now*, she will find herself dropped. Joyce is embarrassing me. F. D. thinks I know all about womens, and here I don't even know where my own woman is at.

"Last night I took F. D. upstairs to see Carlyle who has come back to his wife and baby. I told F. D., 'Carlyle is a young man a year or two older than yourself. He can give you some good advice which has got me stumped to talk over with you. You been running over to Brooklyn a mighty lot these nights lately, spending time with that keen kitty with the leather belt. Carlyle is a married man. He can tell you *how* he got married.' "

" 'Midsummer madness,' " I started quoting.

"That's right," said Simple. "Now, you take F. D. These young peoples nowadays know a plenty and they act like they knows more. But when you come right down to it, sometimes they don't know B from bull-foot—especially when it comes to subtracting the result from the cause. Sometimes it does not even take nine months to have the answer on your hands. Then they are surprised. F. D. is at the age where a boy needs somebody to talk to him."

"Why don't you talk to him? He seems to respect you."

"That's just it. He *do* respect me. And I don't know how to talk about them things without using bad words. That is all right amongst grown men. But F. D. ain't old enough yet to be drafted. Still and yet, he's old enough to do what the Bible says Adam did—and which has been going on ever since. I don't know what to say to a young boy at that age. I gets somewhatly embarrassed."

"So you turn F. D. over to Carlyle for the birds and bees, eh?"

"Carlyle is more near about his same age. But Carlyle's done had experience with which he walks the floor each and every night."

"Do you expect Carlyle's sex vocabulary to be any cleaner than yours?"

"Dirtier," said Simple. "But F. D. do not respect Carlyle."

| On the Warpath

"HAVE you met F. D.'s girl yet?"

"I did," said Simple. "My landlady did also. She passed comment on her, 'Cute as a bug in a rug! Your cousin has better taste than you have, Mr. Semple, being seen in public with streak-haired characters like Zarita.'

"I reminded my landlady that I also knows Joyce.

" 'Which helps a little bit,' she said. 'But I give that young boy, F. D., credit. He did not take up with no trash when he come to New York. Gloria is a real sweet kid. Brooklyn girls is raised. They don't just grow, like they do here in New York. If I was to rear a family,' she continues, 'I would move to Brooklyn—which is a quiet suburb—and leave all you loud-mouthed roomers behind here in Harlem to make out the best way you can. Harlem is no place for a child.'

"Not wishing to carry on the conversation, I did not reply. I were not feeling talkative. Do you know what Joyce wrote me?"

"No."

"Just one word scrawled across the middle of the card like she were in a hurry—*Greetings!* No address, no nothing, but the picture of a beach and some white folks in swimming."

"You could tell from the postmark where it was, couldn't you?"

"It were so pale all I could make out was *AT*—and the rest was hardly there. But it must be Atlantic City, which is where I know Joyce has been before and likes."

"The Paradise, the Harlem, there are some fine night clubs there. Bars, music, dancing."

"I better not go down there and find Joyce setting up in no night club."

"What have you got against night clubs?"

"Nothing. It's what I got against guys who take girls to night clubs. I would not take no woman to a cabaret and spend all that loot on her that I did not intend to take further. A man is always thinking ahead of a woman."

"You have a suspicious mind," I said. "But I am sure Joyce would know how to resist any too intimate encroachments, even if she did accept some handsome stranger's bid for a date."

"'Bang-up good time—I intend to relax,' were the last words she said. It's that very last word, *relax,* that keeps running through my mind. On a vacation, you have to relax *with* somebody. If I go down to Atlantic City Sunday, I better not catch Joyce relaxing on the Boardwalk with no other joker. I will run him dead in the ocean. And he better know how to walk the water because he darest not come back to shore with me on the warpath."

"I am sure an exhibition of that nature would perturb Joyce," I said, "and do no credit to your own intelligence."

"About myself I do not care," said Simple. "As for Joyce, it would be worth a round-trip ticket to Atlantic City just to put the fear of God into her heart. Joyce do not realize who she is messing with, upsetting me like this. Here I am ready to give her the best years of my life, soon as that decree comes, and she cuts out on me for a fourth-night leaving no address whatsoever. *Greetings!* Don't she know no more words than that to write to me? She could say, *Dear Jess.* She could say, *Having a wonderful time, but something is missing—you!* She could say, *Hope you are well!* How much do it cost to go to Atlantic City?"

"Damned if I know."

"Lend me a dime," said Simple. "I am going to phone the bus station and find out. Don't let me catch no other Negro down there on no beach relaxing with Joyce when I get there, either!"

"Think carefully, old man," I said, "before starting on a wild goose chase."

"Wild goose, nothing!" cried Simple. "He'll be a dead duck."

| A Hearty Amen

MONDAY evening Simple greeted me with a grin.

"Did you locate Joyce?" I asked.

"I did not have to locate her. She located me! I have not been nowhere this week end but to East Orange across the river. Joyce come phoning me Saturday from Jersey that she were lonesome and to come over there and take her to a movie. Man, I hopped a bus so fast it would make your head swim."

"I thought you were angry with her."

"When my old landlady call me to the phone and I heard that sweet voice, 'Hello, Jess,' I forgot to be mad.

" 'Where are you, Joyce?' I said. 'Atlantic City?'

" 'No, darling,' she answers, 'just right over in Jersey with my godchild's two parents. Sugar Pie, say hello to your Uncle Jess.'

" 'And don't you know she put that child on the phone and held me up for five minutes. I do not think no child is cute on the phone, especially when it can't hear good. Finally the little varmint dropped the receiver and I got Joyce back. Man, Joyce sounded like old times.

" 'I was just in Atlantic City a hot minute,' she said. 'My friends drove me down there for the day to let me catch some cool breezes. I thought about you, Jess. Come on over here and spend the week end. Willabee and Johnny say you can sleep on the sleeping porch tonight. They got good screens and the mosquitoes are not bad.'

" 'I am poison to mosquitoes, baby. The last one that bit me died himself. I will be there no sooner than it takes the bus to go through the Holland Tunnel.'

"And, man, I really enjoyed myself over there in that small suburban. Joyce's friends make everything so pleasantlike— Budweiser in the ice box, Canadian Club on the sideboard. Righteous, man! Sunday they invited me to church which, to tell the truth, I enjoyed. Setting there with Joyce smelling like a flower, the old folks singing them old-time hymns, I started thinking about my Aunt Lucy and how she used to love Sunday-morning sermons.

"When the minister said, 'Bow your heads and pray,' I prayed I could keep on being good like Aunt Lucy taught me.

"When I raised my head, the sunlight was coming through them pretty colored windows. I put my hand over Joyce's hand. And the choir sung. And the man said, 'May the Lord watch between me and thee while we are absent one from another.'

"I said, 'Joyce, don't you be absent from me too long.'

"Joyce whispered, 'Jess, I'm coming home Tuesday. I'm going to spend half of my fortnight near you.'

"At that point the minister said, 'Amen!'

"I Amen-ed also."

"All of which leads me to the conclusion that you and Joyce are back on an even keel," I said.

"If keel means back in the groove, then there's nothing left to prove. Come seven, manna from heaven! Cool, fool!"

"Dispense with the hep talk. You're not at Birdland. By the way, how's your protégé getting along?"

"My who?"

"Your young cousin."

"More hep than me—F. D. is wearing Harlem for a sport coat. He works, he plays. But he comes home in time to get himself enough sleep to get up and work and play some more. He does not drink. And he has not taken to dope yet, which, according to the papers, all young Negroes do. Neither does he smoke reefers. He says he had rather buy himself some clothes, take his girl to Coney Island, else mambo with his money. Also to Birdland to hear bop. That boy gets around, him and Gloria. But he do not get run down—being's he's an athlete, he's got to keep his wind. He says he got four letters in high school. Now, what does F. D. mean by that?"

"Football, baseball, basketball, and track, I think. They must have a pretty good high school where he comes from."

"Virginia schools is not bad," said Simple. "One thing about his mama, Mattie Mae, was she probably didn't want F. D. in the house much nohow, so she let him stay in school *all day long* every day. She didn't care how much he studied or played, as long as he were away from home, so she could play in her way. F. D. had sense enough to stay in school, and still have himself a little job shining shoes in a hotel, else picking or packing tobacco, making his own money, till he graduated. Which is why he left home, one reason. That big old no-good stepfather of his would whip that boy if he didn't give him half his shine money for board and keep. He also made him be home in bed by ten o'clock, being some kind of religious frantic."

"Fanatic."

"Um-hum! Anyhow, he grabs F. D. and whips him once too often, and F. D. starts thinking about running away. Upshot, I got him on my hands."

"I believe you've handled the situation pretty well, old boy. But you are lucky in that he is such a decent boy, not a juvenile delinquent. Suppose your cousin were one of these tough young jitterbugs you read about, running around in gangs, smoking marijuana, always getting into trouble. What would you have done with him then?"

"Done with him?" said Simple. "Nothing. I'd just call in my landlady and say, 'You let him in here, madam, so *you* get him out.' I bet that boy would have left there flying. My heavy-hipped old landlady can put out bigger mens than I am. I would have no trouble were F. D. inclined to disturbing the peace. Neither would I have to call the law. Just my landlady, that's all."

"But suppose you had to solve the problem of getting him out yourself if he had turned out to be rowdy? How would *you* get him out?"

"Knock him out," said Simple.

"So force would be your only solution for the problems of juvenile delinquency?"

"I would not be trying to solve no problem but my own," said Simple.

| Must Have a Seal

"CHICKEN tender is a mother's love, stewed down with dumplings—that is what we had for dinner Sunday."

"At Joyce's?"

"Sure, at Joyce's. That woman can really mess with pots and pans. Cornbread that melted right out of sight. I didn't leave a piece on the plate. Oh, man, I can't describe that dinner!"

"If Joyce cooks like that now, and you are not even married, what kind of meals will you eat when you set up housekeeping and have your own kitchen?"

"It will be better than cooking in some old landlady's kitchen. Every time Joyce's landlady lets Joyce use her kitchen, she invites herself to eat with us. That's what I was about to tell you," said Simple. "She eats like she never had a pot full of nothing herself. Sunday she slayed that succotash, murdered the beets, completely annihilated the candied sweet potatoes, and drunk a small gallon of coffee. When we got down to the dessert, she was too full to eat more than a ladle of jello, but she put whipped cream on that twice. I'm telling you, it were such a fine dinner, I do not blame that landlady much for scarffing. Joyce buys her vegetables and groceries downtown nearby where she works. The foods is better. Everything is two-three-four cents a pound higher in Harlem. And Joyce likes good groceries. When she gets through salting and seasoning, man, it is scrumptious! That girl is a cook."

"Well," I said, "you have given me an ample description of the dinner. But dinner tables are set as much for conversation as they are for eating. What did you good people talk about Sunday?"

"Politics," said Simple. "November is political times, and Joyce's big old fat landlady took over. She said all them years that she had been persuading all her roomers to vote Democratic, ain't no precinct leader ever presented her with a mink coat, not even a rabbit skin, which is why she switched to Eisenhower. She says, 'The Republicans can bring the country back to normal and keep it there.'

" 'You must think the Republicans is God,' I said to her. 'Back to normal would mean I could ride the bus for a nickel, get a shine for a dime, and buy a new suit almost any old time. You know can't nobody bring them miracles to pass.'

" 'I knows no such thing,' says Joyce's landlady. 'That is what politics is for, to bring things to pass. Building inspectors, health inspectors, all of them never bother me at all, since I'm in politics. They know I helps get out the vote, so they leave me alone —which is a miracle. And when I change my vote, every last roomer in my house had better vote like me, else out they goes.'

" 'That, madam,' I says, 'is against the law. You can't *make* people vote your way.'

" 'Oh, can't I?' she says. 'Now, take you, Mr. Semple, if you was running for Mayor of New York, you'd want me to swing my votes your way, wouldn't you?'

" 'I'd appreciate it,' I said. 'Would you?'

"She leaned across the table and stated in a loud voice, 'No! I would not! Never! No!'

"Which embarrassed Joyce—and made me mad.'

"So that is why you enjoyed the food more than you did the conversation," I said.

"That is one reason," said Simple. "The other reason is that if you don't know anything about anything, like Joyce's landlady, you should not open your mouth."

"Your ruling would practically put an end to conversation," I said. "Almost nobody knows much about anything. Do you want to plunge the world into silence?"

"Only landladies," said Simple, "and wives. Isabel is trying to bug me again by mail. Look what I found on the hall table today from Baltimore!"

He proceeded to read her letter:

"Dear Mr. Semple, My Former Husband,
This is the very last letter you will ever get from me because I have asked you to do something for me and you do not do it, now I will do it myself. I will pay with my own money my own self for

the last installment on our divorce. If I don't, the man I love might get out of the mood of marrying me at all, he has waited so long for you to do your husbandly duty. Jesse B. Semple, I do not think much of you, and have never did. You are less than a man. You marry a woman, neglect her, ignore her, then won't divorce her, not even when your part is only one third of the payment. So you go to hell! The next thing you will get from me will be the Decree, and the lawyer will send that. You do not deserve no gold seal on that paper because you have not put a cent into it and unless a gold seal goes with it free, you will not get one. From now on, you kiss my foot!

ISABEL ESTHERLEE JONES

P.S. *I have taken back my maiden name until I get freshly married as I do not want no parts of you attached to me any longer.*

MISS JONES

"That is an insult," said Simple. "I will not let Isabel get the last word in on me. I will send that lawyer my part of the money tomorrow. Right now I got saved $92.18. Lend me $41.16."

"In the middle of the week? If ever. Are you out of your mind?"

"This is an emergency. But if I can't emerge with it tomorrow, I will on pay day. I'll add my whole pay check to that money I got in my sock and send it off—because when I get that paper, 1 want to be sure mine has a gold seal on it, too. A paper don't look like nothing without a seal."

| Shadow of the Blues

"I GOT IT," said Simple when I ran into him on Saturday.

"Got what?"

"One Hundred and Thirty-Three Dollars and Thirty-Three Cents."

"How?"

"By not paying my landlady, not getting my laundry out of Won Hong Low's, letting my hair stay long, getting no pressing done, neither a shoeshine. And if I don't spend this dollar tonight—which I am about to treat us to a beer with now—I will have One Hundred and Thirty-Four. I am going to send it off to Baltimore early Monday morning, which Money Order will change *Divorce Pending* to *Divorce Ending*—signed, gold-sealed, and delivered. When I get it, it will be like manna from heaven. If you see Joyce, don't say nothing. I want to surprise her with them papers. No more talking."

"Not a word will I say. In fact, I will believe it myself only when I see it."

"You will see it," said Simple. "I have sacrificed for that day."

"So have I," I said.

"You have treated me royal," said Simple, "which is why I am happy to break this One Hundred and Thirty-Fourth Dollar to treat *you* tonight. What will you have?"

"A beer."

"Since I'm busting this dollar, I might as well put a quarter in the juke box. What would you like to hear?"

"If they've got any old-time blues on it, play them."

"Will do," said Simple. "But there ain't no Bessie these days. Do you remember Bessie Smith?"

"I certainly do. And Clara?"

"I bet you don't remember Mamie?"

"Yes, I do—all three Smiths, Bessie, Clara, and Mamie."

"Boy, you must be older than me, because I only heard tell of Mamie. I am glad I am not as ageable as you. You's an *old* Negro!"

"Come now! Let's see what else you might remember, before we start comparing ages. Speaking of blues singers, how about Victoria Spivey?"

"You've gone too far back now if you remember Victoria."

"How do you know how far back she was if *you* can't recall her?"

"I just recall my Uncle Tige had one of her records when I were born which he used to play called 'The Blacksnake Blues.' I almost disremembers it."

"I see. I wonder if you recall when a boy had to be fifteen or sixteen to wear long trousers. Did you ever wear knickers as a child?"

"Knickerbockers," said Simple.

"Then your life span dates back quite a way. Did you ever see Theda Bara in the nickelodeons?"

"My mama told me about Theda."

"Did you ever see *Uncle Tom's Cabin?*"

"Simon Legree, Little Eva, Eliza and the bloodhounds? My grandma told me about all them. But I remember Clara Bow."

"The 'It' Girl of the flapper age."

"She really had *It*. Also I remember Nina Mae McKinney."

"Since your interest in women goes away back, I'm wondering if you remember when girls wore corsets instead of girdles?"

"They didn't wear neither one in them woods where I came from. Besides I didn't start investigating womens until I were eight. Up to then I was playing agates and yo-yo's."

"Oh, so you remember when each youngster had a yo-yo. That's not exactly a recent toy. You were probably in your teens when boys were making crystal-set radios with ear phones."

"If I were making them, I will not admit it," said Simple. "But I do remember when folks didn't have Frigidaires. My mama used to get her ice from an ice-man in town. And Aunt Lucy hung her butter down in the well in the country. In those days a kid would do an errand for a penny—because a penny was worth a nickel. Now it is hard to get one to do an errand for a dime. *Damn* was a bad word then—even without God in front of it. Ladies didn't smoke. And Madam Walker's would lay it down when nothing else would—so slick a fly couldn't get his bearings. When a boy had a birthday, your uncle gave you a dollar watch—an Elgin. Them was the days!"

"Watch out, you're giving yourself away if your memory goes back that far. You're ancient, man, you're ancient!"

"I only heard abut them things."

"Anyhow, to get back to the blues. Let me ask you about one more personality we forgot—Ma Rainey."

"Great day in the morning! Ma! That woman could sing some blues! I loved Ma Rainey."

"You are not only as old as I am, you're older! I scarcely re-member her myself. Ma Rainey is a legend to me."

"A who?"

"A myth."

"Ma Rainey were too dark to be a mist. But she really could sing the blues. I will not deny Ma Rainey, even to hide my age. Yes, I heard her! I am proud of hearing her! To tell the truth, if I stop and listen, I can still hear her:

> *Wonder where my*

Yee-ooo!

> *Easy rider's gone . . .*

Great day in the morning!

> *Done left me . . .*
> *New gold watch in pawn . . .*

Or else:

> *Troubled in mind, I'm blue—*
> *But I won't be always.*
>
> *The sun's gonna shine in*
> *My back door someday . . .*

"One thing I got to be thankful for, even if it do make me as old as you, is I heard Ma Rainey."

| Once in a Wife-Time

"I'M STILL hoping it will get here in time for Christmas," said Simple.

"What?"

"My divorce. But I just got word from that lawyer in Baltimore that he had been held up until he got my money before completing the process. He also writ me concerning on what my wife bases our divorce, now that I have paid. And, don't you know, that woman claims I deserted *her.*"

"Well, did you?"

"I did not. She put me out."

"In other words, you left under duress."

"Pressure," said Simple.

"Then why don't you refute her argument? Contest her claim?"

"That is just why we separated, we argued so much. I will not argue with Isabel now over no divorce. She writ that she did not want to contest. Neither do I. I never could win an argument with that woman. Only once in a wife-time did I win, and I did not win then with words."

"How did you win?"

"I just grabbed her and kissed her," said Simple.

"Why didn't you try that method more often?"

"Because as soon as I kissed her she stopped arguing and started loving. Sometimes it is not loving a man wants. He wants to *win*—especially when he knows he is right. She told me one time that I had forgot and left the front door unlatched when I went to work.

"I said, 'I know I did not.'

"She said, 'I know you did.'

"It were on from there on in. The truth was I left her at home that morning. She was late to work herself, so she was the last one to go out, so she left the door unlatched. But the more I argued, the madder she got. That is the way with a woman when they are wrong. They not only argue, but they get mad. So I just let her rave. When I did not say a word my wife got madder. In fact, Isabel got so mad that night she were shaking. When a woman shakes, you know you got her goat. So at that point, I said, 'Shut up!'

"Do you think she hushed? No, she just started all over again. It took the neighbors from both sides of the project to stop us. Folks wants to sleep and it were two o'clock in the morning.

"But the time that I won the argument, my wife were right, although I would not let her know it.

"Isabel said, 'Jess Semple, I saw you walking down the street with Della Mae Jones when I were passing on the Pennsylvania Avenue bus.'

"I said, 'You's a lie!'

"She said, 'Then my eyes must of deceived me.'

"I said, 'They did.'

"She said, 'I know you. I know her. I know the clothes you wear. I know the way you talk. It *were* you and it *were* she.'

"I said, 'Not me. It might of been she, but not me. Baby, you know I don't care nothing about that girl, not even enough to walk a block with.'

"I grabbed Isabel and kissed her, bam! On the mouth! Then I bit her on the left cheek. After which I kissed her on the ear, and before she could get loose I negotiated her mouth again. By that time, she had done throwed her arms around my neck and would not let me go. So I won that argument.

"The reason was that she was right. If I had argued with her, she would have won, because I do not have the patience to lie and then re-lie again. Lies show in my eyes, anyhow, so I just kept my face so close to her'n she could not see my eyes. Women do not use logic, they just use words. I didn't let her talk. That time I did not even speak. I just bit her on the cheek, hugged her, run my hand down her back, and said, 'Baby!' Which were enough.

"She knowed I had been out with Della Mae Jones, but she did not care after that. She had sense enough to know it would do no good to care nohow. A man is not like a woman. A man can love two, three, four womens at once and still go to work. If a woman loves *one* man, she does not want him out of her sight. She will quit her job and stay home to be sure he comes from work on time. She will miss her lodge meeting to be certain he does not go nowhere. When a woman is a fool about a man, *she is a fool*. But no matter how much she loves you she will *still* argue. Argument is something a woman never gives up, no matter how much she loves you. She still wants to win. If you are in no mood to argue, don't, daddy-o! Just don't! But when you do, do *not* expect to win, not once in a wife-time. If you don't give a wife the last word, she will take it anyhow. That I know! If Isabel says I deserted her in her divorce papers, let it be. Should I argue back, I might never get free. She put *me* out. *Thank God I went!*"

"Now you're about to get tangled up again," I said.

"I am—if the high cost of love don't get me down. Things has changed since I was courting Isabel. Love has done gone way up. It costs me more to take Joyce out now than it does to buy a summer suit or a pair of winter shoes."

"It's all according to where you take her," I said.

"Joyce won't go nowhere but to the Shalimar, Frank's, Mrs. Frazier's. And if she eats a steak, I'm out of a week's work! If she has a bottle of wine (and she won't drink plain old sherry) I am shook. Joyce don't drink nohow, but somebody told her wine goes with dinner when a gentleman takes a lady out to dine—so lately she must have wine—and it has to be some foreign kind like Beergindy or Sawturn, else Keyauntie.

"She says, 'You never take me nowhere, so when you do, I want nothing but the best.'

"I says, 'Baby, after you get the best, then there ain't no *rest.* Sorry! My money is gone.'

"She says, 'Let it go, and make some more.'

"I says, 'Joyce, I believe you is high. I never did hear you talk like that before. You have changed since first I met you. Besides, I don't *make* money. I earns it. I mean the hard way—work. I ain't no numbers man, neither a dope pusher. I ain't no politicianer with a licker store. I cannot afford to take you out more than once a year at this rate.'

"'It has not been but *once* this year,' says Joyce. 'You are my only boy friend, you know that, so if you don't take me out, who will?'

"I said, 'Better not nobody else try.'

"Joyce says, 'Then if you want to keep your exclusive, buy! Baby, buy!'

"'You know I've been saving up for my divorce,' I says as she called the waiter, but I could tell she had larceny in her heart. Somebody must of told her they saw me buying Zarita a beer.

" 'You should of had your divorce long ago,' says Joyce. 'I have nothing to do with your past. I am your future. You should be saving up now to take care of *me*. Don't you love me?'

" 'Sure, I love you, baby,' I says. 'But what makes the high cost of love so *high?* You are my heart throb. But every time my heart throbs in a restaurant these days, it's dollars. You are my all. But when you *take* all, what have I got left to put? I do not want to be embarrassed in the Shalimar, neither Frank's where just plain meat and potatoes costs more than turkey and dressing does in Virginia. Joyce, after all these years, is you trying to play me for a sucker? If you is, lemme tell you—I might look simple, but I definitely ain't no fool!'

" 'Jess, watch your grammar in public. Don't say, *is you*, and *you is*. That is not proper,' Joyce says.

" 'I begs your pardon,' I says. 'Forgive my down-home talk.'

" 'Down-home or up North,' says Joyce, 'such terms is not correct. You know it. You have been to school.'

" 'Colored school,' I said. 'Which is neither here nor there as long as you understand what I am saying. What I am saying is the high cost of living and the high cost of loving together is more than I can take. I don't mind dying for love, but I hate to be broke. I cannot pay my landlady with your affections. I cannot get my laundry out with heart throbs. Neither can I ride the subway with a kiss. I can't even buy a beer with love.'

" 'Beer, beer, beer! All you think about is beer! So go get yourself one of them girls what's satisfied with a hot dog and a bottle of beer. I do not call that going out myself, so I am going *in*. I will thank you to take me home.'

" 'Start walking then,' I said.

" 'Taxi!' she screamed no sooner than she got to the curb, and she wrapped her stole around her. So, daddy-o, I am broke this morning, broke this week, in fact, broke the rest of the month, just from one date. If I didn't love that girl, I would be mad.

"If I had kissed her before we started out, she might of said, 'Let's just stay home and play records.' Then I wouldn't of had to worry about the high cost of love. Love don't cost a thing in private. It's just when it's on display. When women get out they want Beergindy. I do not care nothing about love in public anyhow. I'm a house man, myself."

"Then it's about time you got married again and made a home."

"It is," said Simple, "because love is too high anywhere else. I should of kissed Joyce on the way to her house in that taxi. Now it will take a week to get her back to normal."

Present for Joyce

"*Rowdy*, now that's a nice word. Sometimes I likes to be rowdy myself, but don't like to run with rowdies. Why is that? I like to drink, but I don't like drunks. I don't have the education to mingle myself with educated folks. I don't have a white-walled Cadillac to keep up with sports, numbers writers, and doctors. And not smoking reefers, I can't pal around with hep cats. So who are my buddies? You—and a couple of bartenders."

"The point of such a dissertation at this moment being what?" I asked.

"Nothing," said Simple, "except to offer you a small beer. And to tell you I am tired of working like a Negro all week in order to live like white folks on Saturday night. What I want is a part-time job with *full-time* pay, or else a position where you take a vacation all summer and rest all winter. But I am colored, so I know nothing like that is going to happen to me."

"Color, color, color!" I said. "It is so easy to blame all one's failures and difficulties on color. To whine *I can't do this, I can't do that* because I'm colored—which is one bad habit you have, friend—always bringing up race."

"I do," said Simple, "because that is what I am always coming face to face with—race. I look in the mirror in the morning to shave—and what do I see? *Me.* From birth to death my face—which is my race—stares me in the face."

"Don't you suppose race stared Ralph Bunche in the face, too? And Adam Powell? And Joe Louis? And Paul Williams?

And Dr. Butts? But Ralph Bunche, Negro, became internationally famous. Adam Powell, Negro, went to Congress. Joe Louis, Negro, defeated the world's best fighters. Paul Williams designs houses for Hollywood stars. Dr. Butts writes articles for the leading papers, gets fellowships, speaks all over the country. Suppose they had all just stood at a beer bar like you and moaned about race, race, race!"

"I ain't as smart as Ralph Bunche," said Simple. "I can't holler like Adam Powell, having no microphone in my throat. And I ain't built like Joe Louis. I'm a light-weight. Paul Williams is colleged, and got mother wit, too. And I cannot write no articles like Dr. Butts. But every time Dr. Butts publishes something, Joyce buys it, or else asks me to buy it for her, so my money helps support him. Butts has got some of my money. I bought tickets to every one of Joe's fights in New York, so my money helped Joe get that championship belt. I put my dollars in the box office when I go to the movies which helps them movie stars pay Paul Williams to design them a house. And I vote for Adam Powell. So they all come right down to *me*. And where am I?"

"Through leaders like those we've just mentioned, you will get somewhere," I said. "You have to take the long view."

"It seems like to me this very last week were as *long* as a year. Sometimes I start work on Monday and by the time I get to Tuesday, it looks like I done worked seven days. By the time I get to Wednesday, it seems like a month. And when Saturday comes, I been slaving a year. Some weeks just naturally seems long, I mean, long! No week should seem like a year, but when you're working at something that don't get you nowhere, they do!"

"Some weeks do lengthen out to infinity," I said.

"I don't know infinitive," said Simple. "But there is something wrong somewhere with the way weeks are made. If I was to make a calendar, I would crowd a work-week into *one* day. But I would make a vacation-week stretch out over a month, particularly the week before Christmas on my calendar."

"Your calendar would be most confusing," I said. "Nobody but yourself would understand it—and I fear even you would get mixed up. You cannot change time around to suit your personal feelings. There is something inexorable about time. You cannot hold it off."

"You cannot hold off Christmas either," groaned Simple. "I know if Christmas came more than once a year I could not stand it."

"Don't you like the Christmas spirit?"

"I like any kind of spirits, provided they have alcohol in them. I love eggnog well spiked. What I mean is, if Christmas came *twice* a year, it would be more than a man could bear. Women like to shop. I do not."

"Has your shopping been so extensive this season that it has broken you down?" I demanded.

"It has near about done me in, and all I have got so far is one little old present—for Joyce. And there is no way of being sure she will like what I bought. Womens is funny about presents. Joyce is always yowling and howling over how I never give her nothing—so this time I thought I would spend Ten Dollars and get her something real good, and pick it out my own self, without advice from nobody. So I did. It strained my brain. It also strained my nerves, not to speak of my feet. But I did not want to shuff Joyce off with no easy present this time—since I really aim to marry that girl in June. So, beings as the downtown stores are open late on Thursday nights and, being a working man, I cannot go to *no* store in the daytime, before I even et my supper Thursday I headed for Macy's to pick out Joyce's present.

"Don't you know that store were full, I mean jammed, even though everybody ought to have been home eating dinner! It took me one hour to get to the counter, one more hour to get waited on, another hour to pick out the present, and another hour to fight my way away from the counter. I did not want to get nothing too cheap, neither nothing beyond the cash I had in my pocket. As it was, it used up my carfare for a week after they added the tax onto it that the clerk did not tell me about. By that time it were eight P.M. Then it took me another hour to get the thing wrapped up in a gift box. By that hour I were so weak with hunger and my bunion hurt me so bad that, if I did not love Joyce, I would have said, 'To hell with it,' and give up. But I stuck it out. Now, if she do not like the present, I do not care."

"After all you went through to get it," I said, "she is bound to like it. Certainly I am curious to know what you bought for her."

"A purse," said Simple, "an evening purse, just big enough to hold her lipstick and handkerchief."

"Any purse is big enough to hold money also," I said, "so that is what your gift will remind her of."

"Doggone it!" said Simple. "You are right—money. I have made my first mistake for the coming year! But it is a beautifine purse, genuine imitation rhinestone studded with a silver lock. Do you reckon she will like it?"

"I am sure she will like it if you put a Ten Dollar bill inside."

"Daddy-o!" yelled Simple. "Must I give her my life? Besides, I will *never* open that gift-package to put nothing inside. I couldn't get it tied up again."

"You could put the Ten Dollar bill on the outside," I said.

"I could put the *store bill* on the outside," said Simple, "then she could take it back and get Ten on a refund."

"Joyce would not be so callous on Christmas," I said.

"She'd wait until after Christmas," said Simple.

| Christmas Song

"Just like a Negro," said Simple, "I have waited till Christmas Eve to finish my shopping."

"You are walking rather fast," I said. "Be careful, don't slip on the ice. The way it's snowing, you can't always see it underneath the snow."

"Why do you reckon they don't clean off the sidewalks in Harlem nice like they do downtown?"

"Why do *you* reckon?" I asked. "But don't tell me! I don't

wish to discuss race tonight, certainly not out here in the street, as cold as it is."

"Paddy's is right there in the next block," said Simple, heading steadily that way. "I am going down to 125th Street to get two rattles, one for Carlyle's baby, Third Floor Front, and one for that other cute little old baby downstairs in the Second Floor Rear. Also I aims to get a box of hard candy for my next-door neighbor that ain't got no teeth, poor Miss Amy, so she can suck it. And a green rubber bone for Trixie. Also some kind of game for Joyce to take her godchild from me during the holidays."

"It's eight o'clock already, fellow. If you've got all that to do, you'd better hurry before the stores close."

"I am hurrying. Joyce sent me out to get some sparklers for the tree. Her and her big old fat landlady and some of the other roomers in their house is putting up a Christmas tree down in the living room, and you are invited to come by and help trim it, else watch them trimming. Do you want to go?"

"When?"

"Long about midnight P.M., I'd say. Joyce is taking a nap now. When she wakes up she's promised to make some good old Christmas eggnog—if I promise not to spike it too strong. You might as well dip your cup in our bowl. Meanwhile, let's grab a quick beer here before I get on to the store. Come on inside. Man, I'm excited! I got another present for Joyce."

"What?"

"I'm not going to tell you until after Christmas. It's a surprise. But whilst I am drinking, look at this which I writ yesterday."

XMAS

I forgot to send
A card to Jennie—
But the truth about cousins is
There's too many.

I also forgot
My Uncle Joe,
But I believe I'll let
That old rascal go.

I done bought
Four boxes now.
I can't afford
No more, nohow.

So Merry Xmas,
Everybody!
Cards or no cards,
Here's HOWDY!

"That's for my Christmas card," said Simple. "Come on, let's go."

"Not bad. Even if it will be a little late, be sure you send me one," I said as we went out into the snow.

"Man, you know I can't afford to have no cards printed up. It's just jive. I likes to compose with a pencil sometimes. Truth is, come Christmas, I has feelings right up in my throat that if I was a composer, I would write me a song also, which I would sing myself. It would be a song about that black Wise Man who went to see the Baby in the Manger. I would put into it such another music as you never heard. It would be a baritone song."

"There are many songs about the Three Wise Men," I said. "Why would you single out the black one?"

"Because I am black," said Simple, "so my song would be about the black Wise Man."

"If you could write such a song, what would it say?"

"Just what the Bible says—that he saw a star, he came from the East, and he went with the other Wise Mens to Bethlehem in Judea, and bowed down before the Child in the Manger, and put his presents down there in the straw for that Baby— and it were the greatest Baby in the world, for it were Christ! That is what my song would say."

"You don't speak of the Bible very often," I said, "but when you do, you speak like a man who knew it as a child."

"My Aunt Lucy read the Bible to me all the time when I were knee high to a duck. I never will forget it. So if I wrote a Christmas song, I would write one right out of the Bible. But it would not be so much what words I would put in it as what my music would say—because I would also make up the music myself. Music explains things better than words and everybody in all kind of languages could understand it then. My music would say everything my words couldn't put over, because there wouldn't be many words anyhow.

"The words in my song would just say a black man saw a star and followed it till he came to a stable and put his presents down. But the music would say he also laid his heart down, too —which would be my heart. It would be *my* song I would be making up. But I would make it like as if I was there myself two thousand years ago, and *I* seen the star, and *I* followed it till I come to that Child. And when I riz up from bending over that Baby in the Manger I were strong and not afraid. The end of my song would be, *Be not afraid.* That would be the end of my song."

"It sounds like a good song," I said.

"It would be the kind of song everybody could sing, old folks and young folks. And when they sing it, some folks would laugh. It would be a happy song. Other folks would cry because—well, I don't know," Simple stopped quite still for a moment in the falling snow. "I don't know, but something about that black man and that little small Child—something about them two peoples—folks would cry."

| Tied in a Bow

"WHEN she took that present from the Christmas tree and untied it in front of all them other people, Joyce screamed, cried, danced, whirled around, run across the room, hauled off and kissed me, then cried, 'At last you have crossed the Ohio!' "

"What in God's name did she mean by that?"

"She were thinking about *Uncle Tom's Cabin,* Joyce explained to me later. And all she could say was, 'Free! Free! Free! Jess Semple, you're free!' "

"Do you mean to say you've been granted your divorce?"

"That is what I had hanging on the tree Christmas morning," said Simple, "my divorce. It were all tied up in a big red ribbon with a sprig of holly on it, also a bow. It were beautiful, rolled like a diploma. Did I ever show you my receipt? Look."

> Baltimore, Maryland, 16th inst.
> For legal services rendered Mrs. Jesse B. Semple, received from her late husband, J. B. Semple, the sum of $133.34 re divorce.
>
> (signed) J. Harvey Scraggs
> Attorney-at-Law

"See, I even paid the extra penny—the rest of them only paid One Hundred and Thirty-Three Dollars and Thirty-Three Cents. I put in the most—Thirty-*Four* Cents. But to see how happy Joyce was Christmas morning, it were worth it. Now we can have a wedding this June with a capital *W*— only a year late. Joyce is thinking about who she is going to invite to our wedding right now—fancy with a veil, graved invitations, and two receptions, one before and one after. Also a story writ up for the papers. She says we will call it: 'The Semple-Lane Nuptials,' which is another name for wedding."

"That's going to run into money," I said, "so you'd better start saving again."

"Buddy, I have resolved to do nothing but save from now on in. With New Year's coming next week, and a wedding coming in June, my resolutions is already resolved, and I will not wait until New Year's Day to put them into force. Resolve No. 1: No whiskey and very little beer. For every glass of whiskey I can drink three or four beers. I will drink only four, no more."

"Economics, not morals, will keep you in a milder alcoholic groove," I said.

"So moved," said Simple. "Now, Resolve No. 2: This year I will not talk so much. I believe if I listen more, I will learn more. Also I will get in less arguments, and be more wise than I am. The Bible says, 'A wise man holdeth his tongue.' I will hold mine—especially with women and landladies."

"Excellent! When do you intend to start?"

"Shortly. Resolution No. 3: Whatever I do say, I will not try to get in the last word with a woman. I will let a chick have the last word from now on no matter what she says. A woman can be dead wrong, I will still let her have the last word. I won't let that worry me any more."

"You have turned diplomat in your old age," I said.

"Who's old? I am just tired of arguing with females. Now that I am going to be caged up with one come June, I wants no ruction in my cage."

"You and Joyce are going to make a nest together, not a cage."

"Whatever it is, I want no feathers flying. I want peace and calm, quiet and no arguments, that is, in my private life. There is also one more resolve I have resolved. Believe it or not, buddy-o, and that is this: To let the Race Problem roll off my mind like water off a duck's back—pay it no attention any more. I have been worrying as long as I have been black. Since I have to be black a long time yet, what is the sense of so much worriation? The next time I read where they have lynched or bombed a Negro, I will just shrug my shoulders and say, 'It warn't me.' The next time I hear tell of a colored singer barred out of Constitution Hall in Washington, I will say, 'I ain't no singer.' Next time I hear that colored folks can't eat in the Stork Club, I will say, 'Chitterlings is better than filet mignon anyhow.'"

"The New Year will completely change your character," I said. "You will no longer be yourself."

"I am already changed," said Simple. "Like the camel, I have been threaded through the eye of a needle and come out a new man. Like the sow's ear, I am a silk purse—only it is empty. Like the Liberty Bell, I ring for freedom. I've crossed the Ohio! Lend me a half, since it's a holiday week, and I will buy us both a bottle of Bud."

"That old habit of yours, buying drinks with borrowed money —after all those resolutions!"

"My resolutions don't cover other people's money," said Simple.

| Sometimes I Wonder

"WHAT'S on your mind this evening?" I asked one cold January night when it was quiet at the bar, and Simple seemed depressed.

"I am trying to figure out how to stay alive until I die," he said. "The way things are happening to me, I might not live my time out. I got troubles. It makes me sick to think of them."

"You know what the preacher said, don't you? 'You might get too sick to eat. You might get too sick to sleep, too sick to work, too sick to talk—but you never get too sick to die.' "

"I know a man with all that sickness is liable to wake up some morning and find himself dead," said Simple. "But I blame all my troubles on talking. I did not want Joyce to know I took Zarita to the Bartenders Ball—but telephone, telegraph, tell-a-Negro—and the news is out. The last is fastest—a Negro. I told Joyce's girl friend's boy friend, and the boy friend told his girl friend. His girl friend told Joyce. Then the rumble were on! From here on in, I will never tell nobody nothing again."

"That is a safe rule," I observed.

"I also will not be caught in public with Zarita again. Some womens is all right in private. In fact, fine. But in public they act like they are out of their minds. A crowd excites some folks and the show-off in them comes out, so they have to not only show-off but *show-out*. Zarita were the life of that ball. To tell the truth, she attracted attention."

"Do you mean to say she did not behave like a lady?"

"Less like a lady than usual," said Simple. "More like as if she was being paid to put on a show. She bawled and she brawled. She clowned. And she sounded out when I said, 'Baby, set down!' She got high and wanted to fly. Danced every set. Jived every man she met. That chick didn't miss a bet. Frantic! And me paying for her tickets. Keeping up with her nearly give me the rickets, man. Trying to get her home almost broke me. And if I was to tell you the rest, friend, well, words would choke me! When the musicianers started playing she started doing the mambo, the sambo, and the hambo. She danced twenty mens down, including me."

"You really had your hands full, fellow."

"That I did. Then at four-five A.M., Zarita wanted to stop in every after-hour spot on the Avenue when the ball were over. I thought I knew them all, but Zarita knowed some jook joints nobody I know ever knowed. With licker at Fifty Cents a shot, for the rest of the week what have I got? A big head, and a small purse. It were broad open daylight before we started home. By that time, it were time for me to go to work. Bartenders should have their balls on Saturday so a man can rest afterwards, especially when he goes out with Zarita."

"How could Zarita get an old night-owl like you down?"

"She did," said Simple. "But the worst of it was that news of all this balling got back to Joyce. She lit into me like a house afire. Then ended up telling me, 'I do not expect you to be a saint, Jess Semple, because they stopped making saints when they started putting M–R—period—Mr.—instead of S–T. in front of men's names. But I do know one thing, *if, when,* and *after* you marry me, you had better let Zarita alone. And, *just to get in practice,* you better start now. Don't let me hear tell of you running around with that woman again. Why, you liable to catch the seven-year itches. And from me you'll catch the kind of chastisement you read about only in the Bible. In fact, worse, because chastisements are up my sleeve you have never even read about. Mark my words.'

" 'They is marked,' I said. I could tell Joyce were not fooling. What is a chastisement, anyhow?"

"A castigation, a punishment."

"I do not want no more punishment from Joyce. Last night she were so mad she turned gray. In fact, she were *real* mad."

"Jealous, you mean."

"Joyce says she would not low-rate herself by being jealous of Zarita. But what made her so mad was that Joyce knowed I must have spent some money. She wondered where did I get it, when I had just borrowed Ten Dollars from her the night before. Joyce said if she thought I had spent *her* money on Zarita, she would annihilate me for life. Lucky I could show Joyce my receipt where I paid my rent. It's a good thing I had one from this time last year. My landlady do not put the year on them, just the month and the date. So Joyce thought it was a receipt for now. She don't know I didn't pay my rent this week."

"I call that deceit," I said.

"Better deceit than defeat. Now I have *really* got to figure out how to settle my rent. Can't you lend me Ten Dollars?"

"You know I cannot lend anybody Ten Dollars in the middle of the week."

"Then how on earth am I going to stay alive until I die? I cannot face my landlady."

"Borrow back from Zarita that Ten Dollars you spent taking her to the dance. Rob Peter to pay Paul."

"Zarita's name ain't Peter," said Simple, "and my landlady's sure ain't Paul. In so far as concerning Zarita, who just left out of here, sometimes I wonder why God made womens like her, because I don't understand her at all. I thought I did, but I do not believe I do. Zarita knows I go with Joyce. She knows I *love* Joyce. Zarita does not love me. Yet and still, Zarita is trying to make trouble between us—me and Joyce. Now why would she do that, as good as I am to that girl? I buy her a fifth of licker practically everytime I go to see her, treat her if I meet her, even take her out once in a while if I know Joyce is in bed and won't run into us. Nice as I been to Zarita, she comes telling me tonight she is 'thinking of telling Joyce how close we been.' She's done heard somewhere I'm planning to marry Joyce. Now, why would Zarita want to start some stuff?"

"Probably envious," I said, "because Joyce is going to have a happy home and she, Zarita, will still be on the loose."

"Loose as a goose," said Simple, "which is the way Zarita likes to live. She won't let no man tie her down, she says so herself. Plays the field, been playing it, and means to keep on playing it—no intention of being housebroke. Zarita will stick by a man only until the bottle is empty. Then she says, 'Don't you think we ought to run down to Paddy's before closing time and have a little drink?'

"Once back here in Paddy's, that's the end. Next thing you

know she's found some other fellow who will take her to an after-hours spot. 'Bye, baby!' She's gone. Zarita likes to stay up and out all night long. She would exhaust a working man. When I first met her, she wore me down. Now I don't even see the chick more'n once or twice a month and nothing happens. So why does she want to come bringing up that she believes she'll tell Joyce all? There ain't no *all!* It's done, finished, over with."

"A man's past always lasts. In other words, 'Your sins will find you out.'"

"Truer words were never spoke," said Simple. "But I sure ain't gonna let Zarita come between me and Joyce!"

"Perhaps Zarita is just trying to blackmail you."

"I never will mail her a black cent! She's not much on money, nohow, just licker. That's one nice thing about Zarita, she's not a begging girl. In fact, she's free-hearted. She'll spend her money as fast as she will yours. I do not believe anything will shut Zarita's mouth but to scare her to death."

"Maybe she's only teasing you."

"I can tell when a woman's got larceny in her heart. When I told her I was getting engaged to Joyce formal this spring, I could see her ears go back like a cat looking cross-eyed at milk.

"Then she said, 'Oh, you is, is you?'

"Any time anybody says, 'You is, is you?' they mean you no good, especially if they're smiling."

"Sometimes," I said, "even if a woman no longer wants you in her arms, she wants you in her heart."

"Dog-bite her heart! And she'll never get me in her arms any more. I wish I had never had her in mine."

"If wishes were horses beggars would ride."

"Zarita would ride, too," said Simple, "right out of my life. I would just like not to be worried by her any more."

"For once, race is not your main complaint. I am glad somebody has taken your mind off the color problem. In the past you have talked me to death on that score. Sometimes I wonder what makes you so race-conscious."

"Sometimes I wonder what made me so black," said Simple.

| Four Rings

"I HAVE not seen you for a few days," I said. "Where've you been?"

"Working," said Simple.

"Same place, your old job back?"

"Not yet—but the same place. I'm helping to reconvert. I went down there Monday and said, 'Look here, don't you need somebody to maintain while you converts?'

"The man said, 'I believe they are short-handed, but I don't believe they're employing any colored boys in the reconversion jobs.'

"I said, 'What makes you think I'm colored? They done took such words off of jobs in New York State by law.'

"I know he wanted to say, 'But they ain't took the black off of your face.'

"But he did not. He just looked kind of surprised when I said, 'What makes you think I'm colored?' Then he grinned. And I grinned. He is a right good-natured white man.

"He said, 'Go see the foreman.'

"I did. And I got took on. I got tired of waiting for them to reconvert that plant, so I am reconverting along with them. In six or eight weeks, they'll be ready to open up again. I will know a lots more about the new machines and things they are putting in because I'm watching every move they make and every screw they turn. Maybe I might even get a better job when the plant opens up. We got a good shop steward in my department. I believe he will look out for me."

"I hope so," I said. "You've been there long enough to deserve some upgrading."

"I'm on the up-and-up," said Simple. "I was so happy last night, I kissed Joyce all over the parlor. When we set down on the sofa she thought there was a bear next to her. I were so rambunctious, Joyce says, 'There's an end to this sofa—and

you have got me right up against the end. Unhand me, Jess
Semple. I'm going to make you something to drink.'

"Now that surprised me so that I let her go. Joyce had not
ever made me a drink before—knowing how I drink in the street
—except she's giving a party and serving guests and such, which
must include me. Well, sir, Joyce went on back in the kitchen,
and in a few minutes she comes out with two cups and a pot
just steaming, something with a spicy smell.

" 'Whiskey toddy?'

" 'Guess again.'

" 'Hot rum punch?'

" 'No!' she says, 'Sassafras tea.'

" 'What?' I hollers. 'Sassafras tea?'

" 'To cool the blood,' she says. 'You remember down home,
old folks used to give it to the young folks in the spring? Well,
spring is on its way, dear. And I think you need this.'

"It did look right good, and smelled delicious, steaming pink
and rosy as wine. I had not had no sassafras tea since I left
Virginia when us kids used to strip the bark and bring it home
to Grandma Arcie to dry. Trust Joyce to think up something
different.

" 'You know we got to have out health tested before we can
get married,' she said.

" 'I know it,' I says. 'Let's go tomorrow.' Not really meaning
that, but don't you know that girl took time off from work and
went. Me, too. And we'll have the certifications by the end of
this week."

"This is only March," I said. "June is a long way off. Aren't
you rushing matters a bit?"

"Them little details we wants to get out of the way," said
Simple. "We is busy people. We got to start looking for an apartment. No more rooming from our wedding night on. Then soon
as we can, we gonna start buying a house. Maybe next fall. Do
you want to room with us in our house?"

"What my situation next fall will be, I cannot tell. So may I
delay my answer?"

"You may, just so you're standing up there beside me at my

wedding. You're supposed to hand me the rings. Ain't that what the best man does?"

"I think he does. But I'm rather backward about being your best man. After all, we are only bar acquaintances. A best man is usually a *close* friend, somebody with whom you grew up or with whom you went to college, somebody you know very well."

"I did not grow up with nobody, my folks moved so much. I stayed with fifty-eleven relatives in seven different towns. I did not go to college, and I do not know anybody very well but you. I bull-jive around with lots of cats in bars, and I sometimes cast an eye on different womens now and then. I drinks with anybody from Zarita to Watermelon Joe. But, excusing Zarita, I don't know none of them other folks very well. With them I just jives. Maybe I don't even know you, but with you at least I talk. No doubt, you got some friends you know better. But don't nobody know *me* better. So you be my best man."

"Then I'm supposed to give you a bachelor's party a night or two before the ceremony. Your wedding is going to cost me money, too, Jess! I'm certainly glad you're drinking less these days, so I won't have to stock up so heavy on liquors."

"Just a keg of beer," said Simple. "I mean one *private* one with my name on it. What you give the other jokers, I do not care. And the young folks will need some refreshments. F. D. is also getting married."

"At the same time as you and Joyce?"

"Yes," said Simple. "So he writ me to get him two rings just like ours. Him and Gloria wants everything to be just like me and Joyce's."

"Has that young boy gone and committed another Carlyle?" I asked.

"I asked him that, too," said Simple. "He said, 'No.' Him and Gloria do not want to have no children at all until he comes back from the army."

"From the army?"

"Didn't I tell you F. D. got his draft call? Soon as this college term is over, he has to go to his service. So them kids is gonna get married so F. D. can go with a clear conscience. F. D. and

Gloria are marrying to separate—and me and Joyce are marrying to stay together. There's some advantage in being in a high age bracket after all."

"Love will find a way," I said, "whatever the age. God bless all of you—F. D. and Gloria, and you and—"

"Joyce—my honey in the evening!"

"Yes, all four of you."

| Simply Love

LENT. Tentative sticking of heads out windows pushed up only to be pulled down. It is *not* warm yet, even if the sun is shining and the streets are dry. City Sanitation Trucks sprinkling pavements. Kids at stick ball competing with traffic. Marbles and tops, penny whistles, chalk on sidewalks, jumping ropes. Passers-by duck and dodge handballs against stoops. Children think it's warmer than it is, running like they do.

Joyce is not the only one to brew sassafras tea, but it's hard to find sassafras bark in Harlem. You might have to have somebody mail you a bundle from home. Earliest breath of spring, when the sunrise is bright, landladies open their front doors first thing in the morning to air out the house, bright and early in the day, first thing. Joyce's big old fat landlady, still in her kimono, is sweeping out the vestibule and sweeping off the front stoop before breakfast when she almost drops her broom in amazement as she turns to see a man come running down the steps inside. Mr. Semple!

" 'What are you doing, coming out of *my* house at seven-eight o'clock A.M.?'

" 'Coming out is all,' I says.

" 'Mr. Semple, this is a decent house.' She pauses. 'Was you in there *all* night?'

" 'I were.'

" 'This is the first time! . . . Or is it? . . . I am surprised at you! And doubly surprised at Joyce Lane.'

" 'She is Joyce Lane no longer, madam.'

" 'What?'

" 'She is Mrs. Semple now. March has turned to June—we got married yesterday.'

" 'Ooh-ooo-oo-o!' she strangles.

"You could have knocked that old landlady down with a feather. She looked more surprised than you do."

"You can knock *me* down with a feather, too," I exclaimed. "Do you mean to tell me you jumped the gun and got married *before* the wedding—in March instead of June?"

"We did. Joyce and I did. And it feels like something I never done before."

"But I thought you were going to have a church wedding?"

"We were. But the feeling just overcome us early. So we went down to City Hall and rushed the season. We can get married again in a church any time we want to, when we get the dough."

"But what about the engraved invitations? What about the bridal gown she's having made? What about the relatives coming from down South for the ceremony? And what about the cake?"

"Man, that is where I was going this morning, to Cushman's to buy a cake when that big old fat landlady stopped me. Old landlady was so surprised she invited me right back in the house to call Joyce to come down and have hot cakes with her. She said, 'I'll make you your first cakes.'

"So the landlady fixed our wedding breakfast. It were *fine*. But she asked to see my license first just to be sure I were not there under false pretenses. Then she said it was O.K. that I had stayed upstairs last night."

"Well, friend, I still want to know, what about my dark-blue suit I was buying especially for the wedding, since you said I was going to be your best man?"

"You can wear it to our house to dinner. The invitations, the relatives, the cake, your suit, Joyce with a veil on—I asked her this morning, 'Baby, will you miss all them things? Are you mad or glad?'

"Joyce says, 'Glad, Jess, glad.'

"What happened was I took my first week's salary that I received back on the job and bought the license. I were not taking no chances of being laid off again before the wedding happened. Only thing is, buddy, I did not know where to find you yesterday morning to stand up with me, it being Saturday. We just picked out a couple of strangers who was down at City Hall getting married, too. They was our best people. And we was theirs. They were white. But we did not care, and they did not care. They stood up with us and we stood up with them. That white man were my best man, and I was his.

"We was all so happy when it was over that that white couple hauled off and kissed *my* bride, and I hauled off and kissed his. I did not think anything like that would ever happen—kissing white folks, and they kissing me. But it did—in New York—which is why I like this town where everybody is free, white, and twenty-one, including me."

"What about the wedding rings?"

"Me and Joyce is going to pick out the rings Monday."

"What about F. D. and Gloria, who were going to get married with you?"

"F. D. is grown. He can get married by his self. Joyce and me will stand up with him if he wants us to. But I will write that boy and tell him *I* could not wait. F. D. is young and got plenty of time. His memory don't go back no further than Sarah Vaughan—never heard of Ma Rainey. Besides he's on the baseball team, which will keep him busy pitching till June."

"Well, I did not have a chance to give that bachelor's party for you, which I regret."

"It would be no use to give it now because I have ceased from this day on to be a drinking man," said Simple, "so you'll save your money. Not that Joyce cares too much about me drinking, but I plans to respect what little objections she do have. She will never see me high again. And Zarita will never see me at all. Zarita has done cried, and wished me well, and is thinking about getting married herself—which is one more reason not to drink—with her off my mind."

"But can't I even buy you a beer in celebration of the occasion?"

"*One*—providing you got a stick of chlorophyll chewing gum about you."

"Hypocrite."

"Just kidding," said Simple. "But all kidding aside—and thanks for the beer—I *am* a new man. I intends to act like a new man, and therefore *be* a new man. I will only drink in moderation—which means small glasses—from now on. And this spring I will down as much sassafras tea as I will beer, if not more. What Joyce likes, I like. What she do, I do. Same as in the Bible—'Whether she goeth, I goeth'—even to concerts and teas."

"You are indeed a changed man," I said. "It's simply amazing."

"Simply heavenly," said Simple. "Love is as near heaven as a man gets on this earth."

| Bang-up Big End

"I wonder how come they don't have lady pallbearers?" asked my friend.

"Lady pallbearers?"

"Yes," said Simple, "at funerals. I have never yet seen a lady carrying a coffin. Women do everything else these days from flying airplanes and driving taxis to fighting bulls. They might as well be pallbearers, too."

"Maybe it's because women are more emotional than men," I said. "They might break down from sorrow and drop the corpse."

"Whooping and hollering and fainting and falling out like they used to do at the old-time funerals," said Simple, "has gone out of style now, leastwise in Harlem where the best undertakers has a nurse in attendance. If anybody faints at a funeral now, the nurses stick so much smelling salts up to your nose that you sneeze and come to right away. You better come to—else that ammonia will blow your wig off. They say undertakers' helpers get paid by the hour now, too. They are very busy people, also expensive, so they have no time for nobody holding up a funeral by fainting. And these modern educated ministers do not like their sermons interrupted by people screaming and yelling. Modern ministers is all Doctors of Divinities and such, so too cultured for hollering. But I remember a funeral I went to once down in Virginia where all the mourners delivered sermons, too, and talked and hollered louder than the preacher. And the widow of the deceased asked the dead man why did he leave her.

" 'Why did you leave me, Thomas?' she cried. 'Why?'

"She knew darned well the man drunk himself to death, also that she had put him out of the house more than once, and quit him twice. Yet there she was crying because he had relieved her of his burden once and for all. You could hardly hear the minister who was preaching the corpse to heaven instead of hell, so much racket did his wife and relatives keep up."

"Ways of grieving vary," I said. "In India, for example, the widow in some communities throws herself onto a flaming bier and perishes with her husband."

"Them widows must be right simple," said Simple.

"In some countries widows wear black all the rest of their lives after the husband dies."

"Which saves them cleaning bills," said Simple. "Dirt does not show on black."

"In Ireland they have wonderful wakes the night before a funeral and eat and drink all night."

"I wish I was in Ireland," said Simple. "I could really help drain a bottle."

"And in Haiti they play cards at the wake."

"No," said Simple, "*no cards!* I would not want to lose my money gambling, not even for my best friend. I would not play no cards at nobody's wake."

"In some parts of Asia, they bury the dead standing up."

"Which is better than being buried upside down," said Simple, "or cremated—burnt up before you gets to hell."

"Cremation is a sanitary process, I think. Besides, ashes takes up very little space. Just imagine all the acres and acres of land nowadays taken up by cemeteries. A person's ashes in a jar can be kept on the mantelpiece."

"What old mantelpiece? Where?" cried Simple. "Never no

ashes of no deceased on my mantelpiece. Oh, no! When a person is dead and gone they should be where they belong, in the ground."

"Pure custom," I said. "In some countries folks are not buried in the ground at all. In certain primitive communities the dead are put on a mountaintop and left there. At sea you're dropped in the water. It's all according to what you are accustomed."

"Well, I have not been buried yet," said Simple, "but when the end comes and I am, I want to be decent buried, not dropped in no water, nor left on no mountain, neither burnt up. Also I want plenty of whooping and hollering and crying over me so the world will know I have been here and gone—a bang-up big end. I do not want no quiet funeral like white folks. I want people to hear my funeral through the windows. If not, I am liable to rise up in my coffin myself and holler and cry. I demand excitement when I leave this earth. Whoever inherits my insurance money, I want 'em to holler, moan, weep and cry for it. If they don't, I dead sure will come back and cut 'em out of my will. Negroes don't have much in this world, so we might as well have a good funeral."

| Duty Is Not Snooty

"I REMEMBER one time you told me that you thought that if white people who say they love Negroes really do love them, then they ought to live like Negroes live. Didn't you say that?"

"I did," said Simple, "especially when they go down South."

"That means then that our white friends should ride in Jim Crow cars, too?"

"It does," said Simple.

"Why?" I asked.

"To prove that they love me," said Simple, "otherwise, I do not believe them. White folks that love me and care about my race ought to sleep in colored hotels when they travel—which are mostly not built for sleeping. They also ought to eat in col ored restaurants—which in small towns is generally greasy spoons. They should also wait an hour for a colored taxi in them places where white cabs won't haul Negroes. Also let my white friends what plan to stay in the South awhile, send their children to the colored not-yet-integrated school, which is most generally across the railroad track in a hovel. And when they get on the buses to come home, let them ride in the back of the buses. If the back seats for colored is crowded, then let them stand up, even if some of the white seats is empty—which colored dare not set in for fear of getting shot through the windows. When nice white folks got through with all that Jim Crow, from eating to sleeping to schools to Jim Crow cars, then we would see how they feel for real."

"If you are expecting our good white friends to go through all of that, then you are expecting them to be superhuman," I said.

"I ride in Jim Crow cars and I am not superhuman."

"You ride in them because you have to," I said.

"I believe in share and share alike," declared Simple. "Them white folks that really loves me should share them Jim Crow cars with me, and not be setting back up in the hindpart of the train all air-cooled and everything whilst I rides up by the engine in an old half-baggage car. Also, I want my white friends to experience a Jim Crow toilet. There is nothing like a COLORED toilet in a Southern train station! Half the time, no mirrow, no paper towels, sometimes no sink even to wash your hands. They is separate, all right, but not equal. Let them try one, then them nice white folks, who are always asking me what more do I want since the Supreme Court decided I could vote, would understand what I want. I wants me a train-station toilet with everything in it everybody else has got."

"You know it is against local law for white people to use COLORED waiting rooms down South, or for colored people to use WHITE. Do you want decent white folks to get locked up just to prove they love you?"

"I'd get locked up for going in their waiting rooms, so why shouldn't they get locked up for going in mine? It ain't right for friends to be separated."

"What good would it do us for our white friends to get locked up?"

"It would teach them how dumb it is to have WHITE and COLORED signs all over Dixie."

"Liberal whites already agree that is stupid," I said.

"They would agree more if they experienced it," said Simple. "And if they got locked up a few times, them signs would come down! White folks do not put up with whatever they don't like. Just let a white man get turned down when he goes in a restaurant hungry. He will turn the joint out. If I get turned down, all they do is turn me out. White folks has got a theoretical knowledge of prejudice. I want them to have a real one. That is why I say when these nice white folks from up North goes down to Florida in the winter, let them go Jim Crow. When they get there let them stay at one of them colored hotels where they don't have no bell boys to wait on them hand and foot, also no valet service, and no nice room service for breakfast on a push wagon, and where the elevator is liable to be broke down, if they got one. Let them live colored for just *one* vacation. I bet they will not be so sweet-tempered then. They would not like it. They would be mad! It is not enough for white folks just to be nice and shake my hand and tell me I am equal. I know I am equal. What I want is to be *treated* equal. So maybe if the nice white folks really find out *what* it is like *not* to be treated equal—after they live Jim Crow themselves—I bet you, things will change! You know, white folks would not put up with Jim Crow—if they ever got Jim Crowed themselves. They don't really know what Jim Crow is. But it is their duty to find out, and duty cannot be snooty."

"Your flights of fancy are rather intriguing," I said, "but you know none of what you are saying is going to happen. Good people are not *that* good. To tell the truth, if I were white, no matter how much I loved Negroes, I doubt that I would submit myself to Jim Crow living conditions just to prove my love."

"Neither would I," said Simple.

"Then you would not be very good, either."

"No," said Simple, "but I would be white."

| Bones, Bombs, Chicken Necks

"For the first time since I been married," said Simple, "Joyce has not spoke to me all day."

"Did you speak to her?" I asked.

"I tried," said Simple, "but she did not answer."

"What happened? What's the matter?" I asked.

"She's interfered with my habits," said Simple.

"What do you mean, interfered with your habits?"

"My pleasure, and my ways," said Simple.

"Well, tell me," I said, "if you are going to tell me."

"It were like this," Simple began. "After dinner, I were setting in my front window gnawing on a pork-chop bone, observing Harlem, and I had just got down to the juicy part, when Joyce says, 'Jesse B., why did you take that bone away from the table?'

"I say, 'Baby, to gnaw on.'

" 'But not in the front window,' says Joyce.

" 'It's my window,' I said.

" 'It's also mine,' says Joyce, 'and I do not wish bone-gnawing there in public for the world to see.'

" 'Not even in my own window?'

" 'Most especially in *our* own window,' says Joyce. 'What you are doing is real down-homish—leaning from the window with a meat bone in your hand. You are my husband and I do not wish everybody passing by the street to see you. Eat at the table, and stop eating when you get up. Do not, *please*, carry bones to the window.'

" 'Aw, Joyce,' I says.

" 'Aw, Joyce nothing,' says she. 'You do not see me leaning from a window with a bone in my hand.'

" 'You're a lady,' I says.

" 'And I hope you are a gentleman,' says Joyce.

" 'People eat hot dogs in public in the Yankee Stadium,' I

says, 'and corn on the cob at Coney Island. So why can't I gnaw a bone in my own house?'

" 'Inside the house, yes,' says Joyce. 'But, Jesse B., listen to me! Please do not gnaw that bone in the window! *Please*.'

"Which, when I saw she were so serious I asked her, 'why?' " said Simple. "And you know what Joyce told me? 'Because Emily Post says "DON'T." '

" 'Baby,' I says, 'Emily Post were white. Also, I expect, rich. That woman had plenty of time to gnaw her bones at the table. Me, I work. When I get home, I want to look out in the street before dark and see what is going on. Since I'm married, I don't get out much. At least, honey, let me *look* out.'

" 'Look out all you want to,' says Joyce, 'but not with a bone in your hand. That is most inelegant.'

" 'Inelegant, hell!' I says, and I sat right there. 'Just you try to get this here bone away from me.'

" 'I want Negroes to learn etiquette,' said Joyce. 'Bone-gnawing is *not* etiquette—at least, not in public.'

"I did not answer. And, don't you know, Joyce burst out crying. Do you reckon Joyce is pregnant? They tells me womens act crazy that way sometimes when they is in the family way. Why should Joyce care if I suck a pork-chop bone in the front window or. not? We ain't got no back window. And I do not see why a man can't gnaw a bone and look out in the street at the same time. Nobody is looking up specially to see what I am doing. Nobody in the world cares if I gnaw a bone or not in my window—nobody but Joyce."

"Which should make you happy," I said, "that somebody cares when you commit a *faux pas*."

"What have I committed?" asked Simple.

"A *faux pas*," I said. "It really is not proper to sit in the window gnawing on a bone."

"Is it a crime?" asked Simple.

"It's not a crime," I said, "but it is a *faux pas*."

"It must be something *awful* for Joyce not to speak all day," said Simple. "Write that word down for me, so I can tell her I will not commit it again."

"*Faux pas* is a French phrase," I said.

"Then, now I know how to say 'gnawing a bone' in French,' said Simple.

"*Faux pas*—boner," I said.

"Bone," said Simple, "and there's one other thing which the Lord made and put on this earth almost as good as a pork-chop bone—that is the neck of a chicken. One reason I very seldom like to eat in restaurants is because you seldom get a chicken neck. If they do serve a neck, it is not proper to eat it, so Joyce says, because you have to suck on the bones. Now, why is it not proper to suck a chicken neck in a restaurant?"

"Because it makes so much noise in public, and therefore is bad manners."

"Manners is sometimes mighty inconvenient," stated Simple.

"You may not care about manners," I said, "but your wife does. Certainly Joyce is a woman to be proud of. She tries to uphold the tone of the Harlem community. One reason why white people don't want Negroes in their neighborhoods is because they say we lower the tone of the community. Eating bones in the window just isn't done in high society."

"Who's in high society?" asked Simple. "Not me, and I don't want to be. White folks might not gnaw bones in windows, but they sure do some awful other things. They murders their mothers almost daily. I never read of so many children knocking off their parents as here of late—but you seldom read of a colored child doing such. White folks also Jim Crows colored people, which I do not think is good manners. I had rather they gnaw a bone than segregate us. White folks blows off atom bombs and burns up people, too. It looks like to me it would be better to gnaw a bone than to singe them Marshall Islanders all up, like them pictures that they showed after that big bomb test they had out in the Pacific. Them folks will never have no more hair on their heads, and them atomized Japanese fishermens never will have no more children. I think white folks would do better to set in their front windows and gnaw bones myself, even if they were not so high-tone. Bone-gnawing, to my mind, is better than bomb-bursting. Atom bombs is lowrating the tone of the whole world. When I gnaw my bone or suck my chicken neck, I am not hurting a human soul."

"You're hurting your wife if you make her feel bad," I said. "So for Joyce's sake, if not your own, you could suck your chicken necks and gnaw your pork-chop bones in private. In fact, consideration for others begins at home—which might in a sense explain the behavior of American white folks. They've gotten so accustomed to mistreating Negroes at home in the past that it is hard for them to care about what colored folks in Asia think. And if you keep on gnawing bones in spite of what Joyce thinks, after a while you will not care what anybody else thinks either. From your own selfishness in regard to your wife's wishes, it is only a step to being inconsiderate of everyone everywhere. Consideration begins inside yourself first, right where you are, *at home*. Bones and bombs are not unrelated, pal. And certainly good manners are better than chicken necks or pork-chop bones."

"From whence did you get such wrong information about such good food?" asked Simple.

| A Dog Named Trilby

"Once when I were a child in Virginia, I knowed an old white lady who had a dog named Trilby," said Simple. "Trilby were black with white feet, white around the eyes, and she walked sort of sideways so you did not know if she were going or coming. Trilby and that old lady was both very old and very mean —but Trilby was the meanest. Both were mean, but that dog had her beat.

"Well, another old lady who was colored, named Jenkins, lived just down the block two or three houses away from the white woman. It being a small town, everybody lived in houses. Some houses had yards front and back, and nearly everybody had porches. In summer they kept their doors open and the screens closed. But any dog could easy open a screen door and walk in and out of any house. Now, Trilby never paid no attention to the inside of old lady Jenkins' house until after Mrs.

Jenkins' dog died. Before that time, Trilby would just play with
the Jenkins' dog in the yard, but never go in the house. Trilby
were not too mean to play with another dog, even if it belonged
to colored folks. But with people Trilby only snarled, growled,
also barked at every human, including me. Only at her madam,
Trilby did not snarl—nor at that other dog belonging to Mrs.
Jenkins. Seems like when Trilby was with that other dog she
lost her meanness. Trilby loved that dog.

"Now, the old white lady what owned Trilby naturally did
not associate with old Mrs. Jenkins, it being down South. Neither did she like her dog playing with a colored woman's dog.
But dogs will be dogs, so she could not stop that. When she saw
Trilby in Mrs. Jenkins' yard, though, she would always call her
home.

" 'Here, Trilby! Here, Trilby! Here, Trilby!'

"Then that old white lady would give Trilby something good
to eat to keep her home. Whereupon Trilby would grab her
fine bone, lay behind her screen door, and growl at everyone
who went by. Else that dog would run out and bark when she
got tired of gnawing on her bone. Trilby never did gnaw on me,
though, because I would have kicked that old mutt sky-high to
a firecracker if she had. I loved dogs, but I did not like Trilby.
Nobody liked Trilby except her owner and old lady Jenkins'
dog. Them two dogs got along fine, both being ageable and
shaggy and hair-balls—some kind of spitzes and poodles, part
cur, one black, one white—the white lady's dog being the black
one, and the colored dog being the white one.

"It were wintertime when the white dog died, and old Mrs.
Jenkins were left dogless. Then Trilby did not have nobody to
play with. Trilby's mean old lady-owner were glad that other
dog had died. She did not like Mrs. Jenkins nohow. And with
that other dog gone, she took for granted Trilby would stay
home, not be playing in old lady Jenkins' yard come summer,
nor romping on her porch with her dog. Now, she would not
have to bribe Trilby into staying home with her. But such were
not the case. Meanwhile, Trilby begun to lose her appetite that
winter. Come spring she were a thin old rail of a black dog,
with white circles around her eyes. Trilby looked like she were

made up for Halloween. And she become meaner than ever, snapping and snarling at the mailman, the milkman, and also at me delivering papers. So I took to passing on the other side of the street.

"But that mean old white lady loved her mean old dog. The butcher said she even bought Trilby fresh calf's liver every day to build up her vitamins—which were unheard of in our town where dogs just ate scraps and bones from the table. Not Trilby —she had liver. But, as nice as that old lady treated her, Trilby showed her anatomy. Come spring, as soon as the door were opened, Trilby went down to Mrs. Jenkins' house, spite of the fact that Trilby's friend-dog was dead and there was nobody for her to romp and play with there. But, don't you know, that dog just opened Mrs. Jenkins' screen and nudged herself into the house—which were the *first* time she had been inside—and laid down on the rug where that other dog used to lay.

"Her old mistress would call her from up the street, 'Trilby! Trilby! Hey, Trilby!' But Trilby would not come. Finally the woman had to go right to that other house and holler from the sidewalk, 'You-all send my dog home.'

"No answer, so she had to go up to the door and knock to get results. Trilby caused them two old womens—one white and one colored—to exchange words for the first time in years. But what they said were not Christian on neither side. Trilby's madam had to drag her by the scruff of the neck. Next day, it being warm and the doors being open, Trilby were right back again, nudging at Mrs. Jenkins' screen door with her bony old nose. She went in, and settled down on the rug.

"'Trilby! Trilby! Come here, Trilby!' called Miss White Lady.

"But Trilby did not budge. Trilby had adopted herself a new home in her old age—the run-down old house where her dog friend used to live which her mistress did not like. Every chance Trilby got, she were there. In fact, Trilby did not stay at home at all any more if she could help it. And every time that old white woman would come after her dog, them two old women would say words to each other folks never knowed they knew and which are not in the books. Finally, even I got sorry for that mean old white lady whose mean old dog did not want to come home.

" 'Trilby! Now, Trilby!' she begged.

"But she had to drag Trilby home each and every day. Then she would pet her, humor her, and dine her on fine fresh liver. She even bought Trilby a soft new rag rug to lay on. But as soon as the door were open, off went Trilby back to that other house.

" 'Trilby! Trilby! Please, Trilby!'

"She reached out her hand to pet her, but Trilby commenced to snarl at her mistress what had bought her that expensive liver. She growled, bared her teeth, and growled again each time that old lady come near. Then one day she snapped at her, and a little speck of blood come on that white lady's finger.

" 'Why, Trilby, you snapped at me! *Me*, what loves you! And you done bit the hand that fed you!'

"Well, that old woman did not live very long after that. She taken so low sick she could not come to drag Trilby home no more. And the day she died all by herself, Trilby were laying on that *other* rug in that *other* house inside that *other* door."

| Enter Cousin Minnie

"GUESS who has come to town now?" said Simple, pushing an empty beer glass back from the bar and frowning deeply.

"Who," I said, "has come?"

"Some new cousin name of Minnie," said Simple.

"Minnie? How does she look?" I inquired.

"Like the junior wrath of God," groaned Simple. "Yet, ugly as she is, last week she walks up to my door, all unknown to me, and rings my bell, and states, 'I am your Cousin Minnie.'

"I says, 'Whose Cousin Minnie?'

" 'Yours,' says she, out of the clear blue sky. 'Ain't you Jesse B. Semple?'

" 'I am,' says I. 'But *who* are you?'

"Your mother's brother's youngest child,' says she.

" 'How come I never heard of you before?' says I.

" 'Because I am an offshoot from the family,' says she.

" 'What shot you back at me?' I asked before I thought, because I really did not mean to insult the girl.

" 'Aunt Mamie down in Piedmont, Virginia, give me your number,' says she, 'because Mamie knowed I did not know nobody in New York, and she did not want me to be way up here in Harlem all alone. So I look up you—my one cousin in the world who knows what the North is all about. Jesse, I done come North.'

" 'Why did you wait so long?' says I. 'It is very late now to do any good for yourself. You almost as old as Aunt Mamie.'

"I do not know why I wanted to hurt that girl right off the bat, but she was so ugly she made me mad. Also, I think she were somewhat drunk. She looked like to me she might be most of the time drunk. Did you ever have any relatives what was drunk—or if they was not drunk, they looked drunk?"

"No," I said. "Not relatives. But I have known a few alcoholics. They can be difficult at times."

"That is just what Cousin Minnie is," said Simple, "difficult. Since I have come to know her, I finds that she is a good-hearted girl. But her heart is in a very weak body. Minnie is weak for licker. Just why Aunt Mamie would give her my address in Harlem, big as Harlem is, I do not know, and me married to a woman like Joyce who hates the smell of whiskey, wine, or beer on *my* breath, let alone on a relative's who is distant to me. I says, 'Minnie, don't come around to my house drunk, please, neither come here high. I do not wish to be low-rated in my wife's sight. Joyce thinks my people is somebody.'

" 'I might have been somebody myself,' says Minnie, 'if your uncle had married my mama. But I'm a side child.'

" 'Don't say it,' I said. 'There's none such in our family! But you do look exactly like my Uncle Willie, who were nobody's picture for framing. Minnie, I can see the Semples' spitting image in your features. You sure resembles the family line. But where have you been all these years that I did not know you before?'

" 'They kept me hid. I was a secret child.'

" 'I wish you was a secret now, because I do not know what to do about a woman like you related to me. Why did you come to New York?'

" 'Because I have done got plumb tired of the South,' said Minnie. '*Ebony, Jet,* and the *Chicago Defender* all talks about how beautiful is the North, so I come up here to see. I am plumb tired of Jim Crow.'

" 'Give me your hand,' I said. I shook it. I were proud of her ambition.

" 'Have you got a little drink of any kind around?' says Minnie.

" 'If I had, I would have drunk it,' says I. 'All we keep in our icebox is milk and Kool-Aid.'

" 'Cousin Jess, can you lend me a dollar?' says Minnie.

" 'I do not keep money in the home, neither,' says I.

" 'Aunt Mamie said if I come to New York, you would help me,' said Minnie. 'If I ever needed help, I need it now, Cousin Jess.'

" 'In the middle of the week,' says I, 'even if it were payday, I could not be too generous.'

" 'Then have you got a place I can sleep here in your apartment with you-all?'

" 'God forbid!' said I. 'Don't you know folks in Harlem ain't got no place for relatives to sleep? This is a kitchenette.'

" 'Down South they say Harlem is heaven,' says Minnie. 'Yet you has nowhere for me to rest my head?'

" 'You know that old song,' said I, ' "Rest Beyond the River"? In Harlem, we *all* got one more river to cross before we can rest. Set down and I will tell you about Harlem, Minnie, so you will be clear in mind. In fact, I will tell you about the North. Down South you're swimming in a river that's running to the sea where you might drown but, at least, you're swimming with the current. Up North we are swimming the other way, against the current, trying to reach dry land. I been here twenty years, Minnie, and I'm still in the water, if you get what I mean.'

" 'Ain't you got just a drop of something that ain't water in the house,' asks Minnie, 'to help me swim better?'

" 'Come on, girl, put on your coat,' I said, 'and I will take you out to a bar before my wife comes. I reckon we both need a drink to help us swim better. Let's go see if we can make it somehow or another to dry land right now. Come on, Minnie.'

"And we went. Whilst setting at the bar, I discovered that Minnie is really very partial to what comes in a bottle with a government seal on it."

"I can see where you're going to have a problem with your cousin," I said. "She seems to be an alcoholic."

"Which is a habit Minnie really cannot afford," said Simple, "especially since she always wants to borrow money. Now, you know and I know, money is usually the *last* thing I possess— and in that regard, I falls for no hypes. Setting there on that bar stool, 'Minnie,' I says, 'I give you my love, I give you my cousinship, I give you my welcome to Harlem, U.S.A, but I cannot give you money. You are up here in the free North now where you got to scuffle the best way you can.'

"But Minnie says, 'Jesse, I am a lady, and there are some things I do not do such as hustle.'

"I said, 'I did not mean that you should do wrong, neither did I use the word *hustle*. I said scuffle, which means, work, work, work.'

" 'That is one thing, Jess, I will do, work. But lend me a little something until I gets a job.'

" 'That's what the Relief and Welfare is for,' I says. 'Many a human has been here in Harlem ten years and has not got a job yet, not since they found the Relief Bureau. If you be's lucky enough to get a nice Relief Investigator, you can live awhile.'

" 'I want no handouts, city or otherwise,' says Minnie. 'Also, I really want no advice just now. What I need tonight is five dollars.'

" 'Cousin,' I said, 'if you asked me for the moon, I could reach up in the sky and snatch it down quicker than I could find five dollars. We is poor folks in Harlem.'

" 'Poor it do seem,' said Minnie. 'Why I used to could borrow five dollars most anytime down home in Virginia. You-all Negroes up North is real broke.'

"'Say that again!' says I. 'And of all those that are brokest, I am among the most.'

"'How do you keep your home together?' asked Minnie.

"'By the budget,' says I, 'and Joyce controls that. I do not know a thing about a budget. In fact, I never saw a budget. My wife has got one—but she always loses it before the week is out. Else she keeps it in a Mason jar. Anyhow, I cannot go in the budget and get nothing out for you, not this late in the week, no way.'

"'So I must suffer?' says Minnie.

"'I fears 'tis so,' said I.

"'By coming up North all alone,' moans Minnie, 'I have made my bed hard and therefore I got to sleep in it?'

"'I hope you will not be rest-broken,' says I.

"'When *just* five dollars would take the rocks out from under my pillow?' pleads Minnie.

"'Girl, don't make it hard for me, too! Have mercy on your cousin. Or do you take me to be simple? Do you think you can beg me out of what I ain't got even if I had it?'

"'I'll say no more,' says Minnie, 'except that I wanted freedom, which is why I come up North. You know, I do not like Jim Crow. I likes to drink in joints where people is integrated, like this one. Jesse, help me to stay up North in freedom.'

"Well, pal, that weakened me—that word *freedom!* Don't you know I let that old girl beg me out of five dollars—which I went home and borrowed from Joyce's budget, which never balances nohow, so I don't reckon freedom can throw it off much more than it always is. Minnie is a refugee from the South. America has always been good to refugees. Since Minnie has come to America, New York, Harlem, U.S.A., I just had to lend that girl five dollars. If I never get it back, I have made my contribution to freedom—freedom to be integrated anywhere, at any time, drunk or sober—which really ain't no hype."

| Radioactive Red Caps

"How wonderful," I said, "that Negroes today are being rapidly integrated into every phase of American life from the Army and Navy to schools to industries—advancing, advancing!"

"I have not advanced one step," said Simple. "Still the same old job, same old salary, same old kitchenette, same old Harlem and the same old color."

"You are just one individual," I said. "I am speaking of our race in general. Look how many colleges have opened up to Negroes in the last ten years. Look at the change in restrictive covenants. You can live anywhere."

"You mean *try* to live anywhere."

"Look at the way you can ride unsegregated in interstate travel."

"And get throwed off the bus."

"Look at the ever greater number of Negroes in high places."

"Name me one making an atom bomb."

"That would be top-secret information," I said, "even if I knew. Anyway, you are arguing from supposition, not knowledge. How do you know what our top Negro scientists are doing?"

"I don't," said Simple. "But I bet if one was making an atom bomb, they would have his picture on the cover of *Jet* every other week like Eartha Kitt, just to make Negroes think the atom bomb is an integrated bomb. Then, next thing you know, some old Southern senator would up and move to have that Negro investigated for being subversive, because he would be mad that a Negro ever got anywhere near an atom bomb. Then that Negro would be removed from his job like Miss Annie Lee Moss, and have to hire a lawyer to get halfway back. Then they would put that whitewashed Negro to making plain little old-time ordinary bombs that can only kill a few folks at a time. You know and I know, they don't want no Negroes nowhere near no bomb that can kill a whole state full of folks like an atom bomb can. Just think what would happen to Mississippi. Wow!"

"Your thinking borders on the subversive," I warned. "Do you want to fight the Civil War over again?"

"Not without an atom bomb," said Simple. "If I was in Mississippi, I would be Jim Crowed out of bomb shelters, so I would need some kind of protection. By the time I got the N.A.A.C.P. to take my case to the Supreme Court, the war would be over, else I would be atomized."

"Absurd!" I said. "Bomb shelters will be for everybody."

"Not in Mississippi," said Simple. "Down there they will have some kind of voting test, else loyalty test, in which they will find some way of flunking Negroes out. You can't tell me them Dixiecrats are going to give Negroes free rein of bomb shelters. On the other hand, come to think of it, they might *have* to let us in to save their own skins, because I hear tell in the next war everything that ain't sheltered will be so charged with atoms a human can't touch it. Even the garbage is going to get radioactive when the bombs start falling. I read last week in the *News* that, in case of a bombing, it will be a problem as to where to put our garbage, because it will be radioactive up to a million years. So you sure can't keep garbage around. If you dump it in the sea, it will make the fish radioactive, too, like them Japanese tunas nobody could eat. I am wondering what the alley cats will eat—because if all the garbage is full of atomic rays, and the cats eat the garbage, and my wife pets a strange cat, Joyce will be radioactive, too. Then if I pet my wife, what will happen to me?"

"You are stretching the long arm of coincidence mighty far," I said. "What is more likely to happen is, if the bombs fall, you will be radioactive long before the garbage will."

"That will worry white folks," said Simple. "Just suppose all the Negroes down South got atomized, charged up like hot garbage, who would serve the white folks' tables, nurse their children, Red Cap their bags, and make up their Pullman berths? Just think! Suppose all the colored Red Caps carrying bags on the Southern Railroad was atom-charged! Suitcases would get atomized, too, and all that is packed in them. Every time a white man took out his toothbrush to wash his teeth on the train, his teeth would get atom-charged. How could he kiss his wife when he got home?"

"I believe you are charged now," I said.

"No," said Simple, "I am only thinking how awful this atom bomb can be! If one fell up North in Harlem and charged me, then I went downtown and punched that time clock where I work, the clock would be charged. Then a white fellow would come along behind me and punch the time clock, and he would be charged. Then both of us would be so full of atoms for the next million years, that at any time we would be liable to explode like firecrackers on the Fourth of July. And from us, everybody else in the plant would get charged. Atoms, they tell me, is catching. What I read in the *News* said that if you even look at an atom bomb going off, the rays are so strong your eyes will water the rest of your life, your blood will turn white, your hair turn gray, and your children will be born backwards. Your breakfast eggs will no longer be sunny-side up, but scrambled, giving off sparks—and people will give off sparks, too. If you walk down the street, every doorbell you pass will ring without your touching it. If you pick up a phone, whoever answers it will be atomized. So if you know somebody you don't like, for example, just phone them—and you can really fix them up! That's what they call a chain reaction. I am getting my chain ready now—the first person I am going to telephone is my former landlady! When she picks up the phone, I hope to atomize her like a Japanese tuna! She will drive a Geiger counter crazy after I say, 'Hello!' "

"My dear boy," I said, "what makes you think you, of all people, would be able to go around transferring atomic radiation to others? You would probably be annihilated yourself by the very first bomb blast."

"Me? Oh, no," said Simple. "Negroes are very hard to annihilate. I am a Negro—so I figure I would live to radiate and, believe me, once charged, I will take charge."

"In other words, come what may, you expect to survive the atom bomb?"

"If Negroes can survive white folks in Mississippi," said Simple, "we can survive anything."

| Two Sides Not Enough

"A MAN ought to have more than just two sides to sleep on," declared Simple. "Now if I get tired of sleeping on my left side, I have nothing to turn over on but my right side."

"You could sleep on your back," I advised.

"I snores on my back."

"Then why not try your stomach?"

"Sleeping on my stomach, I get a stiff neck—I always have to keep my head turned toward one side or the other, else I smothers. I do not like to sleep on my stomach."

"The right side, or the left side, are certainly enough sides for most people to sleep on. I don't know what your trouble is. But, after all, there are two sides to every question."

"That's just what I am talking about," said Simple. "Two sides are not enough. I'm tired of sleeping on either my left side, or on my right side, so I wish I had two or three more sides to change off on. Also, if I sleep on my left side, I am facing my wife, then I have to turn over to see the clock in the morning to find out what time it is. If I sleep on my right side, I am facing the window so the light wakes me up before it is time to get up. If I sleep on my back, I snores, and disturbs my wife. And my stomach is out for sleeping, due to reasons which I mentioned. In the merchant marine, sailors are always talking about the port side and the starboard side of a ship. A human should have not only a left side and a right side, but also a port side and a starboard side."

"That's what left and right mean in nautical terms," I said. "You know as well as I do that a ship has only two sides."

"Then ships are bad off as a human," said Simple. "All a boat can do when a storm comes up, is like I do when I sleep—toss from side to side."

"Maybe you eat too heavy a dinner," I said, "or drink too much coffee."

"No, I am not troubled in no digestion at night," said Simple. "But there is one thing that I do not like in the morning—waking up to face the same old one-eyed egg Joyce has fried for breakfast. What I wish is that there was different kinds of eggs, not just white eggs with a yellow eye. There ought to be blue eggs with a brown eye, and brown eggs with a blue eye, also red eggs with green eyes."

"If you ever woke up and saw a red egg with a green eye on your plate, you would think you had a hang-over."

"I would," said Simple. "But eggs *is* monotonous! No matter which side you turn an egg on, daddy-o, it is still an egg—hard on one side and soft on the other. Or, if you turn it over, it's hard on both sides. Once an egg gets in the frying pan, it has only two sides, too. And if you burn the bottom side, it comes out just like the race problem, black and white, black and white."

"I thought you'd get around to race before you got through. You can't discuss any subject at all without bringing in color. God help you! And in reducing everything to two sides, as usual, you oversimplify."

"What does I do?"

"I say your semantics make things too simple."

"My which?"

"Your verbiage."

"My what?"

"Your words, man, your words."

"Oh," said Simple. "Well, anyhow, to get back to eggs— which is a simple word. For breakfast I wish some other birds besides chickens laid eggs for eating, with a different kind of flavor than just a hen flavor. Whatever you are talking about with your *see-antics*, Jack, at my age a man gets tired of the same kind of eggs each and every day—just like you get tired of the race problem. I would like to have an egg some morning that tastes like a pork chop."

"In that case, why don't you have pork chops for breakfast instead of eggs?"

"Because there is never no pork chops in my icebox in the morning."

"There would be if you would put them there the night before."

"No," said Simple, "I would eat them up the night before—which is always the trouble with the morning after—you have practically nothing left from the night before—except the race problem."

| Puerto Ricans

I WAS rushing past the newsstand at 125th and Lenox on the way to work this morning when I bought a comic book to read in the subway. When I got on the train and opened it, that book were in some kind of foreign language. I said to the guy beside me, "What's this?"

He said, *"Español!"*

I said, "What?"

He said, "Spanish—for Puerto Ricans."

I said, "Puerto Ricans? Are you one?"

He said, *"Si,* are you one, too?"

I said, "I am not! I am just plain old American."

He said, "You—*Negro* American."

I said, "You look just like me, don't you? Who's the darkest, me or you?"

He said, "You, darkest."

I said, "I admit I have an edge on almost anybody. But you are colored, too, daddy-o, don't forget, Puerto Rican or not."

He said, "In my country, no."

"In *my* country, yes," I said. "Here in the U.S.A. you, me—all *colored* folks—are colored."

He said, *"No entiendo.* Don't understand."

I said, "I don't blame you. I wouldn't understand color either if I could talk Spanish. Here, take this comic book in your language which, me—*no entiendo*."

So I gave him my comic book and went on to work. On the way I kept thinking about what a difference a foreign language makes. Just speak something else and you don't have to be colored in this here U.S.A.—at least, not as colored as me, born and raised here, and 102 per cent American. The Puerto Ricans come up here from the islands and start living all over New York, Chicago, anywhere, where an ordinary American-speaking Negro can't get a foothold, much less a room or an apartment—and the last place a Puerto Rican wants to live is Harlem, because that is colored. So they live uptown, downtown, all around town, the Bronx, Brooklyn, anywhere but with me, unless they can't help it. And do I blame them? I do not! Nobody loves Jim Crow but an idiot, and I am Jim Crowed.

Español! Now that is a language which, if you speak it, will take *some* of the black off of you if you are colored. Just say, *Sí*, and folks will think you are a foreigner, instead of only a plain old ordinary colored American Negro. Don't you remember a few years ago reading about that Negro who put on a turban and went all over the South speaking pig Latin and staying at the best hotels? They thought he was an A-rab, and he wasn't nothing but a Negro. Why does a language, be it pig Latin or Spanish, make all that much difference?

I have been in this country speaking English all my life, daddy-o, yet and still if I walk in some of them rich restaurants downtown, they look at me like I was a varmint. But let somebody darker than me come in there speaking Spanish or French or Afangulo and the headwaiter will bow plumb down to the ground. I wonder why my mama did not bear me in Cuba instead of in Virginia? Had she did so, I would walk right up to the White Sulphur Springs Hotel now and engage me a room, dark though I be, and there would not be a white man in Dixie say a word. But just let *me* enter and say in English, "I would like a reservation."

The desk clerk would say to me, "Negro, are you crazy?"

I would say, "No, I am not crazy. I am just American."

He would say, "American though you be, you will never sleep in here. This hotel is for white folks."

Then I would say, "You ought to be ashamed of yourself, drawing the color line in Virginia where Thomas Jefferson was born, in this day and age of such great democracy."

Whereupon he would call the manager who would say, "You better get out of here before I have you arrested for disturbing the peace."

I would say, "What kind of peace are you talking about? That is the trouble with you white folks, always wanting peace, and I ain't got no privileges. You are always keeping the best of everything for yourself. All the peace is on your side."

Then the old head desk clerk would say, "Get out of here before I call the law." And the manager would reach for the phone.

Whereupon I would pull my Spanish on him. I would say, "*No entiendo.*"

Then they would both get all red in the face and say, "Oh, I beg your pardon! Are you Spanish?"

But by that time I would be mad, so I would say, "I will not accept a room here." And walk stalking out. I would say, "Where I cannot spend my money if I speak American, I will *not* if I speak Spanish. You white folks act right simple. Good-by!" I would leave them with their mouths wide open. *"Adios!"*

Then, if I was an artist, I would put all that into a comic book. I wonder why somebody don't make comic books out of the funny way white folks in America behave—talking democracy out of one side of their mouth and, "Negro, stay in your place," out of the other. I wish I could draw, I would make me such a book. I would start a whole series of comics which I bet would sell a million copies—*Jess Simple's Jim Crow Jive,* would be the title. I would make my books in both English and Spanish so the Puerto Ricans could laugh, too. Because it must tickle them to see what a little foreignness will do. Just be foreign—then you don't have to be colored.

| Minnie Again

"You know I wish my Cousin Minnie would leave New York and go on back down home to Virginia where she come from," allowed Simple. "Even if she did come North looking for freedom, Harlem is too much for her."

"Why? What's happened now?" I asked.

"Last week Minnie got behind in her rent and was about to be evicted from the house where she rooms at," said Simple. "So she come calling *me* up from a pay phone to ask me am I going to let her get put out in the street."

"What did you say?"

"I told Minnie I has nothing to do with the matter, being as ·I'm neither her landlord, her husband, her father, nor her brother. I am just an off-cousin—not even by marriage."

"Minnie said, 'Jess, I did not waste my time and my dime to call you up to listen to no such talk as that concerning our cousinship, which is by blood, if not by law. I needs me some money.'

"Now, I hate to get too plain-spoken with anybody, least of all a woman. But I had to tell Minnie what I thought she was. After which I told her what I thought she wasn't—which is that she ain't right bright. Minnie ought to could look at me by now and tell I never have no money. I also told Minnie that she is not stable, as the Relief folks says, because to my knowledge Minnie has had four jobs in three weeks and kept none of them.

" 'Furthermore, Minnie,' I says, 'you are not sober. I can tell right now the way you talk on this phone you are not sober. Tomorrow, you will have a hang-over, and cannot go to work again, even if you have a job. Don't bother me about money,' I said and I started to hang up. But before I got the hook from my ear, Minnie called me a name which no man can take on the phone. In fact, Minnie were so indignant she called me *out of my name.* So I was forced to reply. Just then Central said

'Five cents more, please,' which Minnie did not have. So our conversation were cut off on an unpleasant note with the last word being Minnie's. Boy, did you ever have a begging relative?"

"Who hasn't had such kinfolks?" I asked.

"Just when Joyce and me get a phone in our room, after being married almost two years without a phone of our own, who should come to New York and start phoning us but Cousin Minnie! I got a good mind to take my phone out of its socket."

"Then Minnie would probably come to your house and worry you in person," I said.

"Not if my wife put the evil eye on her," said Simple. "Joyce is a good girl, but she can look so-ooo-oo-o mean at times that even me, her lawful wedded husband, am scared to look back at her. Joyce can keep Minnie out of our house. Only reason she has not done so up to now is because Joyce tries to treat the woman right since Minnie is my kinfolks. But Minnie is driving kinship in the ground. Minnie loves money more than she does me, else she would not bug me with that word so much. From the first time I laid eyes on Cousin Minnie she needed money. First, money to stay in town after she got here, then money to buy something to eat (which is what she calls drink), then money to pay for a job at the employment office, then money to get out to her new job in the subway, then money to get another job after she quit the first job because the lady who hired her did not like frozen food, and Minnie said she did not intend to shell no fresh peas when peas come already shelled frozen. Now Minnie wants money to keep from getting put out in the street because she is three weeks behind on her rent. Minnie thinks I am a Relief Station, else God—and I ain't nothing but a man, a working man, and a colored man at that. Do you believe Minnie's in her right mind?"

"I think she is simply uninformed as to our habitual state of impecunity in Harlem," I said. "Many newly arrived immigrants from the South think all New Yorkers are rich. They don't realize that most of us live from day to day, from hand to mouth."

"I have tried to break that sad news to Minnie," said Simple, "but it does not seem to penetrate. I have put my hand in my pocket and turned it inside out to show her that my pockets are empty. I have told Minnie that my wife and me runs on a budget and that the budget runs out before the week does. But I want to tell you one thing, cousin or not, the next time Minnie asks me for money, I am going to sic Joyce on her, and I bet you Minnie will understand then!"

"Why would you bring Joyce into your family affairs?" I asked.

"Joyce is my loving wife," said Simple, "and from her I hides only a few secrets. You know it is nice to have a nice wife. And, so far, Joyce treats all my relatives polite. When Joyce first met Cousin Minnie, newly come to our town from Virginia, to tell the truth I thought my wife might snob Minnie. But Joyce did not snob her. My wife is as nice to Cousin Minnie as if Minnie was cultured—which Minnie is not. In fact, as you know, Minnie drinks. But Minnie had sense enough to come to my house last night almost sober. But she come, as usual, with a purpose. The first thing Minnie said last night was 'Jess, I been caught in the toils of the law.'

"I said, 'Minnie, don't toil me up in no law, because I will have nothing to do with what you been doing. What have you done?'

" 'Well,' said Cousin Minnie, 'I were caught in an after-hours spot when it got raided Saturday, and they took everybody down, including me.'

" 'What was a lady like you doing out so late in a speak-easy?' I inquired.

" 'Ain't you never been out late yourself?' said Minnie.

" 'I admit I were.'

" 'And in an after-hours spot?' asked Minnie.

" 'I have been in such,' I said, 'but I did not allow myself to get caught. Nobody has caught me in a speak-easy, except folks like me that was in there themselves, and they were not polices.'

" 'You been lucky,' says Minnie. 'I been caught two or three times in raids—twice in Virginia where they catch so many Negroes they let us all off easy. But up here in the North, I

been remaindered for a hearing. And it is not prejudice, because
that joint was integrated. There was white folks in the place,
too, drinking, and they got remaindered also. Remaindered
means I might have to pay a fine, and I has no money, which is
why I turn to you, Jess, my only cousin in New York City.'

" 'I wish you was no relation to me,' I says, 'because I has no
money, neither, and I hate to turn a relative down.'

" 'If you are just temporarily out of cash,' says Minnie, 'can't
you borrow some?'

" 'My credit is not good,' I said. 'And were I borrowing for
myself, it would be hard. For you, that is another story. Minnie,
I don't hardly know you, even if you do be Uncle Willie's child.
We was not raised up together at no time!'

"As easy as I can, I says, 'I has no money, never have had no
money and if you looking to borrow what money I get, *I never
will have none.* Do you not remember our Aunt Lucy who used
to say, "Neither a borrower nor a lender be?" That was her
motto. It is also mine.'

" 'That,' says Minnie, 'is a very old corny motto. You ain't
hep to the jive. The new motto now is, "Beg, borrow, and ball
till you get it all—a bird in the hand ain't nothing but a man." '

" 'I ain't coming on that,' I said. 'You sound like a woman I
used to know named Zarita in my far-distant past. But, Minnie,
I'm a married man now. I need my money for my home.'

" 'For lack of five simoleons you would let me maybe go to
jail, your own blood-cousin, here all alone by herself in Harlem
where I don't know nobody. The reason I were in that joint
that got raided was, I was trying to get acquainted. I met a right
nice colored man in there who bought me a drink and seemed
really interested in me until we all got hauled down to the Precinct. Then I asked that man if he would help me to get out.
He said, "Baby, I got to get myself out, I can't be bothered with
you." Peoples is hardhearted in New York City. You are hardhearted, too, Jesse B. Semple.'

" 'Hard as that rock in the St. Louis Blues that were cast into
the sea! Minnie, I regrets this is what big-town life does to peoples. Girl, you had ought to stayed down yonder where you was
in Virginia.'

"'I'll say no more,' said Minnie. 'Have you got some beer in the icebox?'

"'Not with me around the house,' I says. About that time, Joyce come back out of the kitchenette where she was peeling potatoes and says, 'Miss Minnie, could I offer you a nice fresh glass of Kool-Aid?'

"So you know what Minnie says? She says, 'Thank you, I never drinks a drop of no kind of ade, neither nothing else clear colored, such as water. I thank you just the same, Cousin-in-law, married as you is to my favorite cousin, Jesse B., I thank you just the same. And good night.'

"The very word Kool-Aid run Minnie out of the house. When she left Joyce laughed and said, 'I knowed that would get rid of her—Kool-Aid! I would never let Minnie drink up that nice cold can of beer I just bought for you on my ways home from work out of our budget.'

"'Joyce, I don't know which I love the most,' I said, 'you or your budget!'"

| Vicious Circle

"HOUSING, so I hear, is a vicious circle," declared Simple. "If the first colored family did not move into a white neighborhood, the second one couldn't. But as soon as one Negro moves in, here comes another one. After a while, so they tell me, we're right back where we started from—in a slum."

"What do you mean, slum? All colored neighborhoods are not slums."

"I thought that's what slums meant—colored," said Simple.

"You did not."

"Yes, I did, too. Folks are always yowling about colored slums."

"Whatever got you on this subject, anyhow?"

"Mrs. Sadie Maxwell-Reeves, Joyce's club lady friend," said Simple. "She has done moved into a high-class white neighborhood. But no sooner than she got there hardly, than another colored family moved in—which made her mad. Now, six more houses in the block have been sold to colored. Mrs. Maxwell-Reeves is beginning to think that she had just as well have stayed in Harlem and not tried to get outside the circle. Which I reckon she had, because she says it won't be no time now before the candy store on the corner is turned into a bar, and the jukebox will be playing 'Jelly! Jelly! Jelly!' "

"Surely Mrs. Reeves does not object to living next door to Negroes does she, being colored herself?"

"She shouldn't, but I am afraid she do. She's been telling Joyce for a year that she was moving out into a nice white neighborhood in the suburbans. She has moved. But by this time next year, she'll find herself in a nice *colored* neighborhood. Only Mrs. Maxwell-Reeves is afraid it won't be so nice by then—when all her own peoples gets out there. She says we is caught in a vicious circle. I asked Joyce who's to blame. Who started that neighborhood to turning colored? Answer: Mrs. Maxwell-Reeves herself! If she hadn't broke the ice and overpaid the price to move in, that block would still have been white. But when them white folks looked out the window and saw Sadie Maxwell-Reeves they started packing to leave. Real-estate prices went way up the next day. The agents saw Negroes coming, so they charged double to even inspect a house. Still Negroes buy, no matter how high. Now, Mrs. Maxwell-Reeves is no longer by herself."

"What do you mean, by herself?" I asked. "Negroes in white neighborhoods are not by themselves."

"They are colored, though, ain't they?" said Simple.

"Isolationist," I said. "Self-segregationist! What do you want Negroes to do, never expand, never spread out?"

"Spread out all they like," said Simple. "But don't get mad if some other Negro spreads out with you. If Mrs. Maxwell-Reeves wants the whole white neighborhood to herself, with no other colored in it, then she ought to buy the *whole* neighborhood, the whole suburbans, not just one house. Mrs. Reeves got mad because when she moved in the block, here come some more colored folks moving in. Now one house has already got a

ROOMS FOR RENT sign up, so she told Joyce. 'Roomers run down property,' says Mrs. Reeves. Which they do. Me, myself, to tell the truth, if I had a house, I would not want a roomer in it."

"You were a roomer yourself for years," I said, "before you got married."

"I know it," said Simple, "but now only until Joyce and me can find ourselves an apartment. I want to get as far away from roomers as I can—just once in life. Roomers dips into a man's business. They eye your wife—the mens do. Sometimes even a female tempts *me* myself, if she's pretty. Joyce has done warned me about that chick on the third floor where we room now."

"Then you can sympathize with Mrs. Maxwell-Reeves' position," I said. "Rooming houses do lower the tone of a residential section, overpopulate an area, and cause it to cease to be exclusive. But often, Negroes who buy in exclusive neighborhoods have to have roomers to help them pay off the mortgage and keep up the high taxes. Not everyone is as well off as Mrs. Reeves."

"Mrs. Maxwell-Reeves is so well off she never did have no roomers even in Harlem, Joyce says. Just a whole house to herself! Some Negroes *is* rich."

"That is why she wishes to be exclusive," I said.

"Then she will have to move again," said Simple. "She paid the price to break the ice to get colored folks into that neighborhood first—now it is no longer exclusive—and when it gets crowded, it won't be suburban. So I guess she will just have to move again."

"Yet, if she does, the same thing may happen."

"That is what Mrs. Maxwell-Reeves calls a vicious circle," said Simple, "when Negroes move in. Listen, daddy-o, are Negroes vicious?"

"Do *you* think Negroes are vicious?"

"No," said Simple, "it must be the circle."

| Again Cousin Minnie

"You see that little old joker down at the end of the bar?" asked Simple, pointing with his beer. "Well, that Negro's been in jail so much he ought to belong to the Bail-Bond-of-the-Month Club."

"What's his claim to fame?" I requested.

"He's a numbers writer," said Simple. "But he's also got political influence. The cops take him down, but next thing you know, he's back walking the streets again. And fight! That little cat can fight, man, anybody! Hard as nails! I do believe he would fight his own papa."

"It's too bad he can't turn his energies to better purpose," I said, "such as the field of race relations where militancy is needed."

"He would be a Mau Mau," said Simple. "Was he in Montgomery, he would turn Rev. King's love feast upside down— and the buses, too. 'Love thy neighbor as thy self,' would not mean a thing to him. He do not love colored folks, let alone white. All that man loves is to fight. But the womens like him. See them girls all around him now down there at the end of the bar? When my Cousin Minnie was in this bar last, she asked me who he was and could I introduce her to him. I told her, not me! She would have to meet that man at her own risk, I said, and if she got hurt in the process, don't come running to me for help because I would not want to be mixed up in the rumble. But I told her last week:

"There is many a slop
'Twixt the lip and the chop.

"You are liable to get gravy on your chin before you get the pork chop in."

"What in the world do you mean by that?" I asked.

"Cousin Minnie," said Simple, "is still slipping and slopping

around in them Lenox Avenue bars looking for a chump with a pot of gold. I told Minnie when she first come here that the rainbow with the pot of gold at its end arches right on over New York City. It must terminate somewhere out in the Atlantic Ocean, because it sure do not end in Harlem.

"Minnie said, 'Oh, as many rich old Negroes as there are around here, particularly West Indians, I am bound to find me a man with beaucoup loot and a Cadillac to boot. I never was a woman to play myself cheap.'

"Minnie has now been in Harlem a right smart while, and she is still trying to borrow five or ten dollars from me ever so often. But not if my wife knows it. Relatives or no relatives, Joyce does her best to balance me and the budget, and if I lent Minnie money every time she asks for it, nobody's budget would work out right."

"I gather your Cousin Minnie did not find her pot of gold as yet in New York," I said.

"No," said Simple, "but she thought she had found a rainbow. Minnie come telling me last month about some well-to-do old Negro she had met who had eyes for her like crazy, even spending seven or eight dollars to take her to Frank's for dinner, to the Palm Café for drinks, and to Small's to hear music. Then if she still was not ready to go home, down to that after-hours spot where they used to have the golden key and where drinks is a dollar a throw, even plain sodas with a cube of ice, and where the chicks are fine. I told Minnie she better keep that old geezer out of that speak-easy, else he might latch onto one of them pretty models and put her down.

"Minnie said, 'All that glitters ain't got what I got. I knows how to handle this old goat, myself. I am going to propose to him that we get married.' And don't you know, Minnie did. She proposed to the man herself."

"What did the man say?" I asked.

"That is where the slip came," said Simple. "But there was no use in Minnie's crying—because she proposed to the man. He did not propose to her, so there was no breach of promise nor promises breached. Just a clop betwixt the lip and the chop, that's all! That old man told Minnie, said, 'Daughter, I been married four times, and I think it will be a long time before I try it again.'

"Minnie said, 'But what about all your houses you owns over in Brooklyn and Corona, and them six lots full of potatoes out in Long Island? Where will they be? Who's gonna benefit from all that when you gone?'

"That old Negro told Minnie, 'Don't worry about when I'm gone because, barring poison, I will be here awhile. And it takes all them potatoes on all them lots to feed my children I got, without taking on another wife. Wife Number 1 was O.K., and Wife Number 2 did do. Wife Number 3 quit me, and Wife Number 4 ain't no more. And all of them cost me money's mammy. But with what dough I got left, I intends to look out for myself. No jive, as long as I am alive, there will be no Number 5.'

"Whereupon Minnie hollered, 'Why, you old rat, you! You got one foot in the grave and the other one on the brink. I don't want you, nohow. I will put you down, and now—soon as you pay for this steak.' They was setting in Frank's when the blowup came and everybody in society heard what Minnie said. You read about it in *Jet* last week, didn't you? Only *Jet* did not mention no names. It just said an elderly Harlem real-estate man were embarrassed by a loud-mouthed, mad, brownskin woman. That were my Cousin Minnie. *Jet* did not repeat what Minnie said. She said, 'You are just a rat, that's all, an old rat!'

"But that man were not fazed. He just told Minnie real quiet-like, whilst he chewed on his diet, 'You are kinder old yourself—and an old ship can always leave a sinking rat.' "

| Name in Print

"Just look at the front pages of the newspapers," said Simple, spreading his nightly copy of the *Daily News* out on the bar. "There is never hardly any colored names anywhere. Most headlines is all about white folks."

"That is not true today," I said. "Many headlines are about Negroes, Chinese, Indians, and other colored folks like ourselves."

"Most on the inside pages," said Simple, blowing foam from his beer. "But I am talking about front-page news. The only time colored folks is front-page news is when there's been a race riot or a lynching or a boycott and a whole lot of us have been butchered up or arrested. Then they announce it."

"You," I said, "have a race phobia. You see prejudice where there is none, and Jim Crow where it doesn't exist. How can you be constructive front-page news if you don't *make* front-page news?"

"How can I make front-page news in a white paper if I am not white?" asked Simple. "Or else I have to be Ralph Bunche or Eartha Kitt. That is why I am glad we have got colored papers like the *Afro, Defender, Courier*, and *Sepia*, so I can be news, too."

"I presume that when you say 'I' you mean the racial I— Negroes. You are not talking about yourself."

"Of course I am not talking about myself," said Simple, draining his glass. "I have never been nowhere near news except when I was in the Harlem Riots. Then the papers did not mention me by name. They just said 'mob.' I were a part of the mob. When the Mayor's Committee report come out, they said I were 'frustrated.' Which is true, I were. It is very hard for a Negro like me to get his name in the news, the reason being that white folks do not let us nowhere near news in the first place. For example, take all these graft investigations that's been going on in Brooklyn and New York every other week, unions and docks, cops and bookies, and million-dollar handouts. Do you read about any Negroes being mixed up in them, getting even a hundred dollars of them millions, or being called up before the grand jury? You do not. White folks are just rolling in graft! But where are the Negroes? Nowhere near the news. Irish names, Italian names, Jewish names, all kinds of names in the headlines every time Judge Liebowitz opens his mouth. Do you read any colored names? The grand jury don't even bother to investigate Harlem. There has never been a million dollars' worth of graft in Harlem in all the years since the Indians sold Manhattan for a handful of beads. Indians and Negroes don't get nowhere near graft, neither into much news. Find me some Negro news in tonight's *News*."

"I would hardly wish to get into the papers if I had to make news by way of graft," I said. "There is nothing about graft of which any race can be proud."

"Our race could do right well with some of that big money, though," said Simple, signaling the barman for another beer. "But it does not have to be graft, in unions or out. I am just using that as an example. Take anything else on the front pages. Take flying saucers in the sky. Everybody but a Negro has seen one. If a Negro did see a flying saucer, I bet the papers wouldn't report it. They probably don't even let flying saucers fly over Harlem, just to keep Negroes from seeing them. This morning in the subway I read where Carl Krubelewski had seen a flying saucer, also Ralph Curio saw one. And way up in Massachusetts a while back, Henry Armpriester seen one. Have you ever read about Roosevelt Johnson or Ralph Butler or Carl Jenkins or anybody that sounded like a Negro seeing one? I did not. Has a flying saucer ever passed over Lenox Avenue? Nary one! Not even Daddy Grace has glimpsed one, neither Mother Horne, nor Adam Powell. Negroes can't get on the front page no kind of way. We can't even see a flying saucer."

"It would probably scare the wits out of you, if you did see one," I said, "so you might not live to read your name in the papers."

"I could read my name from the other world then," said Simple, "and be just as proud. Me, Jesse B. Semple—my name in print for once—killed by looking at a flying saucer."

| Minnie One More Time

"Do you know what?" asked Simple.

"No, what?" I said.

"Cousin Minnie's knees is farther apart than necessary. In

other words, she is bowlegged as she can be. In fact, so bow-legged she could not catch a pig."

"Say not so!" I said.

"Minnie is also homely, squat, shot, beat and what not," said Simple, "yet there is something about that chick that mens admires. To tell the truth, if Minnie were not my cousin by blood—as well as by fooling around—I might kinder like her myself. Minnie is not pretty, but she is something else not pretty—which is I do not know how to explain by sight—but which must be good."

"Never having laid eyes on your Cousin Minnie, I can't imagine what you are talking about in exact terms, but I think I understand. Minnie is an ugly woman who has pretty points, a homely dame who hypes men, a sad sack who signals back when it comes to the Male Code, not the Morse Code. Am I right?"

"No more righter could you be than in what you say about Minnie! There is something about Minnie that carries her through this world without work. That broad has not worked three weeks in six months, yet she lives, drinks and enjoys life. How does she do it? Answer—some chump called a man lays it on the line for Minnie. To look at her, you would never think that Minnie could attract a chimpanzee, let alone a chump. But she do. Now, me, I have to work for a living. Does Minnie? I'm ugly. But Minnie's uglier. Still and yet, when Minnie flashes that big old smile of hers on some simple-minded man on payday—his payday is her heyday. Minnie can cover her rent for a month—and the chump is out of his week's salary. And does Minnie care about the square? She does not! Not Minnie! She'll let the poor man go home so broke he don't have a nickel for church on Sunday morning. I told Minnie some-day some man is going to give her a good old New York head-whipping if she don't watch out.

"Minnie said, 'Don't you believe it. I can take care of my-self,' which I do believe she can. Anyway, I am glad Minnie is getting some acquaintanceship in Harlem and knows some-body else besides me, because when Minnie first come North she like to almost worried me to death coming around every other day or so to borrow a dollar, or borrow five, or something. Now that girl knows so many folks, she borrows from me less often. I am not afraid to answer the bell at my house no more as I used to be, for fear it might be Minnie. A begging relative can be a nuisance.

"I told Minnie once, 'Girl, you got to learn to stand on your own two feet in Harlem, because up here in the free North it is every soul for himself. Even if you are too bowlegged to catch a shoat, you better catch a number or something and get yourself some money.'

"Minnie said, 'I am going to catch a man. But until I do, Jess, I depends on you for help. You are my very first cousin.'

" 'As often as you run to me, your first cousin, for money,' I said, 'I must be your last cousin, too.'

" 'You know I ain't got nary another relative in New York, Jess Semple, besides you. And if I had, I would be too proud to ask them for anything. I asks you because you be's my favorite cousin, also you come North in search of freedom, too. You got brains.'

" 'Thank you for the compliments,' I says. 'But I really cannot afford to pay for none. Minnie, I cannot lend you even a dime tonight.'

" 'Then make it a quarter,' says Minnie."

"Has Minnie ever offered to pay you back any of the money you lent her when she first got up here from Virginia?" I asked.

"Minnie believes it is more blessed to give than to receive— providing the man is the giver. No, Minnie has not yet offered to pay me back anything, and I am too much of a gentleman to ask her. But some day I am liable to get high and say, 'Minnie, I hate to insult your ladyhood, but I need my money which I have lent you in the past.' Not that I will expect to get it, for I learned long ago never to put my trust in relatives."

"Not all relatives are like your Cousin Minnie," I said.

"Thank God for that!" cried Simple. "Minnie takes after me —she's a lickertarian. But in drinking, I cannot keep up with her. Miss Minnie claims she is drowning her sorrows since she arrived in Harlem. Well, they sure ought to be well drowned by now! That woman can go, Joe!"

"You should be the last one to condemn her. I've known you to be quite intoxicated in your heyday."

"My heyday is over," said Simple. "This is my stay-home day —now that I'm a married man. But Minnie! She can drink a poor boy friend under the table and not bat an eye—still be setting on her stool sober as an owl. Last Saturday night I watched a stevedore trying to get Minnie drunk so he could make his point. That man's whole week's salary went into Minnie—and she still sat there unhugged, unkissed, and untouched. She has done got hep to big city ways now, too. Minnie don't just drink plain whiskey no more when she is being treated. She orders Scotch—which is ninety cents a throw. It do not take a working man long to unbalance his budget at that rate, before even the week end is over, let alone before next week's expenses begin. A wise man would at least save something out for subway fare and for facing the landlady. But many a joker in this world is not wise, do you know that? Facts is, I can remember when I had so little sense myself as to let chicks like Zarita drink me up. But Minnie is another story. You know, she come around to my house Sunday whilst Joyce was at church."

"Wanting money again?" I asked.

"Not this time," said Simple. "This time she wanted some kind of jive protection from her latest boy friend who threatened to knock her on her anatomy."

"Why?"

"Minnie says she does not know why," said Simple, "but I think I know. Minnie has done asked that man for money one time too many, and he knows she does not do anything with money but pour it over a bar. Minnie has been in Harlem, New York, mighty near all winter and has not got herself a warm coat yet. Coming from a mild climate like the South, she is liable to catch her death of pneumonia and go into a decline. Yet to tell the truth, Minnie has not even had a cold. Licker is good for something, as I know myself. It is good for cold."

"Then you cannot blame Minnie for wanting to keep warm," I said.

"No," said Simple, "but she cannot wear licker when she

goes out. I like to see my kinfolks dressed up, not looking like Gabriel's off ox when they strolls the Avenue. Minnie is no beauty, so she needs clothes to set off what she ain't got. I know I used to drink considerable before I got married, but I do not like to see a woman drink much—unless she is some old gal I am trying to make a quick point with—and then licker is on my side. But Minnie makes bars a habit. No wonder her boy friend has got to the place where he is about to draw back and teach her a lesson. And if Minnie thinks I am going to get mixed up in that rumble, she is wrong. No, not I!"

"You mean to say, you would not protect your cousin from force and violence on the part of a man?" I asked.

"In the first place, Minnie is not my full cousin. In the second place, I did not know she was in the world until she showed up here in Harlem claiming cousinship. In the third place, I do not know what Minnie might have done to provoke that man. Minnie might have done more than you or me can imagine. Women can drive a man sometimes to force and violence."

"In my opinion," I said, "there is no excuse for a man to hit a frail helpless woman, and do you mean to tell me you did not go to her rescue Sunday?"

"No."

"Well, have you heard what happened since? Aren't you worried? Today is Wednesday and Minnie might be annihilated by now."

"I saw Minnie in Paddy's Bar last night, solid as ever, setting on a stool spending somebody's good money. I did not linger, being married, but just got a quick beer and whilst I was drinking my beer, I asked Minnie how she were.

"Minnie said, 'Fine! Fine as wine and twice as mellow.'

"I said, 'What about the boy friend?'

"Minnie said, 'Oh, that old Negro is in bed asleep. The only times he comes out is Saturday night, which is the time he wants to ascertain his prerogative to fuss and fight. That is why I came to you Sunday for protection. Saturday night in Harlem ain't no different from Saturday night in Virginia, which is everywhere the night for mens to get rambunctious. But I never did like to be threatened with no force nor violence.

Of course, one of the nice things about this man is that he will
tell you in front what he is liable to do. Some mens just haul
off and hit you.'

." 'Suppose that was to happen to you?' I asked Minnie.

" 'Cousin Jess, I would phone you to come and go my bail,
because I would be in jail, and the man would be in Paradise,'
said Minnie.

" 'Then why come running to me Sunday for protection since
you can take care of yourself?' I asked her.

" 'Because I hates, if threatened, not to be a lady,' said Minnie. 'But if ever some man was to hit me, Jesse B., I would
wear my ladyhood like a loose garment, with my sleeves rolled
up. Bad man or no bad man, as sure as I am setting on my anatomy this evening, I would be setting on it tomorrow, too. When
push comes to shove, Jesse B., I am one woman who can take
care of myself, married or unmarried. Listen, I learned long ago
that when a man slaps a woman, that is the time for a woman to
make a stand—the very first time she gets slapped. If she don't,
the next thing you know, that man will hit her and knock her
down. If she lets him get away with that, next thing, he will
kick her—slap her first, kick her, then stomp her. Next thing,
he'll cut her. If a man gets away with cutting a woman and she
don't stop him, he will shoot her. Yes, he will! If a woman lets
a man slap her in the beginning, he is liable to shoot her in the
end. I say, stop him when he first raises his hand! My advice to
all women is to raise theirs, too! Raise your hand, women! Protect yourself—then you won't have to bury yourself later!
That's my theory.' "

"Then you won't have to worry about your Cousin Minnie's
physical well-being while she is in New York," I said.

"I don't," said Simple. "To tell the truth, I would be scared
of that woman myself were she not related to me."

| An Auto-Obituary

"I WILL now obituarize myself," said Simple at the bar. "I will cast flowers on my own grave before I am dead. And I will tell people how good I were, in case nobody else has the same feeling. Even if you are good in this life, when you are gone, most people think it is a good riddance. So, before I become dust to dust and ashes to ashes, I will light my own light—and not hide it under no bushel. My light will be lit now."

"I believe you are well lit already," I said.

"I have not had a drink today," said Simple, "except these beers in this bar."

"Then what gives you this flow of morbid thoughts?" I asked. "And why is death so prevalent this evening in your conversation? You do not look like a man who is about to die."

"Cold weather has got me," said Simple. "I swear, when I went out to work this morning, I thought I would freeze to death. This cold wave is nothing to play with. Hawkins is talking like the rent man does on the fifteenth, when you should have paid your rent on the first. I have not done nothing to the weather, so I do not know why the weather should be so hard on me. But I am so ashy in that mirror I look like ashes, and so cold I feel like ice. That's why I'm talking about death this evening—because if I do die of cold, I want some FINE words said over my body—which is why I think I had better say them myself right now, then I know they will be said, because my wife may not have enough money to pay the minister to state what I want stated. I wants to be praised to the skies, even if I do go to hell."

"Such a desire is understandable," I said, "so go ahead, preach."

"I wants myself," said Simple, "a sermon preached by a good minister something like this: 'Jesse B. Semple, born in Virginia, married twice for better or for worse—the first time for worse the last time for good. Jesse B. Semple, he were a good man. He were raised good, lived good, did good, and died good.'

"Whereupon, in my coffin, I would say, 'Rev, you have lied good. Keep on!'

"And my old minister would preach on: 'Jesse B. Semple deserves to rest in peace, deserves to pass on over to the other shores where there is light eternal, where darkness never comes, and where he will receive a crown upon his noble head, that head that thought such noble thoughts, that head that never studied evil in this world, that head that never harbored harm —that head, that head, oh, that head of Jesse B. Semple that receiveth his crown. And slippers! Golden slippers on his feet with heelplates of silver to make music up and down the golden streets. Oh, Jesse B. Semple, walking on the golden streets, hailing a celestial cab to go whirling through eternal space down the Milky Way to see can he find some old friends in the far-off parts of heaven! Angel after angel passes and he does not know any of them. He does not know this angel, nor that angel. But here, oh, here at last is an angel that knows him.'

" 'Rev! Rev!' I would whisper from my coffin, 'You will have to tell me the angel's name, because I don't recollect who it is. I think all my friends must have gone to hell.'

"Rev would preach on: ' 'Tis an angel from your youthhood, Semple, a young angel you grew up with, but whom you cannot recognize since this angel died before the age of sin, but is now whiter than snow, as all are here in heaven. No matter how dark on earth you may be, in heaven you are whiter than snow, Jesse B. Semple, whiter than snow!'

" 'Aw, now Rev,' I would say, 'with me you do not need to go that far.'

"But old Rev would keep on, because that sermon would be getting good to him by now: 'Though your sins be as scarlet, in heaven, I say, Jesse B. Semple, old earthly Semple, down-home Semple is whiter than snow. White! White! White! White! Oh, yes, you are whiter than snow!'

" 'Then, Rev,' I would have to holler, 'I would not know my own self in the mirror, were I to look.'

" 'In God's mirror all are white,' says Rev, 'white wings, white robe, white face, white neck, white shoulders, white hips, white soul! Oh, precious soul of Jesse B., worth more than words can tell! Worth more than tongues can fabulate, worth more than speech can spatulate, than throat can throttle, than human mind can manipulate! This soul, this Jess B. of a soul! This simple soul, this Semple! Gone to glory, gone to his great reward of milk and honey, manna and time unending, and the fruit of the tree of eternity.'

" 'Rev,' I would be forced to say laying there in my coffin thirsty, 'your words are as dry as popcorn and rice. You have mentioned neither beer nor wine—and I am *paying* you to preach this sermon.'

" 'The juice! Sweet, sweet juice of the vine! Juice, juice, juice,' Rev would say. 'Oh, yes, Jess Semple is partaking today of the juice of the vine, and the fruit of the tree, and the manna of time unending, and the milk and honey of the streets of gold, and the wine of the vine of timeless space in that blessed place beneath his crown of gold, wrapped in the white robes of his purity, with white wings flapping, and his immortal soul winging its way through immortal space into that eternal place where time shall be no more, and he shall rest in peace forever and forever, ever and forever—for Semple were born good! He were raised good! He lived good, did good, and lied—I mean, *died*—good. Amen!' "

Jazz, Jive, and Jam

"It being Negro History Week," said Simple, "Joyce took me to a pay lecture to hear some Negro hysterian——"

"Historian," I corrected.

"—hysterian speak," continued Simple, "and he laid our Negro race low. He said we was misbred, misread, and misled, also losing our time good-timing. Instead of time-taking and money-making, we are jazz-shaking. Oh, he enjoyed his self at the expense of the colored race—and him black as me. He really delivered a lecture—in which, no doubt, there is some truth.'"

"Constructive criticism, I gather—a sort of tearing down in order to build up."

"He tore us down good," said Simple. "Joyce come out saying to me, her husband, that he had really got my number. I said, 'Baby, he did not miss you, neither.' But Joyce did not consider herself included in the bad things he said.

"She come telling me on the way home by subway, 'Jess Semple, I have been pursuing culture since my childhood. But you, when I first met you, all you did was drape yourself over some beer bar and argue with the barflies. The higher things of life do not come out of a licker trough.'

"I replied, 'But, Joyce, how come culture has got to be so dry?'

"She answers me back, 'How come your gullet has got to be so wet? You are sitting in this subway right now looking like you would like to have a beer.'

" 'Solid!' I said. 'I would. How did you guess it?'

" 'Married to you for three years, I can read your mind,' said Joyce. 'We'll buy a couple of cans to take home. I might even drink one myself.'

" 'Joyce, baby,' I said, 'in that case, let's buy three cans.'

"Joyce says, 'Remember the budget, Jess.'

"I says, 'Honey, you done busted the budget going to that lecture program which cost One Dollar a head, also we put some small change in the collection to help Negroes get ahead.'

" 'Small change?' says Joyce, 'I put a dollar.'

" 'Then our budget is busted real good,' I said, 'so we might as well dent it some more. Let's get six cans of beer.'

" 'All right,' says Joyce, 'go ahead, drink yourself to the dogs —instead of saving for that house we want to buy!'

" 'Six cans of beer would not pay for even the bottom front step,' I said. 'But they would lift my spirits this evening. That Negro high-speaking doctor done tore my spirits down. I did not know before that the colored race was so misled, misread, and misbred. According to him there is hardly a pure black man left. But I was setting in the back, so I guess he did not see me.'

" 'Had you not had to go to sleep in the big chair after dinner,' says Joyce, 'we would have been there on time and had seats up front.'

" 'I were near enough to that joker,' I said. 'Loud as he could holler, we did not need to set no closer. And he certainly were nothing to look at!'

" 'Very few educated men look like Harry Belafonte,' said Joyce.

" 'I am glad I am handsome instead of wise,' I said. But Joyce did not crack a smile. She had that lecture on her mind.

" 'Dr. Conboy is smart,' says Joyce. 'Did you hear him quoting Aristotle?'

" 'Who were Harry Stottle?' I asked.

" 'Some people are not even misread,' said Joyce. 'Aristotle was a Greek philosopher like Socrates, a great man of ancient times.'

" 'He must of been before Booker T. Washington then,' I said, 'because, to tell the truth, I has not heard of him at all. But tonight being *Negro* History Week, how come Dr. Conboy has to quote some Greek?'

" 'There were black Greeks,' said Joyce. 'Did you not hear him say that Negroes have played a part in all history, throughout all time, from Eden to now?'

" 'Do you reckon Eve was brownskin?' I requested.

" 'I do not know about Eve,' said Joyce, 'but Cleopatra was of the colored race, and the Bible says Sheba, beloved of Solomon, was black but comely.'

" 'I wonder would she come to me?' I says.

" 'Solomon also found Cleopatra comely. He was a king,' says Joyce.

" 'And I am Jesse B. Semple,' I said.

"But by that time the subway had got to our stop. At the store Joyce broke the budget again, opened up her pocket purse, and bought us six cans of beer. So it were a good evening. It ended well—except that I ain't for going to any more meetings—especially interracial meetings."

"Come now! Don't you want to improve race relations?"

"Sure," said Simple, "but in my opinion, jazz, jive, and jam would be better for race relations than all this high-flown gab, gaff, and gas the orators put out. All this talking that white folks do at meetings, and big Negroes, too, about how to get along together—just a little jam session would have everybody getting along fine without having to listen to so many speeches. Why, last month Joyce took me to a Race Relations Seminar which her club and twenty other clubs gave, and man, it lasted three days! It started on a Friday night and it were not over until Sunday afternoon. They had sessions' mammy! Joyce is a fiend for culture."

"And you sat through all that?"

"I did not set," said Simple. "I stood. I walked in and walked out. I smoked on the corner and snuck two drinks at the bar. But I had to wait for Joyce, and I thought them speeches would never get over! My wife were a delegate from her club, so she had to stay, although I think Joyce got tired her own self. But she would not admit it. Joyce said, 'Dr. Hillary Thingabod was certainly brilliant, were he not?'

"I said, 'He were not.'

"Joyce said, 'What did you want the man to say?'

"I said, 'I wish he had sung, instead of *said*. That program needed some music to keep folks awake.'

"Joyce said, 'Our forum was not intended for a musical. It was intended to see how we can work out integration.'

"I said, 'With a jazz band, they could work out integration in ten minutes. Everybody would have been dancing together like they all did at the Savoy—colored and white—or down on the East Side at them Casinos on a Friday night where jam holds forth—and we would have been integrated.'

"Joyce said, 'This was a serious seminar, aiming at facts, not fun.'

" 'Baby,' I said, 'what is more facts than acts? Jazz makes people get into action, move! Didn't nobody move in that hall where you were—except to jerk their head up when they went to sleep, to keep anybody from seeing that they was nodding. Why, that chairman, Mrs. Maxwell-Reeves, almost lost her glasses off her nose, she jerked her head up so quick one time when that man you say was so brilliant were speaking!'

" 'Jess Semple, that is not so!' yelled Joyce. 'Mrs. Maxwell-Reeves were just lost in thought. And if you think you saw *me* sleeping——'

" 'You was too busy trying to look around and see where I was,' I said. 'Thank God, I did not have to set up there like you with the delegation. I would not be a delegate to no such gab-fest for nothing on earth.'

" 'I thought you was so interested in saving the race!' said Joyce. 'Next time I will not ask you to accompany me to no cultural events, Jesse B., because I can see you do not appreciate them. That were a discussion of ways and means. And you are talking about jazz bands!'

" 'There's more ways than one to skin a cat,' I said. 'A jazz band like Duke's or Hamp's or Basie's sure would of helped that meeting. At least on Saturday afternoon, they could have used a little music to put some pep into the proceedings. Now, just say for instant, baby, they was to open with jazz and close with jam—and do the talking in between. Start out, for example, with "The St. Louis Blues," which is a kind of colored national anthem. That would put every human in a good humor. Then play "Why Don't You Do Right?" which could be addressed to white folks. They could pat their feet to that. Then for a third number before introducing the speaker, let some guest star like Pearl Bailey sing "There'll Be Some Changes Made"—which, as I understand it, were the theme of the meeting, anyhow—and all the Negroes could say *Amen!*

" 'Joyce, I wish you would let me plan them interracial seminaries next time. After the music, let the speechmaking roll for a while—with maybe a calypso between speeches. Then, along about five o'clock, bring on the jam session, extra-special. Start serving tea to "Tea For Two," played real cool. Whilst drinking tea and dancing, the race relationers could relate, the integraters could integrate, and the desegregators desegregate. Joyce, you would not have to beg for a crowd to come out and support your efforts then. Jam—and the hall would be jammed! Even I would stick around, and not be outside sneaking a smoke, or trying to figure how I can get to the bar before the resolutions are voted on. *Resolved*: that we solve the race problem! Strike up the band! Hit it, men! Aw, play that thing! "How High the Moon!" How high! Wheee-ee-e!' "

"What did Joyce say to that?" I demanded.

"Joyce just thought I was high," said Simple.